ONE LAST HOLD

by

Angela Smith

One Last Hold
Copyright © 2014 by Angela Smith

First edition, published October 2014

Interior Layout by Author's HQ
Cover Art by Steven Novak

DEDICATION

To my family, who never gave up on supporting me.

In memory of my mother, Kristina, who may not have had the chance to see her dreams come true, but gave birth to a new generation of dreamers.

Chapter One

WESLEY WEBB TURNED his wheel to face the front straight, beginning the last lap of the race.

"You're looking good," his spotter, Derrick, affirmed through earplugs that had long-since burned a hole in his head. "Don't push it. You need a good finish."

Derrick knew him well enough to know he'd punish himself on the last lap and take chances he shouldn't take. But a good finish wasn't what it was about for him. It was about winning, and heading into turn two, Wesley was confident the win was his.

"Watch Armstrong to your left."

Wesley's palms sweat as he gripped the wheel. He imagined his car racing through the finish line—first. A few more seconds and that would become reality. His heart pounded and every beat seemed to pull Chad Armstrong closer. He held his breath, his pulse thrummed low as his mind reeled with all the consequences of all possible moves. He quickly exhaled, every exertion an effort to slow his rival's advance.

"Focus, focus," Wesley said as he let out a breath and took another one in, this time through his nose. Every nerve ending tingled in adrenaline and anticipation.

He was so ready to get out of this cage.

He bit his lip, concentrating in order to out maneuver Chad's tricks as Chad nudged him closer to the wall. This game was getting old.

"You're almost there," Derrick cued. "Watch the wall."

"Stay with me," Wesley said to his car, to his spotter, to God, and to whoever the hell else wanted to listen.

He only needed to maintain the lead a few more seconds.

Derrick's warning shrill was too late. Chad clipped the left quarter, spinning Wesley's car out of control. He frantically tried to steer out of the skid. For a moment, control was within reach, until the tire's sidewalls dug into the soft earth of the infield.

The car flipped.

Over and over.

He skidded to a stop upside down and watched Chad cross the finish line. Something he wouldn't have a chance to do tonight.

"You okay?" That damned voice in his earplugs again, reminding him people were freaking out because he hadn't come out of the car.

"Yeah." No. Fury was a molten hole in his gut, eating its way into his throat.

He crawled out of the cage and pitched his helmet and earplugs to the ground. Firefighters rushed to douse the blaze, and troops surrounded him to assist him and his car out of the infield.

Fisting his gloved hands, he pushed through the men and focused on his main goal: get past that finish line.

Even though he'd be footing it tonight.

Adam, his crew chief, advanced on him. "Do you need an ambulance?"

"No." He didn't need an ambulance, he didn't need sympathy, and he damn sure didn't need anyone trying to comfort him with words.

Right now, vengeance was his only fuel.

Wesley was fed up with Chad's selfish moves that endangered fellow racers Tired of the blatant disrespect to the racers and the sport, and tired of Chad looking good in front of the media and making everyone else the bad guy.

Wasn't hard to make Wesley into the bad guy. He was a blackguard to the media, an easy *bad-guy* target.

As he approached the stands, the merger of boos and applause as Chad was carried from his car joined the ringing in Wesley's ears.

Chad sneered at Wesley from across the throng of people and hailed a mock salute. Wesley sprung towards him, camera flashes blaring applause. He'd gladly brawl in front of the cameras and take a fine if it meant giving Armstrong a black eye.

Adam planted a fist in Wesley's chest, stopping him. "Stand back, man. It's not worth it."

He retreated and pushed his way past the media circus as the flashes continued. They followed him and thrust their microphones in his direction. The last thing he wanted to do was explain his feelings to them.

"Do you have a comment on what happened tonight?"

"How do you feel about not finishing the race?"

"Do you have something to say to Chad?"

Their badgering continued. Wesley stopped and glared, aiming for a smartass retort, but Adam's hand against his back pressed him onward. He couldn't afford to make more enemies of the media.

How in the hell did they think he felt? How would they feel if the situation was reversed?

In times like these, he hated the media, people who didn't recognize or care when someone was in pain, in mourning, and needed to be left alone. Wesley mourned the loss of first place. He'd hoped to gain some much needed points and get a lead on Chad. Instead, Chad kept him from even crossing the finish line.

And for that, he wanted to kill the sonofabitch.

***

Caitlyn Daniels was stuck in traffic so thick, it hadn't moved once in the past fifteen minutes. Thankful for the solitude within the confines of her car, she didn't care if it took a lot longer to escape this cluster.

Her pen scratched against paper to the whims of her thoughts and if she stopped now, all would be lost.

Glancing up long enough to check her surroundings, she once again focused on her writing, giving Wesley the credit he deserved while remaining neutral in her words and in her feelings.

Neutrality was hard to accomplish. She wasn't sure if she wanted to hug him or kill him.

The wipers scrawled against the windshield and jolted her from her writing. The rain had come in an icy cold gush as soon as the race ended, but it was now a drizzle, the temperatures barely high enough to keep it from freezing.

Caitlyn switched off the wipers. She wished it was as easy to turn off her memories. Like the memory of seeing Wesley, his car flipping and flipping. The fear of witnessing his almost-death. And the oh-so-long-ago memories of them together.

Her cell phone rang. The crazy song reserved for her boss grated on her nerves. She made a mental note to change Beethoven's Fugue to something more soothing, especially because talking to Blake was enough to rattle her.

"Did you get anything good?" Blake Rogers never wasted time. Foregoing niceties and useless chatter, he struck right to the point.

"No luck with an interview on Wesley this time." Caitlyn rubbed the knot of tension in her neck and remembered standing with the other media who longed to get a comment from Wesley. He only glared and turned away and since she stood near the back, covered from head to toe to keep warm, he wouldn't have recognized her.

"Did you speak with Chad?" Blake asked.

"I did. He had no remorse for what he did."

"He didn't do anything wrong."

"He almost killed Wesley."

"Wrecks happen all the time in racing. It wasn't Chad's fault. What did he give you?"

"If Wesley is as talkative as that man, I'll have his whole life story in one interview. Chad told me things I didn't need to know." Caitlyn didn't bother telling her boss that wasn't about to happen. Wesley didn't like to share ten years ago. He damn sure didn't like to share now.

"Anything that might prove beneficial to our story?"

"Only if you want a story on Chad," she said.

"Not unless you have anything new. There are already

plenty of stories on Chad."

"We knew this wouldn't be easy. Wesley isn't as friendly with journalists as most of the other guys. You know that."

"You'll have to try harder."

An ongoing battle between Caitlyn and her boss. Wesley, despite his celebrity status, liked to stay below the spotlight and when it did fall on him, the media reports were rarely nice. He came across as surly and antagonistic. Blake hoped that since she grew up with Wesley, she'd be able to convince him to grant her an in-depth interview, something he'd never granted any reporter.

"I expect something good in my email come morning." With that, Blake ended the call.

She closed her eyes and leaned back on the headrest. She pictured Wesley's face, his deep green eyes, the warmth that used to linger when he looked at her. Then the wreck, the car flipping, flipping, flipping as she watched in horror and waited for him to emerge. Collapsing relief when he did emerge. *Alive.*

Yet, she might as well have been dead to him.

Her eyes opened, darkness surrounding her as a mix of rain and sleet fell again, rapping against her windshield.

She'd have something to Blake by morning. Her article was already good. But she'd have to rewrite it, take out her emotion at seeing him again—even if it was only from a distance—yet still stir her readers with emotion.

Caitlyn grabbed her phone and checked social media.

She'd worked for Blake before graduating from college, just as he got his magazine business off the ground. When digital took over, his magazine had remained successful, in part because his employees used social media and blogs to track their current stories, and in part because Blake was good at what he did.

Blake had bragged about how he created it all on his own with merely a few dollars to his name. A weekly entertainment magazine focused on everyday people, with a touch of famous. A 'how-to', a 'hot- off- the- press', a 'rumor mill' containing ideas on entertaining people, oneself, hobbies, and exclusive biographical interviews by some of the most exceptional people.

Wesley Joel Webb defined exceptional. A handsome stock-car racer with a license to practice law. A shaded past most people could only speculate.

Except for Caitlyn, because she had been there.

***

"I think the engine is salvageable."

Adam wiped his greasy hands on a towel while Wesley continued to stare into the abyss of the garage shop, gripping what was left of his car's frame to stand upright. Vertigo dominated his thought process as he saw himself sliding across the track, this time from a spectator's perspective and not a participant.

The scent of burnt metal left an acrid taste in Wesley's mouth that not even two quarts of water could ease. The taste lingered, making his tongue thick, corroding his gut.

"The guys and I will have to check it over, but I think we can save a few things," Adam said.

Who the hell cared about the damn engine, anyway? They had more where that one came from. It was Adam's way of trying to lessen their frustration level. Plus, Adam liked to tinker with things, which made him one hell of a crew chief.

"You okay?" Chad approached and slapped Wesley on the back like they were old friends.

His hackles rose at the familiar voice, and he tightened his grip on the mangled frame. Of course Chad wanted to rub his nose in the win. Just like him.

"No thanks to you." He ignored the handshake Chad offered and focused his attention on the car. A safer route than doing what he really wanted, which was to wipe that smug smile off Chad's face and beat the holy shit out of him.

He couldn't afford another fine. He couldn't afford another damaging news article. Like it or not, he had to play nice.

When he felt like this, the best thing to do was ignore the cause and focus on the car—the means of his escape. The car was his catalyst, the ignition for the release of anger, dread, fear, depression. Its magic had worked for years whether he worked on it or inside it.

"I'm sorry about what happened." Chad's arrogant face displayed a smirk larger than the track at Talladega.

Being sorry meant regretting what happened and wishing for the possibility to change it. Despite all the warnings, Chad continued to take excessive risks in order to win, and that was unforgivable. Wesley doubted Chad felt sorrow for anything he did.

"That was one hell of a wreck though, wasn't it?" Chad needled. "It'll give YouTube viewers enough fodder for days. Hell, it probably has thousands of views already. I've watched it a dozen times myself."

Enough was enough. Hands cranked, Wesley turned and aimed his glare on Chad, cracked his knuckles as he stepped toward him. Every muscle in his body ached at the long hours spent in his car. Landing a few punches in Chad's face might help stretch out the kinks in his body.

Chad retreated and held up his hands. "Yo, hey, you trying to make the news again, or what?"

"You'd like that, wouldn't you?"

"I mean no harm. This'll probably make you famous and have fans screaming your name. Speaking of fans, I met an old friend of yours earlier."

"Come on Wes." Adam grabbed him by the elbow.

God, he hated to withdraw, but he hated to be fined or banned from next week's race even more. Chad would gladly flaunt an injury for the crowds and show everyone what a bad guy Wesley was. Last month's article after a bitter public dispute made him look like a sore-loser-asshole. His sponsors urged him to make better choices. Landing a bruise on Chad's face was definitely not the better choice.

"This chick said she went to school with you. She was hot. Dark hair, blue eyes. She asked about you."

Whatever. He grew tired of his games and wouldn't give him the pleasure of reacting. That's exactly what Chad wanted. He returned his attention to the car, but the engine swam in front of him.

Plenty of women asked about Wesley. Women with dark

hair and blue eyes. Anyone could change their hair color, but he usually avoided all women with blue eyes because they reminded him of a woman he'd spent ten years trying to forget.

"That girl was hot," Chad repeated. "Wish I'd gone to school with you, bud." Chad whacked Wesley on the back, laughed, and stepped away. "If there's anything I can do to help, let me know."

Wesley pocketed his fists and leaned against the car lift's post. "Stop cheating to win."

"What? I hope you don't think it was intentional."

"Yeah, right. The only way you can win is to cause your opponents to crash. Typical dirty takedown."

"It was an accident."

"Those *accidents* are happening more and more frequently. This time, I'm reporting it to the officials."

"You go ahead." Chad landed a stream of spit near Wesley's feet. "You wouldn't have won anyway."

***

The dim glow of a nightlight shadowed the walls of the RV. He slithered his way through the rooms in search of the documents. Find them and make a hasty departure. That was his mission. But the thrill of being in the trailer surpassed the need to escape before the owner arrived.

He stroked the marble-lined counters, his gloved hands making the texture indistinguishable. But it still turned him on. Everything about this turned him on.

The owner had eaten bacon for breakfast. The smell lingered and made him long for his mother's home-cooked meals. But she had been gone for years now and he couldn't boil water, much less fry bacon.

He opened the stove and microwave to see if any bacon remained. No such luck, though a plate lined in bacon-greased paper towels was left out. He didn't bother checking the refrigerator.

A floor lamp illuminated the bedroom. Blue velvet on the bed, and he'd bet on satin sheets underneath. The guy was proud of this room, if rumor had it right.

He didn't see any frills to indicate a woman, but his curiosity got the best of him. He turned down the comforter. The sheets weren't satin. What a disappointment. Regular cotton sheets but, judging from the stains on them, either the guy jerked off or he had a girl visit from time to time.

He'd bet on both.

He approached the closet door, wide open, and rummaged through a plastic file bin. Ahh, there it was, exactly what he was searching for. He took it but didn't leave. Not yet. If there was anything else he could nab while he was here, he would.

He heard a key in the lock and the door clicked open. Frozen in the shadows, he touched the knife he carried. He hadn't necessarily planned on killing, but when he saw the owner, intense loathing charged him. He wanted the guy dead. He could try to escape, or exact revenge.

But God didn't allow him to choose an option. The owner noticed him before he could slip away and think on his decision.

"What the hell?" the owner muttered. Realizing what the intruder came for would not be pretty, the guy turned to run. It was too late.

The blade sank into the man's ribs. The smell of blood fed the killer's senses and caused his own blood to pulse in his gonads.

Ah, it'd been a long time, but the sensation of a kill hadn't changed.

Chapter Two

CAITLYN WAS BRUSHING her teeth and preparing for bed when Chad Armstrong's name on the television caught her attention. She scrambled into the narrow hotel room and peered at the TV, curious to know what the news would report about his win tonight. Her article had been written and submitted, but using all avenues of the press to spread social media was another aspect of her job on assignment.

Police lights flashed across the screen. Caitlyn bolted to the bathroom, spat out her toothpaste, and rushed back to the TV.

"The police are investigating a possible homicide of Chad "Strong Arm" Armstrong. Armstrong was found dead—"

"What?" She grabbed her phone as words scrolled across the screen, depicting tonight's events. Chad Armstrong, stabbed while entering his RV.

"Oh God. Oh God," Caitlyn muttered. All she could think of was Wesley. Was he okay?

She punched in Blake's number. She didn't know Chad Armstrong, barely knew anything about him or the sport, but this was crazy. Although most of the press seemed to eat up his words, she considered him a self-absorbed jerk.

When Blake learned Caitlyn had gone to school with Wesley, he hadn't listened to all the arguments of why she shouldn't be assigned to this story. She knew nothing about racing. Wesley didn't consider her a friend. But Blake hadn't wanted to assign Patricia, and Caitlyn stopped fighting. Patricia wasn't right for the job. Why? Jealousy maybe, but mostly because Patricia wouldn't let up until she had the story Blake wanted. Sure, the story could make her famous, but she wanted to protect Wesley from Patricia's type.

She wanted to be the one to write Wesley's story.

Caitlyn paced the room and dreaded each ring. "Come on, Blake, answer." This was big news, and she needed to know how he wanted her to handle it.

"Hello?" Blake's groggy voice shook Caitlyn. He'd obviously been sleeping and hadn't seen the news. She'd have to be the one to tell him.

She asked anyway. "Have you seen the news?"

"What? No. What time is it?"

"Chad Armstrong has been murdered."

***

"Damn, damn, damn, this shouldn't be happening."

Wesley kicked gravel as he paced the grounds and listened to the murmur of his companions. It was almost his turn to talk to the cops, but he had no idea what he'd tell them.

As much as he disliked Chad, Wesley wouldn't wish this on anyone. The fact that Chad was stabbed as he entered his RV scared the shit out of the people who stayed on the grounds. The park, where most of the racers and their families stayed, was considered safe, monitored by security guards, and no one else could get past the entrance.

Most racers disliked Chad. Wesley had imagined terrible scenarios that would put Chad out of racing for good. But murder? Never.

And now he felt guilty about wanting the S.O.B. dead.

"I brought you something to drink." Adam handed Wesley a cup of steaming coffee and Wesley nodded his thanks. He sat next to him, on the steps of a nearby trailer where everyone clustered.

He may have been burning up earlier, but now Wesley was literally freezing his balls off. He clenched his coat tight and held the cup close to his lips to inhale the steam and absorb the heat from the drink into his body. The buzz of conversation around him intensified as people wondered who it could have been and what would happen next. They waited as, one-by-one, they were questioned by the cops.

He considered calling an attorney. He was the one who had the most motivation, at least tonight, but everyone was being questioned and to call on an attorney would only make him appear guilty.

"Wesley Webb?" an officer called.

"Here." Wesley set his cup on the steps and stood as an officer approached.

"We need to speak with you now." The officer spun around, expecting Wesley to follow. Wesley winked at Adam before following, a sign between his crew that all was fine.

The cop appeared to be in his late forties. He hobbled as if he'd practiced the heel-to-toe test one too many times, or his coveted baton was stuck up his ass. A black beanie hid most of his face.

The officer stopped at a makeshift room designed to question people and didn't turn to face him or introduce himself. The wind shifted and shook the barriers of the canopy tent-room, which was still exposed to the elements and onlookers, but cordoned off by anyone who might attempt to sneak in. Thankfully, the media was not allowed within the confines of the RV Park without permission.

"How long have you known Mr. Armstrong?"

The officer could at least introduce himself, but his gaze was bonded to a pint-sized notebook. He didn't look up, not even when Wesley chose to wait a few breaths before answering. Call it rebellion, but Wesley didn't like the cop's attitude. Respect was a two-way street.

He'd play their game for now.

"We've worked together awhile now," Wesley replied. "I'd say...four years."

"Do you know anyone who would want him dead?"

"No, I don't."

"Would *you*?" The officer finally looked up and leered, his voice rising in a vain attempt to expose his sarcasm.

The name Landers imprinted his name badge.

"No, Officer Landers, I would not."

"He gave you a motive tonight, didn't he?"

"I wouldn't call that a motive," Wesley retorted, never breaking contact with those smug-filled eyes. "If it was, then every damned racer in this field would have a motive against each other."

"Weren't you angry at Chad? You blamed him for what happened. He caused you to wreck. Caused a lot of damage to your car, and you didn't finish the race."

"Happens all the time." The anticipation still lingered within him on the final turn, when he tasted victory.

"You were furious with Chad for what he did. That alone gives you motive."

This guy already pegged him a killer. "I was mad, yeah, but when that kind of shit happens, you have to deal with it next week, on the track."

"You didn't deal with it last time, did you? With that public display?"

"We had an argument that some of the press caught. It was nothing."

"Do you have an alibi for where you were when Chad Armstrong was murdered?"

***

Caitlyn felt hung over the next morning, but she hadn't had an ounce to drink. Probably would have helped her sleep if she had. Blake's early morning phone call annoyed her. She needed coffee before she dealt with her boss. Her head pounded, but the cheap motel offered no in-room coffeepot. The lobby's promise of coffee didn't entice her either. The entire hotel smelled foul, she could only imagine the coffee tasted no better.

Every time she'd tried to sleep, Wesley's car flipped over and over in her mind. His smoldering green eyes watched her from the background, abating into smoke when she'd finally managed to latch her gaze onto his. His gaze was the only way to keep her grounded, to keep her from imagining him trapped in the burning car. She dreamed of cars wrecking and burning so much last night that she'd actually smelled smoke.

"I want you to meet with someone this morning," Blake said. "He works for Wesley and can get you in to see him."

She swung her legs to the floor. "You have someone on the inside and you want *me* to do a story?"

"His name is Adam. He's Wesley's crew chief. He'll take you to your interview with Wesley."

She pressed a hand into her stomach and gulped. Wesley had agreed to an interview with her? Wesley was expecting her? Was he just as nervous?

Oh God, could she do this?

She chugged in a silent breath and slowly exhaled as old insecurities came rushing back. They'd been so close at one time, but she'd spent the last ten years with a huge hole in her heart.

Wesley. She was going to see Wesley.

"I'll do it," she said. "But you've got to find me a better hotel."

After a quick shower in a grimy tub, she checked out of her room with the intention of sleeping at the airport if she had to and found a Starbucks where she ordered a tall caffeine laden cappuccino laced with cinnamon, sugar, and cream.

A decadent cinnamon roll was not on her list of healthy choices but at this point, she didn't care. An overload of carbohydrates would fuel her chaotic nerves.

A man waited for her at the door of a large garage. Average, a tad younger than Caitlyn, with honey blond hair and amber eyes that gleamed when he shook her hand.

"You must be Adam."

"Caitlyn." He kept a firm lock on her a second too long. "I would appreciate it if you didn't tell Wesley it was me who set this up. He doesn't like unarranged meetings with reporters, but I heard you once knew him."

Caitlyn freed her hand, unsure what to think. Did that mean Wesley had no idea she was coming? Her thighs shook as she surged forward, into the surprisingly clean garage. Machinery and equipment echoed in the steel building and though it was noisy, it was organized cadence. She wondered how many people were employed to keep it clean and how many levels of insulation it took to keep it quiet.

They stopped at a car, and she fished for her phone but decided against pictures until she had permission.

"I'll go fetch Wesley." Adam halted his steps mid-strike. "If Wesley doesn't work out for you, I'll grant you an interview. I never had a reporter as beautiful as you ask me anything personal." He winked before turning away, and her fake smile landed on his back.

Caitlyn wasn't seeking any type of relationship. Wesley had shaded her view of men so much that she was afraid she'd never find the right one when she was ready. She hoped this assignment would help purge Wesley out of her memory so Mr. Right would be easier to identify.

Yeah right. Mr. Right didn't exist.

Wesley had been a friend. Her best friend since childhood. Why couldn't she just remember that?

Because at one time, he had been Mr. Right.

Her fingertips tapped together as she waited for him. Times like these, she wished she smoked, to give her hands something to do.

Wesley emerged from upstairs, his focus on Adam as they chatted. Caitlyn struggled to maintain her composure. Composure? What composure? She'd never had any composure when it came to Wesley, so why would she have it now? She was a stick figure fused together by tape and glue, her speech cut and pasted in her mind so many times she no longer knew what to say.

His hair was thick, dark, mussed. A five o'clock shadow lined his cheekbones, grease dotting his face like freckles. She admired the way his black shirt hugged his shoulders, his jeans snug against his ripcord ass.

God, at one time, she'd take that grease and swipe it across his face. Laugh and run while he chased her across the shop. And once he caught her, she'd pull up his shirt and...

Stop it.

He continued to speak as he stepped off the stairs, without noticing her. She wondered if Adam had told her she was waiting, or if he had any idea who he was about to meet.

His long strides carried him toward her, but he remained deep in conversation with Chad. Had he always been that tall? That overwhelming? His presence took up the entire garage, stifling her breath, stifling her words, stifling her thoughts. Her pulse thrummed low.

Remember him as a friend. Remember him as a friend.

His radiant smile, something she thought to never see again, faded when he noticed her. His green eyes suffocated her as she observed the only man she'd ever loved.

He stopped in front of her and pinned her with a hard glare. His mouth tightened. She stood, transfixed, unable to speak. She'd look like a fool if she turned and bolted.

"Caitlyn."

Shivery tendrils of longing shot down her spine at the way he spoke her name.

"What are you doing here?"

***

Wesley was a grown man, so why did his heart slam against his ribs as soon as he looked into Caitlyn's baby blues?

His reaction to her annoyed him. Caitlyn stood before him, soft and petite and full of curves he didn't remember. His mind spun across the track of Daytona Speedway as he drank in her appearance. Her hair tumbled in waves down her back, smelling of coconut and something else.

Something feminine.

Something *familiar*.

Of all the women who'd ever approached him, one glance from her and he was rock hard. Just like always.

She hadn't answered his question yet, so he asked again, this time more abruptly. "What the hell are you doing here?"

She still had the habit of drumming her fingers together. She once told him it was because she needed something to do with her hands.

He'd given her plenty of things to do with her hands.

He swallowed his desire and blinked hard.

"I was sent here...on assignment." She tucked a stray hair behind her ear and licked her lips. He tore his gaze away from her kissable mouth. In his older days, he'd move in and taste her. She'd cling to him and offer him everything.

"On assignment?" he asked. What was she, a cop? Wouldn't that be ironic if she were the one to arrest him?

"I'm a journalist now, Wesley."

He recoiled. Thoughts of tasting her lips vanished. Un-fucking-believable.

He turned away. He'd give her no chance to explain. Now he knew why she was here.

Reporters couldn't be trusted. If Tim's experience hadn't taught him, his own encounters were bad enough. Caitlyn could air his dirty laundry in public with one story, or hit him where it really hurt by hanging it out to let everyone watch it dry, egging it on for weeks.

"Wait!" She reached out to him, her touch seared his arm.

"What did you think?" he asked, turning to face her. "That since we used to fuck, I'd give you a story I wouldn't give anyone else?"

Chapter Three

CAITLYN STORMED OUT of the garage, fuming. Anger shielded her hurt.

When had Wesley become such a *jerk*?

Maybe spending too much time with his uncle had lessened his compassion. Tim had never liked Caitlyn. She'd always tried to avoid him and the one time she'd asked Wesley why Tim didn't like her, he'd blamed it on her imagination. Tim was just *intense*. Wesley had worshipped Tim then, probably more so now. And now, now Tim had even more reason to hate Caitlyn.

She'd killed his sister.

She swiped her tears, the words to her next article already etched in her mind. Hopefully, she wouldn't forget once her anger ceased.

Racecar driver Wesley Webb wasn't too keen on doing an interview the day after his rival's murder, but he and his team were working hard preparing for next week's race.

She wouldn't write it of course, but oh the things she could say.

She locked herself in the rented vehicle and phoned Blake to tell him the interview was a no-go at this time but he'd have a story regardless. She'd think of something. She always did. And she could do it without insulting Wesley.

She wanted to insult Wesley. She wanted to wrap him in hurt as she was hurting now.

But she'd given him enough hurt to last a life time. Why

should he ever forgive her?

"He'll be signing autographs tomorrow at Tim's Race Shop," Blake told her.

"How do you know all this?"

"Well, it's all over the news."

"How did you manage to get me into the garage?" she asked. She remained in the parking lot, unmoving, as cars rushed over the nearby interstate. Did Blake have a plane ticket home for her, or not?

"Uh, what do you mean?"

"Do you know his crew chief?"

"Not personally, no."

"Then how in the hell did you manage to convince him to take me to Wesley? Wesley obviously didn't know I was coming." She hadn't known it was Tim's shop, and thank God he hadn't been around. If she had known, she wouldn't have gone. She would've flat refused.

Yeah right.

"Oh, I didn't know he wasn't expecting you. Do you still have your hotel room?"

"No, I don't still have my hotel room. I refuse to stay there again."

"I'll find you something. Hold tight and I'll call you back."

The silence indicated he'd hung up. "Blake! Asshole," she barked. "Ugh."

She glanced at her phone and considered calling him again but that was a lost cause. Instead, she opened the browser to research her geography.

From what she'd learned so far, Wesley didn't live too far from here and Charlotte was his uncle's hometown. Tim had opened a racing museum to the public along with Tim's Race Shop, a store with a large garage and fun center next to the race team's private garage. The private garage was rarely open to the public. Blake had lied. Otherwise, Adam would've never let her in. Maybe she should just take Adam up on his offer, ask him to dinner, and find out how the hell he knew Blake.

That was one plan.

She considered marching back into the shop and telling them all how it was going to be but started the car and drove away instead. The door was probably locked anyway.

She'd drive to the airport and buy a ticket home. Blake could just pay her back later. But when Blake called with an address for her a better hotel, she resolved to stay one more night. The ticket could wait until morning.

***

"What in the hell was that all about?"

"Sorry, Wes. Didn't know she was a journalist. Hell, I thought she was family the way she insisted on speaking with you."

"How long have you known me? And you just let someone waltz in without running it by me first?"

Adam shrugged. Wesley studied his friend, wondering if he should be troubled by Adam's shortsightedness. Adam had never in his life tried to interfere in Wesley's business, but lately he had voiced his concern over Wesley's lack of interest in women. He wondered if Adam knew more about his past relationship with Caitlyn than he was letting on, but quickly discounted the notion.

"I don't know all your family," Adam defended.

"You know the important ones, and you know not to let just anyone in here."

"She didn't seem like just anyone."

"Why? Because she's pretty?"

Adam raised his hands and stepped back, warding off the next verbal attack. "Sorry, man. How many women have begged me to meet you? And how many times have I let them? I thought she was family. It won't happen again."

Wesley nodded then turned and walked away. No sense in talking about it anymore. No sense in vocalizing his pain. The pain clustered in his gut even now. The pain of seeing Caitlyn. The memories she generated. It'd been so long, so long ago, but it still felt like yesterday.

She *was* family. She *was* his everything.

But that was the past. Now, they were two different people.

He'd fought hard to keep his gaze from landing on her ring finger. Was she married? Maybe she had kids? Frustration rose in rebellion at the thought.

They had planned on having kids together at one time.

Caitlyn was more beautiful than ever, and Adam could have easily been swayed by those stark blue eyes. Wesley had been swayed by them plenty of time in his past. He'd almost given up everything for her. Might have given up everything for her if things hadn't gone differently. And now she was a reporter.

She could destroy him with merely a blink.

***

Caitlyn placed her hand on the door to Tim's Race Shop and jerked away. Heat, cobwebs, or scary childhood stories of what lurked behind these doors would incite less fear.

She worried Tim would be here today. He hadn't been yesterday, but today Wesley was making an appearance and signing autographs, so it was only expected that he owner of the race team would be here, too. He couldn't turn her away as a fan.

Blowing out a deep breath, she rejected her fear and pulled the heavy door towards her. She wanted to do this. She had to do this. And Blake wouldn't take no for an answer.

She'd spent years looking over her shoulder, expecting Wesley to come back. The simple fact was, he hadn't. When he'd emerged in the racing circuit, she'd tracked his career but never made a move to contact him—until now.

She couldn't walk away yet. If she did, she'd never see him again, and she needed closure.

Even if it was ten years too late.

She could write about Wesley's past and hurt him. Blake would be happy and she wouldn't be forced to spend any more time than necessary with Wesley. She could seek revenge for her broken heart and sell her story to someone way more notable than Blake.

But she'd never stab her family in the back. Wesley, as much as she hated to admit it, would always be family.

Racing memorabilia for sale occupied the waiting area, enticing visitors. She bought a t-shirt to give her hands something to hold when she approached him. Besides, she needed something for him to sign other than her journalist's notebook.

She worked her way to where a throng of fans stood in line waiting to meet him. Wesley sat at an autograph table, his race car placed strategically behind him. He ruffled young children's hair, posed for pictures, and took time to talk with everyone. His prideful glow revealed how important he considered his fans.

Her insides lurched. She shouldn't be here, stirring up bad memories. Not for her, but for him. He'd gotten on with his life. He was happy, well-adjusted, and oh so successful. She would never do anything to destroy that. But her presence could destroy that. She should turn and run.

But she didn't run. Instead, she moved to the back of the line in case she changed her mind. When they cut off the line, she realized she'd made a huge mistake. Last. Great. If someone had been behind her, he'd have to be nice. For show. Right?

He was dressed in his racing uniform. His dark hair mussed enough to be sexy but not haggard. Stubble shadowed his jawline.

Waves surged over her, flooding her in fear and doubt and insecurity. Why was she doing this?

The young boy and his mother ahead of her stepped up. She forced air out of her lungs and straightened her spine.

Wesley posed for a picture with the boy and his mother then ruffled the boy's hair before they left.

Caitlyn hobbled forward on wobbly legs.

Wesley glanced at her. She clutched the shirt to her chest. His smile tightened but didn't fall as he returned to his seat and grabbed his marker.

Too late to run now.

"May I have your autograph?" Her hands shook as she handed Wesley the t-shirt and dropped her purse to the floor. His fingers grazed hers as he took the shirt.

She hadn't expected a smile. Even if it was fake-as-hell.

"Certainly. Where do you want it?"

She fumbled with the button on her jacket and gave a

stupid grin. His friendliness was unnecessary. Nobody was around to impress.

"Whoa, wait a second. Maybe you should show me later." He held up his hands, his smile wide across his handsome face. Caitlyn's cheeks flamed. Not only her cheeks, her entire body. For a moment, she forgot his act was all a game.

He signed the t-shirt and handed it back to her as if that would end their connection, but she didn't leave.

"Looks like that's everyone," Tim said, stopping beside Wesley. He folded his fingers over the back of the chair and studied Caitlyn, his presence dominating the room.

The two were so much alike they could have been brothers. Tim's face was fuller, ripe with deeper lines, a lighter complexion and thinner mouth but then that could have been the sneer he wore as he perused her.

Wesley rose to greet his uncle. Caitlyn hid her trembling hands behind her back.

"You remember Caitlyn?" Wesley asked.

Tim smiled, sending a slow burn of dread into her belly. A caustic smile, like shards of glass fused together for the sole purposes of nicking its recipient. She cocked her head and returned his scowl. She'd be damned if she'd retreat.

"To what do we owe this honor?"

"She's a journalist now," Wesley accused. Caitlyn cringed, feeling like an idiot for not speaking. Tim would like that news even less than Wesley. Why did he feel it was necessary to tell Tim?

"Obviously now isn't a good time to talk," she said to Wesley, her words raspy from holding them back for so long. "Maybe we can meet up later?"

"What's wrong with now?" Tim's voice pierced her spine like the shards of glass she'd imagined on his face.

"This is very awkward," Caitlyn replied. "And I didn't come to make an already awkward situation worse."

"Then why did you come?" Wesley asked.

Instead of force-feeding Wesley politeness, she glared into his eyes and let the emotion they held over her erupt into anger.

"Look, I already have enough shit on you from your

childhood to write a novel. If I wanted to do that, I would have. I have no control of what assignments my boss gives me. He wanted me to interview you. That's what I'm attempting to do whether you like it or not. Instead, I could write what I already know and save myself a huge headache."

"Wesley's at the pinnacle of his career and doesn't need you to screw it up again," Tim interrupted. "Stay in his past."

His words bit into her. She wanted to retort. Wanted to tell him she hadn't screwed up his life. But that would be a lie, so she swallowed the lump in her throat and pretended his words hadn't hurt.

"He wasted four years in law school after what happened, thinking it was a sign," he continued.

"From what I've heard, he spent those four years racing on the side and getting better. I wouldn't call that wasted. Plus, now he has a professional degree to fall back on, which is not a waste."

"He was going to forfeit his dream for you and you would have let him."

"He didn't forfeit anything for me," Caitlyn spat. Wesley's glower dug into her skin. She couldn't believe he was letting Tim treat her like a child. But then again, Tim always had treated her like she wasn't good enough and Wesley had never noticed.

"He was angry, hurt, and a hell of a lot of other things when he was driving that night. He was distracted and that's why he wrecked."

"Tim, that's enough," Wesley scolded, surprising Caitlyn.

Caitlyn still remembered it like it was yesterday. Still had nightmares. And she still blamed herself. Hearing it from Tim's mouth didn't help. He damn sure didn't need to tell her what happened or why.

She'd been there. He hadn't.

"Maybe that dream you say was his wasn't really his." Caitlyn ignored the fact that Tim's frame loomed over hers as she stepped forward to aim a finger at his chest. The table stood between them, but that didn't stop her. "Maybe it was *your* dream. You're obviously the reason he became a race car driver."

Wesley cleared his throat and skirted the table to grab

Caitlyn's elbow before she sliced Tim open with a lone fingernail. "Excuse us," he said to Tim.

Caitlyn pulled out of his grip and gathered her purse from the floor. "Don't bother. I know my way out. And I'll write the story my boss wants. I came here to give you a chance so I could leave out the bullshit of your past life. But I don't know why I bothered giving you a chance."

Wesley snagged her purse and settled his hand on her lower back, ushering her out the door and away from Tim's comeback. He wouldn't even give her a chance to graciously walk away.

Her thighs trembled. She wanted to wiggle out of his touch, but she'd not dare let him see how he affected her. She refused to cry. Anger would leave her more content in the long run, so she let the anger fuel her.

She wouldn't write the story that would condemn him, but he didn't have to know that. Let him worry and fret the way she'd worried and fretted over the years.

"So now you're going to threaten me?" Wesley asked once the door slammed behind them.

She stepped away from his burning touch. "I'm not threatening. Just stating the facts."

"Tim's right," Wesley said. "I don't need this. And with Chad's death, the last thing I need is the media on my ass."

"Right now might be a good opportunity to get someone in the media on your good side. Maybe if you played nice, they'd write nicer things about you."

"I don't have a problem with them writing bad things about me. I'd prefer they not write anything at all."

"If they aren't writing anything, it means you aren't getting noticed. If you want to succeed, you have to be noticed."

"That's not true."

Caitlyn flicked her hair aside and tempered her nostalgia. "How so?"

"I'm already successful. My talent has gotten me noticed. Not brownnosing reporters like you. I'm at a different place in my life. I don't need you trying to pick up things where we left off."

"I didn't come here to start where we left off, you egotistical jerk." Caitlyn yanked her bag from his grip and cradled it to her chest. The way things were going, it wouldn't be hard for this assignment to be her cleansing. Purge Wesley and realize she no longer needed an excuse to avoid other relationships. What she felt for him was in the past. *A past love*. Nothing else.

He was nothing like the man—the boy—she'd loved.

***

The smell of construction tickled Wesley's nostrils as he entered the door to his new home. Sawdust carpeted the entryway and the scent of fresh pine lingered in the air. Not much longer before the house was move-in ready.

He climbed the wooden staircase to the open loft and stepped outside onto the deck. The scene paid homage to the feelings raging within his body. Peaceful, yet conflicting, emotions. Pine trees whipped in the wind. Unrelenting snow nipped at the mountain tops. A deep and restless energy plagued Wesley, yet at the same time he wanted to fall on his bed and sleep.

Unfortunately, his bed wasn't set up and he had no electricity, so it'd be out to the travel trailer for him.

The last few days had been stressful with Chad's funeral and Caitlyn's appearance. Images of Caitlyn still haunted him.

He wondered if he should call her to make amends before she slandered his name all over the internet. The timing couldn't be more perfect. Like she said, he could use a friend in the media after Chad's death. He'd kept checking to see if she'd made good on her threat, but so far he hadn't found any defamation of his character. Didn't mean she wasn't working on it.

Caitlyn had been his inspiration in the beginning of his career. When he began racing, he used the fire that consumed him when he thought of her and their past together to become better until thinking of her no longer benefited him. She became a memory. A painful, distant memory.

Born in North Carolina, Wesley moved to Texas when he was six, where he met Caitlyn. They quickly became friends, lovers, and he'd planned to stay in Texas until he learned life couldn't be planned or bargained with. Now, he moved around constantly and was happy that way.

The orange glow of the sun, piercing in its intensity, skimmed the snow-kissed mountainside and left a trail of incandescent light filtering through the trees. The panorama was beautiful, but the cold seeped into the cracks of Wesley's jacket and became unbearable. The crack in his soul had been unbearable at one time, but racing had mended him.

As he headed inside, a police car pulled up and two offices exited. He lumbered down the steps to meet them and remained by the door as they approached.

He dreaded another encounter with the cops, but the one in his head involved handcuffs. So far, he hadn't seen any.

The first officer flashed his badge. "I'm Sergeant Sikes and this is Detective Brew. We're here to ask you questions about Chad Armstrong."

"I've already spoken with an officer about this. I don't have anything else to give you."

"We have more questions. May we come in?"

Tension knotted his gut. "Do I need an attorney?"

"Not unless you're guilty," Sikes asserted.

The long-legged officer smirked at his partner, and Wesley bit back a retort.

He shuffled aside and let them enter. He should deny them, hire an attorney before he spoke to anyone, but that would only make him look guilty in the media's eye. Besides, he still held his law license. He knew what to say and not to say. "My house isn't finished yet and the electricity isn't installed."

The cops stepped past him and into the house. Sikes glanced around and stopped at the kitchen bar. "This'll be fine." He laid his bag on the counter and removed a handful of pictures. "Can you tell us why Armstrong had a file folder with your name on it?"

Wesley took the photos and studied the file folder in question. It was an accordion folder, somewhat frayed, and his name was sprawled on the front with a black Sharpie.

"No idea," he muttered. "What was inside?"

"We hoped you could tell us that."

Wesley's gaze snapped to the officers and back to the photo, trying to decipher what the picture was telling him. "Was it empty?"

The officer didn't reply, and a sinking sensation in his gut told him he'd already been marked as guilty.

"Where did you find this?"

"Armstrong's residence."

"His RV?" Wesley glanced up, Sikes nodded, and he resumed his study of the pictures.

"It was empty," Sikes admitted. "We believe whoever killed Armstrong took out the contents of that file. We have no idea why they didn't take the entire folder. Could you think of any reason?"

"What's this?" Wesley ignored the question and waved a photo.

"The crime scene techs took that photo. It's a diagram of your family tree. Found on the floor, underneath a table, spattered in blood. Must've fallen out of the folder."

Wesley stared at the pictures while a cold, damp hand squeezed his chest. He gasped for breath. He didn't know what this meant and why Chad had this, but it couldn't be good.

"We think whoever murdered Chad Armstrong took that folder of information about you."

"So I could be the next target?"

"Or the suspect, however you look at it."

Wesley bit back a retort as he returned the pictures to Sikes. Why would he be a suspect? Because there was nobody else? That was a possibility even if the hadn't found a folder with his name. "Have you seen this diagram?" he asked.

"I don't need to see it to know it looks suspicious. They're dusting for fingerprints, testing the blood. We want you to come by the police department so we can get yours."

Wesley glanced at the other detective, who hadn't said a word. What was he, a bodyguard? He stood with his hands at his sides, guarding his gun, ready to strike.

Wesley stepped back and raised his arms. "So I'm a suspect now?" he asked.

"Should you be?"

"No, but neither am I an idiot. I don't know why he had it, but I'd like to find out just as much as you. Maybe he kept a file on all of his competitors."

Sikes shook his head. "No other file of any kind. Some bills and pictures and what have you, but nothing to indicate he was interested in any of the other racers."

"None that you found, anyway. Maybe whoever took it wanted to frame me."

"Maybe," Sikes remarked.

Wesley glanced out the window. The last vestiges of sunlight tumbled past the mountain, hope sinking with it.

"Are you going to get every racers' prints?" Wesley asked.

Sikes slammed his notebook shut, the sound reverberating throughout the vacant house. He grabbed his bag, signaled his bodyguard, and faced Wesley.

"If you can think of anything we need to know, or any reason someone would murder him for a file on you, let us know."

Wesley nodded.

"Other questions might come up later."

Wesley grit his teeth as rebellion welled inside him. He hated these stupid games. "You know where to find me."

Chapter Four

"FANS LOVED YOUR interview with Chad on the night he died. You did a great job."

"Here we go," Caitlyn muttered as she straightened a wall photo before sliding into the vinyl chair across Blake's massive desk to listen to his speech. Rumor had it the reason his office was barely decorated was because he spent all his money to secure the building's prime location in downtown Austin and the rest of his money went on frames for his wall. Six employees were cramped amongst two rooms and Blake's was larger than both of those rooms put together.

Photos and awards of past assignments littered his walls, and since the only time anyone was allowed access to his office was when they were summoned, it was a joke amongst the employees that they had to straighten one wall hanging before leaving and maybe eventually they'd all be straight. Although Caitlyn was pretty sure she'd straightened the same one several times.

Four large file cabinets bracketed two small ones, supposedly storing every article ever printed though no one had access to the cabinets and couldn't test that theory. Blake kept all his secrets behind lock and key.

"Our subscriptions have doubled since your article," Blake continued. "We've received thousands of emails and followers, fans begging for more."

Caitlyn waited, her posture rigid against the seat's edge. Blake wasn't finished.

"But people are begging us for more on Wesley. We're posting teasers on our blog, but they want more."

"So? I won't do it."

She was still plucking the nettles from her heart at her last visit with Wesley. Did he have to be so cruel? Did he have to pretend what they shared hadn't been special, at least at that time in their life?

I'm at a different place in my life. I don't need you trying to pick up things where we left off.

He thought she was after a reunion. Like she was that desperate.

The vinyl chair crackled as Caitlyn settled back and studied her boss. Blake's chair engulfed him and he sat like a reigning king. Fingers steepled, elbows rested on his massive desk. Light purple drapes and dark-colored wood complimented his imperial but sparse design, a decor Caitlyn considered hideous.

"Should I send Patricia instead?"

Blake used the trick that worked on other employees, resorting to reverse psychology to get them to do what he wanted. If *she* didn't do it, he'd send someone else. Someone else would receive the fame, the recognition, and may even gain a reward and a raise.

She wasn't seeking fame or recognition, but she could definitely use the raise he'd promised. Her rent had increased and she hated the thought of moving. The house was near enough to work it didn't take her an hour to commute. Plus, her gas-guzzling car was eight years old, and Blake was stingy when it came to raises.

This should have been an easy job. Approach Wesley, get an interview, and walk away.

"If you think she can get something none of the other reporters have managed, maybe it's a good idea."

"Some men prefer blondes."

Caitlyn brought a hand to her own coffee colored hair and twisted it into a ponytail, but let it go since she didn't have a holder to secure it.

Did Wesley prefer blondes? He never had before. "If you

say so." She was accustomed to Blake's tactics by now. "I'll give her all the information I know so far and she can go next time."

"Is that what you really want?" Blake popped an antacid into his mouth.

"Would you stop?" Caitlyn seized the bottle he'd dug out of his desk. "I don't know why you're addicted to antacids and I don't know what's worse. This," she shook the bottle in front of him, "or nicotine. You're going to kill yourself. If you wouldn't insult people and try to hurt them in the meanest way possible, you might not need these to get you through your day."

Blake muttered a curse as he replaced the cap and stored the near-empty bottle in his drawer. Sometimes, Caitlyn missed the acrid smell of smoke lacing his office.

"I'm not sending Patricia. I've already promised the fans more. You'll go and you'll write a story on Wesley after each of his races, no matter what it says. A tweet here, a picture there, minor stories on the blog with longer weekly ones for paid subscribers. Building up to something better, like an exclusive interview from him. We'll play this by ear for now but I expect it to take a least a month, maybe longer."

"He wasn't happy to see me, even told me to stay out of his life. It doesn't help that I'm a journalist now."

"Hmm, you should write about that, too. Write about his childhood. Here's your plane ticket."

Caitlyn waved it away. "No. No, I can't do it. I won't do it."

Blake ignored her pleas and dropped her stack of papers to the desk. "Your press pass and money. Oh, and I've made a reservation for you."

"Where? The Hellacious Inn?"

She'd never told him no. They battled, they talked things over, she gave him her opinion and he listened, and sometimes she convinced him to do something different, but never had he forced her to do an assignment she couldn't handle.

Until now.

"It isn't the Hilton, but it'll do," Blake said. "I even obtained Wesley's personal number for you."

"How'd you manage that?"

He shrugged. "Connections."

"You have connections yet you can't use them to get your own story, or to get a better hotel?" Caitlyn rose from the chair. She should quit. Walk out. Find another job that wouldn't punish her.

"My connections aren't enough to get me anything other than a phone number. Your job is to get more."

Caitlyn stopped and eyed a crooked picture. "You've placed me in an impossible situation. How do you expect me to do this?"

"You'll do like you always do," Blake replied. "Nobody has ever denied you before."

"Yeah, well most people enjoy the spotlight. He doesn't."

"Well, it's up to you to find out why."

***

Caitlyn unlocked her apartment and stepped inside, dumping her keys and purse on the table beside the door. She'd prematurely ended her date with her best friend, Rayma, to prepare for her trip.

Besides, she didn't want to sit there like a third wheel with Rayma and her newest boyfriend, Keegan. And who wanted to watch them bump noses and kiss all night while whispering to each other? Not her.

Although, she really needed a friend to talk to right now. Rayma would understand her anxiety and urge her to go for it. Rayma would pick up the phone, dial the number, and hand it to Caitlyn.

Rayma wouldn't give her a choice.

Forewarning might help his attitude. She'd never dare show up out of the blue and ask for an interview with anyone else, so why do it to him? She always called her subject to arrange a meeting over the telephone so both parties were prepared.

Caitlyn bit down on her breath, exhaled, and dialed Wesley's number, pressing send before she had a chance to back out.

Her pulse pounded as she questioned what she'd say.

"Hello," he answered.

Hesitating, she swiped a sweaty palm on her thigh and

prayed her voice would not shake. "Wesley?"

***

Wesley knew who it was the moment he heard her voice. Smooth like tequila going down but with an aftertaste that bit you in the ass. It wasn't her voice that was hard to endure, but its effect on him.

No woman ever caused his heart to sink so far, so fast. "Yes?" he answered.

"It's Caitlyn. I hope I didn't disturb you." She paused, and he imagined her drumming her fingers together, one of her quirks despite her grit. Then, he imagined her drumming her fingers across his chest. "Damn," he muttered, then realizing he spoke aloud, said, "How did you get this number?"

"I was wondering if we could meet up sometime after your race on Sunday, or Monday if it'd be better."

"How'd you get this number?" he asked again. This was his private number, reserved only for his team.

Caitlyn ignored him and ploughed on like she was reading a speech she'd written and rehearsed. "This is strictly professional. The magazine I work for is a weekly entertainment magazine based in Austin and the surrounding areas. Every few months, we focus on at least one, sometimes two, major celebrities and usually a mainstream personality also. Sometimes we join them in their daily schedule and write about it. If not, then we join them in whatever function they will allow us and they grant us an interview on their day-to-day living."

She paused, and he detected a note of hesitancy in her voice. He didn't mean to make this hard on her, but what did she expect? Wesley didn't know what to think of Caitlyn and her sudden arrival in his life at the most inopportune time. And she'd threatened to write the story that could destroy him. How did he know she hadn't already?

Maybe she and Chad were involved with each other and were going to blackmail Wesley. He had no secrets from her since she'd been such a big part of his life. She could have shared them with Chad even knowing how important it was to keep those secrets just that—a secret.

No, Stupid. He knew Caitlyn better than that. Didn't he? Sometimes, things changed. People changed.

He'd have to ask Adam if he'd given Caitlyn his number. If not, maybe Chad had it and gave it to her before he died.

"So which one am I?" Wesley asked. He couldn't imagine Caitlyn harnessed enough evil to kill. He didn't imagine her popping up ten years later, out of the blue, with a motive other than what she described.

Unless it was true about a woman being scorned. And if it was, shouldn't he find out?

"Do what?" she asked.

"Am I major or mainstream?"

Judging by the websites out there, you're pretty major."

"Don't think that just because we know each other that I'll give you information I haven't given the other journalists."

"It's not hard for anyone to find out anything about you if they truly wanted to. The thing is, with such little information out there, it's easier for people to make up stories about you."

"You know talking with the paparazzi causes made up stories."

"I'm hardly the paparazzi."

Wesley didn't reply. Caitlyn knew his deepest, darkest secrets. She should understand why he was afraid and thanks to Chad's antics before his death, the media generally hated him.

It hadn't taken much to find out about her. She'd never been married, never had kids. It appeared her career was her life. Maybe his story was the spike in her career she was searching for. He'd be damn if he allowed his past mistakes known, no matter how much he owed her, and he feared that would happen.

Wesley shifted and pulled the phone a fraction from his burning ear. Her breath fluttered through the line. He shut his eyes, imagining her breath on his skin, and swallowed.

"Humor me, Wesley," Caitlyn demanded. "I'll come to every race for the next few weeks to appease my boss. You couldn't prevent that from happening anyway. Then you promise to meet me sometime afterward to give me a short interview, so you can prevent the wrong information from being printed."

***

Wesley thrust his right leg into the driver's side window of his black and yellow racecar, pulled his other leg through and guided his body into the cockpit.

Everyone had shared a heartrending moment of silence in respect to Chad. Colorful banners displaying 'Strong Arm' flew across the stadium in tribute.

With Adam's help, Wesley fastened his safety harness, tugging on it a few times to make sure it was as unforgiving as possible. He reached for his helmet, hooked up his fresh air blower, connected his earplugs and put on his gloves—all a customary procedure by now but one done with careful precision. His crewmembers' diligence outside ensured nothing went wrong.

Wesley closed his eyes and shook off the images of Caitlyn, Chad, his past life, his fears, and a murderer on the loose. Now was no time to allow interferences.

He opened his eyes and petted the steering wheel. "Come on, baby."

A disembodied voice came over the loudspeaker. "Gentlemen, start your engines."

Wesley flipped the ignition and his 750 horsepower engine roared to life. The hum of the motor rumbled his gut and the odor of the engines plugged the air. A protective cocoon enshrouded him and he pulled on his safety harness one last time.

As he followed the pace car around the warm up lap, he held onto a deep breath, willing all his anxieties out with its release. The next few hours would be rough. If he didn't get thoughts of Chad and Caitlyn out of his head, things could get dangerous inside his cage. *Shake it off. You got this.*

His fans would expect a victory tonight, and he was going to give them what they wanted. And what he needed.

The green flag dropped and he stomped on the accelerator with full force. The track whizzed by. He paid careful attention to the turns, other cars gaining force on him, the track, and his spotter speaking to him through his earplugs. Despite everything he had to concentrate on, Caitlyn's image skittered into his head again. She was out there today, watching him race.

Racing was the love of his life. He always wanted to win. With Caitlyn, his first love, out there watching him, his eagerness to win soared.

He wanted to prove to her that he was doing just fine without her.

Chapter Five

CAITLYN SNAKED HER way through a throng of people who'd braved cold weather to watch the race. The cars whizzed by on the track, muffled by her earplugs but reverberating low in her stomach. Whiffs of concession food blubber, mustard, and vinegar mingled with grease from the track, making her queasy. Even if she had been hungry, the thought of seeing Wesley after the race left her too anxious.

She returned to her seat and watched Wesley's car. When he was in the pit stop, she zoomed in her camera's lens and snapped pictures. When the white flag was raised, she stood along with the rest of the crowd, her bag with notebook forgotten.

After talking to racing aficionados and taking notes, she had a great idea for her next article from a fan's perspective. She'd write a piece on the excitement in the air, the buoyancy from hoping the fan favorite won, the choking stench of burning rubber, the importance of at least cotton balls in the ears, and the people who braved the wind, cold, traffic and crowds.

The yells of the fans intensified during the last lap. Caitlyn stood with the crowd, screaming Wesley's name as his car flew past the finish line.

First place.

To her own surprise, she jumped up and down and hugged the two people next to her. Obvious fans of Wesley judging by the signs they carried. Pride infused her as she snapped photos of him performing his victory lap.

Oh God, this was going to be harder than she thought. She longed for the right to say "that's my man," but that right had long since passed. This wasn't just some stranger; this was the man she used to love.

Caitlyn flashed her press pass to enter the press box and was milled through the crowd. She was tiny in comparison to some of the people who vied for his attention, but was somehow thrust close enough that his presence assailed her. Colorful confetti rained down, but was soon drenched with champagne as Wesley's crew sprayed first him, then the crowd.

All but her face and hair managed to avoid the majority of the champagne spritz. She shivered, but the excitement of the moment left her immune to the effects of the cold. Wesley grabbed a bottle, took a swig, and spewed the rest over his crew's head.

A smile stretched across his face. Her heart turned over and over, like a car's engine on a cold winter day. Any fool could see how important this was to him, how happy it made him. Even if she'd never known him, his smile could make her fall in love.

Remember why you're here, she chastised herself as she reached for her camera. *You're here to do a story, to take pictures, not to drool over Wesley.*

And definitely not to fall in love with him again.

A mixture of sweat and champagne poured from his face, but it didn't seem to faze him. Her skin tingled in anticipation.

They'd be alone soon. And then what? What would she say? How would he treat her? And why did she even have to wonder?

"This is what it's all about," one of his crewmembers responded to a reporter's question that Caitlyn hadn't heard. "Winning."

"To what do you owe this victory?" another reporter asked and slammed the microphone as close to Wesley's face as possible.

"This isn't only my victory," he replied. "It's also my owner's, my teammates', my sponsors' and my fans'. I owe this victory to everyone who has helped me throughout this season and beyond, and I can only hope there's more to come. They have all helped to make this race successful."

"What do you have to say about Chad Armstrong?"

A shadow crossed his face. "What happened to him was an atrocious crime. I pray for his family and hope for the person responsible to be found."

***

Although Wesley sometimes resented the media, it was because of them some fans were able to see their favorite drivers. He owed it to his sponsors and to his fans to grant interviews. The crowd cheering for him when he was carried from his vehicle was overwhelming and filled him with fierce pride. No matter what he really was, no matter what made up his life, no matter what happened, his fans rooted for him.

Of course, they didn't know everything about the man they applauded, and he hoped to keep it that way.

The press crowd crushed each other, but somehow Caitlyn's face stood out in the crowd. She could've done anything with her life. But a reporter?

She clutched her coat. Covered in champagne, hair drenched, confetti plastered all over her. She was a mess.

And damn well the most beautiful thing he'd ever seen.

The intense pressure inside his body dominated the cold. The long day in the car and the adrenaline from winning kept him warm. He told himself it had nothing to do with Caitlyn, but that was a lie.

When his crew shuffled the press away, Caitlyn glanced back at him. Wesley nodded and motioned for Adam to bring her to him. She moved toward him with a bag propped on her shoulder and a camera dangling from her neck.

A smile softened her features. He took her bag from her shoulder, more as a way to regain his equilibrium than to ease her load.

"Congratulations, Wesley."

"Thank you." He glanced at his watch. "I have a meeting in twenty minutes but I thought you'd like to wait for me in my RV."

"That'd be great," she said.

"Follow me."

As they strolled past the other RVs, Caitlyn oohed and aahed over the impressiveness of the set-up. He had to agree it was pretty amazing. Most of the racers and their families spent at least three nights at a race track and more time in their trailers than in their homes. Some of them didn't even have homes. Christmas was over, but the wintry season still sported lights and wreaths donned the exterior.

"Here we are." He unlocked the door and stepped aside to allow her to enter first.

She stepped beside him and stopped, hesitating at the entry.

His nerves tingled with the need to touch her, flick her hair aside and taste the crook of her neck, find that familiar spot behind her ear that used to drive her crazy. Before he took that chance, she moved away.

He clenched his hands and swallowed.

She wandered through the living room and down a tiny hallway, turning her head to see if it was okay. He nodded.

"Go ahead, look it over. Make yourself at home." His voice sounded guttural, even to his own ears, but he got that way around her. Even after all this time.

Trailing behind her, he watched as she touched his things and imagined her hands on his body. She opened the door leading to his bedroom, which held a queen-sized bed and wooden dresser, then traced the dresser with her fingertips and stroked the painting on the wall.

"Wow." She fingered the luxurious comforter while he imagined her sprawled atop his bed. "This is bigger than it looks from outside."

Yeah, he thought, *wow.*

He straightened his spine against the doorway, watching her as his emotions skyrocketed. Caitlyn stood in his bedroom, looking hot with her disheveled hair trailing out of her beanie. Most of the confetti had fallen off, but a bright yellow piece still stuck to her waist.

Her gaze traveled over his furnishings, then to him. She smiled and continued her perusal. Warmth flooded him and he wiggled his fingers, chasing away the urges he couldn't afford to feel.

She moseyed out the door, and he closed his eyes after she passed him. His posture grew rigid as he fought for control. Control not to touch her, to taste her, to breathe in her scent. The scent of cinnamon cookies and spicy champagne. His stomach bottomed.

Caitlyn returned to the living room, oblivious to her effect on the house. But Wesley noticed. It was the way his bedroom changed when she walked in, like she'd stamped it with her femininity. She only touched some of his things, but he wondered if his room would ever dispel her presence.

Shaking such stupid thoughts out of his mind, he moved into the kitchen. "Help yourself to drinks and food in the fridge."

"I didn't expect these RVs to be this big. This is incredible. Some people don't even have real houses that look like this."

"You've never been in one of these before?"

"Well, I've been in RVs, sure, but not like this." Caitlyn dropped onto the couch and unzipped her boots, sinking her feet into the carpet. "Aah. This couch is more comfortable than the one I have at home."

"Don't get too comfortable."

Caitlyn jerked up and grabbed her boots, her gaze falling to the floor as she yanked them on. "Sorry. I was caught up in the moment for a second, I guess."

"Caitlyn?"

"What?"

"I was joking. Take your shoes back off."

"What am I doing here?" She strode to the table and grabbed her bag, clutching it to her chest. She stood there, gorgeous as she tore the beanie from her hair, slipped it into the bag, and ran her fingers through her mess of hair.

His body stirred. He'd like to be the one to tear that beanie from her head, to run his fingers through her hair. She kept her gaze downward, lips pursed. Guilt ate at him. He'd made her feel awkward.

"I thought we'd have a second to talk and then I'd be on my way," she said.

He stomped toward her and stopped, plucking the yellow confetti from her waist. Her gaze narrowed.

"You're here because you called me, begging me to grant you an interview. I have some sponsors and stuff I need to deal with and I'm already late. I wanted you to be comfortable while you waited on me, unless you're ready to go home."

"You just told me not to get too comfortable."

"I was kidding."

"Were you really?" She'd always been good at making him feel like a jerk.

He stepped back, away from the lure.

She twined her hair around her hand. "I want you to understand this assignment is coming from my boss. He asked me to do a story on you, so I'm following you around. That's all."

"Relax," he said, although the words were meant more for him.

"I'm excited..."

Excited? Hell, so was he. Oh, she was talking about a different excitement. What was she saying?

"I love to travel and write stories," she continued. "But I'll only report about the race, what's been going on and that sort of thing, and whatever information you care to include. But that's all. Nothing personal. I really hate that you don't trust me."

"That's bullshit, Cait. If I didn't trust you, do you think I'd leave you alone in my house?"

***

He had a point. He let her in his house then left for a meeting. She wasn't sure how to feel about that and didn't know what to do when he was gone.

He'd told her to make herself comfortable...*at home*...but she felt she was interfering just by being there. Sitting on the couch, she folded her hands in her lap and examined the quaint and simple décor. Where scores of pictures adorned her walls, his were bare.

He'd offered his shower to her, but no way. Her hair was

mostly dry, albeit frizzy, and she put the beanie near the heater so it'd be dry any moment.

This was too weird for her, this feeling of not knowing what to do. This feeling that things were normal between them, when they were anything but. For a moment, it felt like the old times. She'd plopped into his couch, and he'd swiftly brought her back to reality.

Don't get too comfortable.

Reality was they were not the same people. Reality was she wouldn't have an opportunity to talk to him like she had before their lives fell apart.

Caitlyn glanced around, trying to get a sense of what he was like now, how he'd changed. A table held a vase of picturesque flowers exuding color and warmth. A bookcase displayed books, magazines, and awards but no other personal items. Nothing to reveal what kind of person he was or what kinds of things he liked to do besides race. No pictures to make someone ask questions.

A large TV occupied the living room, a laptop computer set on the desk in the corner, and the kitchen held the basics, along with a stocked bar perfect for entertainment. She wondered how many women he entertained and a pang, fierce and hot, hit her.

Her nerves tapped along the inside of her skin, like an itch she couldn't scratch. She shot up from the couch and paced, drumming her fingers against each other. She loathed feeling vulnerable and insecure.

A light rap on the door made her jump. At first, she thought Wesley had returned and was being polite by knocking. But when she peeked outside, two uniformed officers stood side by side, watching the door.

She dropped the curtain and shuffled aside, ducking in an attempt to hide before they noticed her. Should she answer?

They knocked again and she opened the door a crack. Better to get them out of here as soon as possible. Surely when they found Wesley wasn't home, they'd leave.

"Can I help you?"

"We have a warrant to search the motor home and its premises." The officer handed over a document.

A search warrant? What did that mean?

Lord, what should she do?

She ignored the warrant. "I'm sorry. This isn't my house. You'll have to come back later."

"No can do," the burly one stated, barreling past her.

"Excuse me." Caitlyn swirled around to face the officer. "A man was murdered last week in his private trailer and you want to come in here when I have no idea who you are?"

"Sorry," the tall one, who seemed to have the most manners, stated. He presented his ID and she studied it, glancing between him and his badge. His picture swam in front of her and she couldn't concentrate long enough to figure anything out. Her mind reeled in fear and confusion.

"I think you should come back when Wesley is here."

"The warrant lays out exactly what we can do," he told her. "We'll do it and be out of your hair."

"I don't see where the warrant gives you permission to be forceful and discourteous," Caitlyn said.

"I'm sorry, miss," the man continued, but didn't leave.

Caitlyn clutched the screen door, trembling as she watched outside, urging Wesley to come home. She glanced behind her several times to watch the officers—and her back—and prepare to run if need be. Their badges appeared real, their IDs matched, but after what happened to Chad one could never be sure. She didn't know what else to do and had nowhere else to go.

"May I ask you what you're looking for?" she asked.

"Anything leading to Chad Armstrong's murder."

***

Post-race inspections sucked, at least for most people. Adam, unlike the others, thought it something akin to a sexual experience. Taking cars apart, putting them back together. It was like a puzzle, and he usually got in trouble when his hands weren't doing something. It was better for all involved to keep his hands and his mind busy.

Adam was a stickler for seeing the car was tight and official and if he so much as suspected someone of messing with the parts, he was all over them. His job was his mistress and one he took seriously.

Wesley was the kind of man he would have strived to be if his life had been different. When he first started working for the racecar driver, he didn't expect to like the guy as much as he did, but he'd grown to admire and respect him. They had worked together a few years now and Wesley never suspected Adam had been anything other than good at his job.

Everyone had a past they kept secret.

Some more than others.

Wesley had a past he wanted to keep hidden. His lips were sealed. He had no desire to tattle to the reporters no matter how they tried to beg or seduce him to give them dirt. As far as Adam was concerned, his past had no dirt. He'd just received some rotten luck in life. Having Johnson Webb for a father was a prime example.

"How're things going here?"

Adam glanced up to find the man in question. He'd taken the pretty brunette back to his trailer and Adam thought he might be getting lucky tonight. Guess not.

Wesley's weariness was unusual even for a demanding day like today. Adam suspected something else was wrong with him. Had the brunette already rebuffed him?

"Just about to tie it up. You okay?"

"Yeah," Wesley said, but his tone of voice spoke otherwise.

"Want to go have a drink?" Adam asked, thinking he might need a cold beer to wash away his troubles.

"No, Caitlyn's waiting for me."

"Is that why you're in such a hurry to get there?"

Wesley snickered. "Yeah, yeah." He picked up a wrench, fumbled with it, and set it down. He picked up a screwdriver, tapped it against his head a moment, and dropped it.

"You trying to break my tools, man?" Adam asked as his friend picked up another one.

"Sorry," he said, ditching it with the rest.

Adam packed away his tools and closed the toolbox.

"I had a meeting with a sponsor," Wesley said. "I get the impression he wants me to meet his daughter."

Adam chuckled and continued to put away his things. "You never did have trouble meeting girls."

Wesley groaned. "No, I can find them on my own. It's the people trying to set me up with someone I have a problem with."

"Wish I had that problem," Adam muttered.

"You're married."

Adam rolled his eyes, doubting he came in here just to tell him that. "Is something else on your mind?"

Wesley stood there. Whatever it was must be bothering him a great deal. He scanned the area, checking to see if anyone loitered, but they were the only two in the garage.

"I received a visit from a couple of cops the other day," Wesley said. "They found a file folder of information supposedly about me, though everything was missing except for a copy of my family tree."

Adam concentrated on keeping his mouth in a straight line, maintaining eye contact, and keeping his breath centered.

"Can you think of a reason Chad would want my family tree?" Wesley asked.

"I can talk to Gene about it if you want." Adam knew Chad's crew chief pretty well and he'd probably ask even if Wesley didn't want him to.

"No, no. I don't want to make a big deal out of it. Actually, I don't want anyone else to know."

"You know I won't say anything if you don't want me to," Adam lied.

"I know, bud." Wesley thumped him on the back. "If you can find anything out without mentioning that, I'd appreciate it."

"Not a problem."

They shook hands and Adam watched Wesley go. No doubt his friend was in some deep shit.

Chapter Six

AN IMAGINARY PACE car kept Wesley's steps to a slow crawl. His heart idled, anticipating the green flag to drop at any moment.

He didn't want to hurry. Hurrying meant he had to see Caitlyn again. She was in his RV, waiting for him. He should hurry. He should get this over with and her out of here. Before he did something *really* stupid.

Spotting her at the door, his pulse performed a stop n'go in his chest, stopping in the pit for one second to accept his penalty.

He'd loved her a long time ago. She was his first love. He'd accepted that and moved on. But seeing her again shot him with pain and regret for everything he'd lost and everything he'd caused. He'd run from her without a backward glance, but he'd been running from something far more intense than his love. He'd been running from his loss, the death of his mother, and the guilt he still held on to.

When he noticed Caitlyn clutching the door and a car parked in front, he flew toward the RV, counting all the reasons he should be angry at himself. He shouldn't have left her alone in his trailer. Not after what happened to Chad. It happened a week ago today. What was he thinking? The killer was still out there somewhere.

Could be after Wesley next. Could be in there, with Caitlyn, waiting for his return.

Maybe he was overreacting. Maybe she was just wondering

when he was going to get back. Maybe she was tired of waiting. Besides, a killer wouldn't park right in front, would he?

"Everything okay?" He yanked open the screen door and pushed past her as he noticed the officers. He wondered why they were in an unmarked car. "What the hell's going on?"

An officer thrust a piece of paper towards him. "We have a warrant to search the premises. We'll be out of your hair as soon as we're finished here."

"What?" He studied the search warrant, unsure what to do next. He didn't want to overreact with Caitlyn so near and give her any fodder for a story. But if there was ever a good time to overreact, this was it.

He should make them leave. Call an attorney. Instead, he paced and told Caitlyn this was standard procedure since someone close was murdered. But it wasn't. They found one tiny slab of information about him in Chad's trailer and now searched for a scapegoat so they could close the case as quickly as possible.

Caitlyn sat on the overstuffed couch. Pale. Shivery. He brought her a blanket and wrapped it around her shoulders, then rubbed her ice cold hands in his.

"Are you okay?"

She nodded, but he wasn't sure if she was aware of what he said.

When they were finished with the search, Wesley shepherded the officers out then returned to sit beside Caitlyn. "Hey, don't be so concerned," he said, trying to lighten her mood. "I'm not being arrested for murder." *Not yet, anyway.*

"I...I didn't know what to do." She looked up at him. Stark blue eyes dazed from shock stared at him, framed by lashes matching the color of her chestnut hair. Hair he'd sunk his face into many times in his youth though it'd changed somewhat over the years. Darker, richer, longer. Laden with the most luscious curls he'd ever seen that right now framed her oval face and tickled his arm.

He kneeled on the floor in front of her and lost his fight to touch her hair. He caught a strand and rubbed the softness between his fingers. "I'm sorry that happened."

"You couldn't control it," she whispered.

Could he? He was being investigated for murder and yet all he could think of was trailing his mouth along the crook of Caitlyn's neck. Of bringing her hair to his lips and breathing in her scent. Pushing her back against the couch and making wild love to her.

But he could do none of those things.

"You're not going to put that in your article are you? I don't know if some of my fans would understand."

She shook her head and lifted her chin, offering cherry red lips ripe for tasting.

He dropped her hair, stood and stepped back, tampering the urge to take her right there on the couch. Chances are she'd push him away. No telling what she thought of him. First his mom and now Chad? Did she consider him a killer?

"You did the right thing, Cait. Everything's fine. They're gone. They'll bother somebody else now."

She offered a fragile smile, meant to convince him she was okay. His heart twinged.

That and something else, lower.

"I need to take a quick shower and get out of these clothes. Then we'll talk."

"S-Sure."

As he showered, he stood under the spray and let the water pelt him. He imagined his concerns like marbles on a racetrack, water washing the debris away. He switched the water to cold. It hurt, but it hurt a lot less than his hard-on. Whoever claimed cold showers were the cure-all obviously hadn't had his kind. The longing to wrap Caitlyn in his arms and remind himself of everything he'd lost was almost more than he could bear.

How was he going to get this ridiculous assignment to end without hurting her? He had to get her out of his life before the situation nose-dived. Before he did something stupid enough to make him believe they could pick things up where they left off.

Wasn't going to happen. And no matter how strong his desire for her, he had to stay focused. Sleeping with her, losing her all over again, could harm the carefully controlled life he'd made for himself. Losing his mother wasn't the only thing that had almost ruined him.

Losing Caitlyn had almost killed him. He couldn't go through it again.

He braced both hands on the wall and turned the temperature up, welcoming the heat as water poured over his face and down his torso.

He would stand here as long as it took to convince himself his feelings for Caitlyn were memories—only memories—and that it was impossible for him to have feelings for her now, except friendship. Not a deep, abiding type of friendship but a here-and-now kind. He would always care about her as a person.

And what would happen when she realized the cops were here because they considered him a suspect?

Could he trust her not to write anything about the police searching his RV? He could just picture tomorrow's headlines: 'Wesley Webb Accused of Murder.'

He didn't want to believe that about her, but he couldn't afford to believe anything else.

***

"Why's your boss so hung up on me?" Wesley grabbed a couple of beers from the fridge, twisted the top, and handed one to Caitlyn. He hovered over his beer, his biceps taut and flexed as he placed both elbows on the bar and propped one ankle behind him on the stool's bottom ring.

She repressed the urge to rise up beside him so his height wouldn't overwhelm her, but she'd probably fall on her ass in her attempt to stand.

He'd taken a shower and came out wearing black athletic pants, a white t-shirt, and dark wet hair.

Dear Lord.

Water trickled down his neck and colonized his shirt, emphasizing his ripped chest. The cologne she sprayed on her sheets—the bottle of musk, vanilla, and nature she'd have to throw away when she got home if she planned to expunge him from her memories—assaulted her senses.

Calvin Klein smelled better on him.

Caitlyn lowered her gaze, took her pen and clicked it open once or twice, swinging herself back and forth on the barstool. Even after all these years, she'd sprayed his cologne on her sheets, claiming it helped her sleep at night. *God, what an idiot.* No wonder she wasn't over him yet.

"Blake is infatuated with racing." She stopped spinning her chair and opened her notebook to write today's date. It was a start. "Off road, drag racing, stock cars. Even motorcycles. You can imagine his excitement when he found out I once dated Wesley Webb, the elusive race car driver."

"How did he find out about us?"

She glanced up and his gaze slammed into hers, rocking her world. Reeling away, she latched onto the counter and swung her barstool to and fro as if she'd meant to lose her balance.

"I don't know."

"You never thought to ask?"

"Of course I asked. He didn't say, only implied it was through my school. I'd talked about going to my high school reunion, and I guess he put two and two together. I don't know."

"Why did you agree to it?"

"I need my job."

"I don't see how he would fire you if you didn't take an assignment."

"I told you earlier, Wesley, he'd send somebody besides me who wouldn't care how painful your past was. The reporters you hate so much because you claim they make up stories? That's who he'd send."

Wesley took a swig of beer. Caitlyn followed suit.

Where did this anxiety come from? She'd interviewed basketball players and movie stars and never felt this crazy flutter all the way down to her toes. Her skin tightened, reservation rebelling in her mind.

What was her problem?

She could list several reasons for her problem. One, she'd never slept with those other subjects, two, she'd never been in love with any of them, and three, she'd never been in their home, her body burning with the hope he'd take her in his arms and ravish her body.

"You want to know something interesting about me?" Wesley asked, pulling her out of her fantasy. "I drink one or two beers after my Sunday night race. Rarely any other time."

She wrote the words slowly, ignoring the shivery little tendrils of want his voice triggered. Not just his voice but his scent, his body, his gorgeous green eyes. God, it was like she was a teenager in lust for the first time. She could get lost in his gaze forever.

She finished writing and tapped the pen against her lips. "Do you realize you've never talked about yourself unless it relates to racing?"

"Why should that matter?"

"Maybe Blake sees it as a challenge, I don't know."

"So you're going to be the first to write about my past life, my past mistakes?"

"That's not my intention." She dropped the pen to the counter and wiped the condensation from the bottle, thankful for something to do with her hands besides clicking the pen or fumbling fingers. "He made a mistake when he sent me because I'm only going to report back to him about the race, your accomplishments, and whatever else you might want me to. I'm going to keep him happy by giving him good stories, but that's it."

"And why is that?" he pried.

Those gorgeous green eyes studied her, the intensity almost knocking her off her stool. She fumbled with the bottle before chugging the beer. At this rate, she'd be too drunk to finish their conversation. That might not be a bad thing.

He didn't move except to take a drink. He didn't fumble with words. He was calm. Intense, but calm. Her presence didn't affect him. And why should it?

"The past hurts me, too," Caitlyn admitted. "I would never print it without your permission. As much as you distrust me, I do care about you as a person." God, why did she say that? The beer wasn't at fault. She wasn't even halfway done with it. She took another long pull, needing to give her mind a reason for delirium.

"I don't distrust you, Caitlyn." He fondled a strand of her hair. Heat splashed in her belly and smoldered in her groin. "I just don't completely trust you."

"Oh, that makes perfect sense."

His hand fell away, thank God. His touch burned her, promising a hope she couldn't afford to consider.

"So you're doing this to avoid horrid assignments, and protect me from Blake's nosy reporters who may dig up my past. Is that it?"

"You should've been a lawyer," she muttered.

"Well, no worries, darling, I've had plenty of reporters nose into my life. I think I can handle any Blake might send."

"I need the raise. My rent has gone up," she blurted.

"Destroying my life is all about money?"

"I'm not here to destroy your life," she defended. Why couldn't he accept that?

The truth niggled at her. Should she admit her reasons? Not that she was here as a means to get over him—she'd never tell him that—but the other idea that had materialized.

"Actually, I considered asking you to let me do a biography on you one day," she admitted.

"You what?" He pushed back from the bar. His brows twitched, his jaw tightened and his chest, though covered by his shirt, appeared to be carved from steel.

She sometimes wondered if what he had underneath his chest, where his heart should be, was carved from steel.

"I have no intention of doing it without your permission."

"You'll never have it."

"Why not?"

He flung his empty bottle in the trash and got another one. He used his foot to shut the refrigerator door and leaned against it.

"You just said you weren't here to destroy my life."

"Right."

"So writing a biography would destroy me. My reputation. My career. It would destroy everything."

"I don't believe that."

He twisted the top off. His muscles flexed as he brought the bottle to his lips. She watched his Adam's apple as he drank and swallowed the longing to taste him. He held onto the neck of the bottle with his fingers, letting it dangle by his thigh.

She did *not* look at the bottle next to his thighs. Ignored the way his pants outlined his shapely ass, legs, groin.

She weaved her fingers through her hair and tightened her fingers on her strands. "I think your fans would love you even more for seeing you're a human being with problems and mistakes."

"No. My fans would hate me."

"And I think it'd help you to talk about it."

"No."

A shadow crossed his face. She'd been wrong. He didn't have steel under his chest, where his heart should be. Maybe it was just rubber, taut and unbending at times, vulnerable to fractures at other times.

She dropped the grip on her hair and let her fingers fall to the notebook, grabbed a page, and crinkled the corner. She'd said too much. He wasn't ready for this. She wasn't even sure she was ready for this.

"You're using Blake as much as he's using you, aren't you?" Wesley drained his beer and tossed it in the trash. "You want to become a famous author and make a lot of money, possibly quit your job so you can write. Your boss merely wants information about the elusive race car driver."

"It has nothing to do with becoming famous and making a lot of money. If I wanted to do that, I could have done exactly that. And technically, I'm not a reporter. I'm a journalist for a very popular magazine and one I'm proud of. I don't report on the news, I write personality pieces. True ones."

Wesley rolled his eyes and sidled next to her at the bar. He didn't sit. She looked away. "As true as your subjects say they are."

"What is your deal with news media anyway?" She whirled her chair around so her knees were even with his upper thighs. *Big* mistake. He stood in front of her, his already powerful body looming over her. Her legs parted, her feet rested against the bottom of the chair. And all she could think about was pulling him into her.

In between her legs, where she burned for him.

"News media?" he scoffed. "It's all about sensationalism. Most of the ones I've met are corrupt. They'll lie, cheat, probably even steal to get their story. They end up hurting people to get what they want and they just don't care."

"We're not all like that. I don't mean to hurt people, but there are some stories out there people deserve to know about."

"Like mine, for instance."

"Your fans care about you. They want to know more about you."

Wesley didn't reply. He didn't need to. The intensity of his gaze made his opinions on the subject clear.

Wesley closed the gap between them, leaned forward, and stopped just shy of her lips. His strong arms caged her in. Her back pressed against the bar. His breath, warm against her check, incited chills along her nape.

"I've always wanted to write a book," Caitlyn blabbed. At least if she was talking, she wasn't focusing on him, on the now. "Something fantastic, something startling, something everyone just *has* to read."

"Yeah, like my biography," he bit out.

"Unfortunately," she continued, trying to ignore the essence of him and the sucker-punch of his scrutiny. Her pulse tripped so hard, she was sure he would hear it. "I have to have a full time job to support myself. You know, a house, food, clothing?"

"Well." Wesley's gaze dipped across her skin. "I don't know about the clothing part."

Her body flamed hot. Neither of them moved. What was he trying to do anyway?

She glanced down, but it didn't help. Now his chest was in full view.

"And I do enjoy my job as a journalist." She pushed against him but he didn't budge. The sensation of his skin, though covered in that minuscule white tee, burned her hand. She gulped, trying to lengthen her shallow breath, and wondered if he'd worn it on purpose.

"There's more you can do with your writing skills. Like write a book."

"You could give me that opportunity."

"No." Wesley stepped away, taking her sanity with him. He rested his back against the fridge and propped one foot on the frame. Angry, jerky movements.

"I love my job," she admitted. "I've learned so many things, grown into so many things, and I've seen so many things, good and bad. Inspiring. I needed that more than you'll understand."

"Why?"

Caitlyn snatched her pen and clicked it closed, then used the tip to doodle circles in the condensation on the bar. She didn't want to answer, didn't want him to know, but she longed to talk and besides, how would she have her closure if she didn't tell him everything?

"There were a lot of things I needed to learn about life," she murmured, remembering him as the friend she once had so she wouldn't feel so uneasy. The friend she could tell anything to, the first person who knew when she started her period. The friend she felt comfortable with before sex and the friend she felt passionate about *after* sex. "I couldn't deal with things for a while. I blamed myself for what happened because Samantha took her seatbelt off to comfort me. I thought I wasn't good enough for you, I thought you blamed me, too." Tears swam under her lids and her voice cracked, but she kept her head down.

"I went to college," she continued, "not only to get an education but also to be with people. *Different* people. I took self-defense lessons, to protect myself if need be, but also to learn how to focus my body and my mind away from my troubles. I took piano lessons until I realized I wasn't any good. And I worked hard while going to school. I even saw a therapist."

He caught her chin in his hand and tilted her face to meet his. She hadn't meant to tell him any of this, hadn't meant to talk about the past at all. Her body grew heavy, fatigued, and she longed for him to wrap her in his arms. But that would never happen. In the end, he'd leave. Just like before.

It'd hurt when he left. She was young, naïve, and so much in love she thought she'd die.

His hand remained under her chin and she wanted to move her head so it cupped her face. She didn't dare. What would be the point? No sense in dragging up old ghosts.

Wesley was no longer the person she grew up with. He was a stranger now.

"I'm sorry if I ever made you feel that way." Wesley cradled her chin and thumbed a tear from her eye. "I never blamed you for what happened. I've always blamed myself, not you, so please understand that."

She shrugged and his hand fell away from her chin but his gaze remained on hers. Eyes holding cavernous layers of green, allure and ambiguity. He'd found a way to hide behind those eyes, as if he always wore shades. She wished she could unveil him. Before that horrible night their lives changed, he had no bad memories. No reason to hide.

"It doesn't matter anymore," she said. Of course she didn't mean it. It would always matter. The memories would always leave a gaping hole. "I will always blame myself, but I can't let that keep me from living my life. You see, I've learned to accept myself for who I am, and I've learned to accept my circumstances for what they may be."

"Then why couldn't you accept me?"

Chapter Seven

WESLEY DROVE CAITLYN to her car and fought back the emotions he'd censored long ago. Talking about it tore him apart inside, which is one of the reasons why he'd left in the first place. He never wanted to revisit the memory of that night, to dredge up memories. Talking didn't help the memories or the guilt. He couldn't dwell on what happened, couldn't fall into that trap again.

Wesley chided himself on not being able to face accountability for his mother's death head on like some people might, but four years of law school should have been ample punishment. He enrolled out of pure guilt. If his parents hadn't been fighting about his future that night, his mother would still be alive. His dad wanted him to go to law school and when he sprung the news on them he was going to race with his uncle's team instead, Johnson was livid.

His mom wasn't as concerned and only wanted the best for her son. She always encouraged whatever made him happy, and he did not want to be an attorney.

Samantha had been in the backseat with Caitlyn, trying to console her because it was just as big a surprise to her, the girl he'd wanted to marry. All the while he argued with his dad in the front. He was driving, and driving fast because of the anger at his dad and his resentment towards Caitlyn for not supporting him.

He never blamed Caitlyn. He only blamed her for turning on him in his time of need. He blamed himself for that too, because if he was the kind of man he should have been, he would have told

Caitlyn first, when they were alone. He wouldn't have sprung it on her with his parents around. He had no intention of ending their relationship; he truly thought she would support him and go with him.

But Caitlyn blaming herself? He'd never known

He'd been too consumed by his own guilt. Remorse tightened his skin, rolling in his gut. She'd blamed herself. Never did he mean for her to blame herself.

His father had done everything he could to cover up what happened that night. Wesley wasn't sure how he'd done it, but any research in his past only mentioned his mother dying in a car accident. The reports made it appear it was a one-vehicle, one-person accident, and Wesley never admitted the truth. The first officer on scene knew. He was *there*. But nothing was said...ever. However much it'd cost for his father to cover the accident up, thinking about it sickened him.

Wesley stopped his car beside Caitlyn's and agonized over what to do next. The temptation to lean over and kiss her almost won, but she opened the door before he had the chance to move.

He snatched her arm before she could exit. He should do something, say something. He shouldn't just let her leave.

She turned her head towards him. "Thank you for the ride." His pulse dipped as she pulled away and climbed out.

He watched her leave, waiting a good five minutes afterward just sitting in his car and staring into the dark.

Caitlyn. How could he have treated her like that? How could he have left without looking back when she'd been the constant in his life? He'd been so young, so stupid. All these years she had blamed herself, and he'd done nothing to prevent it.

The past was the past. She had her life, he had his, and there was no rekindling what they once had.

Even if it had been the best thing that ever happened to him.

***

Wesley carried the last of the boxes into his house and placed it in the corridor along with the others. Movers had already come and gone, but he chose to bring these up himself.

The scent of construction tickled his nostrils, and he reveled in the clean fresh smell. His nerves throbbed in excitement at his first night in his brand new home.

Roaming the house, he stopped to admire the immense windows drawing the outside in. The windows offered such an amazing view that he could imagine he was stepping in the snow that laced through the mountains, could sense the cold on his cheek.

Stepping outside, he checked the pork searing on the grill. The air was crisp and tight, but the news cautioned a wintry weather mix for later this evening

He lumbered up the stairs that snaked the side of his house to the deck outside his bedroom. Although he didn't need such a big house for himself, maybe one day he would. It'd be a great place to raise children, even though children never crossed his mind until now. Now, when he was about to hit the thirty-year mark, he wondered what it would be like to come home to a family of his own.

Opening the door to his bedroom, he jogged down the stairs, fetched a box, and proceeded up again. Back and forth, moving boxes from out of the corridor into their respective places and imagining ways to make his home cozier. He found his trophies, old and new and ones since high school. His mother had saved them, insisting he should always remember his accomplishments. He sat on the floor, lifting trophies out of the box, and stopped at one he'd received for track.

Earning that trophy had been a cornerstone for him. It'd been the day he'd finally decided running wasn't for him, track and field wasn't for him, and law school definitely wasn't for him.

He was an auto racer, through and through.

A knock at the door startled him. He dropped the trophy into the box, stood, and jogged downstairs.

He opened the door and frowned when he recognized the officers, Sikes and Brew. "Can I help you?"

Sikes flashed his badge and a piece of paper.

Fuck.

"We have a warrant to search this house and the premises."

Wesley swallowed the air that furled in his cheek. They hadn't found a suspect. They were still looking at him. "What?" He clutched the door tighter and took the warrant from the detective. Words swam in front of him. The first time worried him but not too severely. This time had to mean he was a potential suspect, probably because they had no others.

"If you'll move aside, Officer Brew and I will get started."

Not knowing what else to do and having no other options, Wesley stepped aside. Dread fissured cold in his blood. "I just moved in today and I'm not all the way unpacked yet."

"This won't take long."

"I'm calling my attorney," Wesley said.

"Go ahead. Won't stop us from searching your house, though."

The officer thumbed through one of the boxes that Wesley hadn't moved from the corridor yet. The box held racing memorabilia, and Wesley's gut clenched as they haphazardly filched through his belongings.

He'd play their game...for now. They wouldn't find anything here. But in the back of his mind, worry gnawed at him. They'd found enough to secure two search warrants: one for his RV and one for his home. It was time to stop ignoring the problem.

He called an old friend from law school. Jacob had gone into criminal law and they'd kept in touch over the years. Jacob promised he'd look into things for him, but Wesley had a hard time trusting anyone. The last thing he needed was the media alerted about the search warrants.

Pissed him off. This wasn't the way he wanted to spend the first day in his new house. Though he'd still spend most of his time on the road and in his RV, this was his home, built with his hard-earned money, something to relax in and enjoy when he wasn't working. And these officers were tainting it with bad memories.

After Sikes glanced through a box laden with DVDs and video games, Wesley took the box into the den and unloaded them. He rarely had time for television, but lounging in a dark room with a movie or video game was one of the best ways, besides sex, to relax.

One of the officers tromped upstairs. How much should he trust them not to plant evidence, anyway? He didn't trust them. Didn't trust anyone at this point.

"Mr. Webb?" Wesley unfolded his legs from their position on the floor.

"Yeah?"

"That'll be it for now," Sikes said.

"Find anything of interest?" Wesley asked, making sure to express his derision.

"We'll keep in touch."

***

The sun gleamed with hatred for the cold, touching everyone with vivid warmth at an attempt to melt the last vestiges of snow. The wind whipped Caitlyn's coat open as she hastened to the rental car.

She dug in her purse for Wesley's address as defrost began its work. The car idled as she entered the address in GPS, then made her way down snow-slicked streets.

The scenery of cars and buildings soon became trees and mountains. Patches of snow covered the roads outside the city limits and her slow drive gave her a chance to revel in the greenery of the pines and the picturesque beauty of the mountains.

Snow was rare in Austin, and if the city was blessed with it, it lasted only a few hours and rarely more than once every few years.

She turned onto a mountainous road and up a gradual incline. White ornamented the trees, the thread thickening as the elevation climbed. She longed to get out and play for a while, to feel the soft powder on her hands.

As she drove, she second guessed her bravado. *Turn back,* she thought as the roads narrowed. She fought her way up through vales of trees. Canyons plunged beyond her sight until another mountain picked them up on the other side. If the car slipped off the road into the gully below, she'd never be found.

How far up this mountain did he live? GPS alleged ten more minutes but at her pace, she doubted its accuracy. She shivered as images of her car buried deep in the snow with her in it anchored her mind in doubt.

She wasn't confident in her ability to drive if the roads got worse. She tried one last time to reach him on her cell, but he still didn't answer. *Shit.* Adam had told her Wesley was home today, but what if he wasn't?

Flakes of snow fell as she spotted a house in a clearing of trees. She parked in the driveway, praying it was Wesley's home. He had company and smoke rose from the grill, indicating he was cooking barbecue. Caitlyn, suddenly uneasy in her decision to come here, sat in the car.

Two men emerged from the house, with Wesley right behind them. Although they wore plainclothes, she recognized the badges hanging around their neck.

Wesley glanced her way and frowned. She shut off the engine and opened the door, stepping out as Wesley shook one of the officer's hands. She stood by the door a moment, waiting for him to finish his conversation and using the time to study her surroundings.

More cops? She didn't understand.

He couldn't have chosen a better site for his new home, creviced between gently sloping hills plunging into deep fertile valleys threaded with silken snow. Pine trees loomed above, ahead, and beyond her scope and fragments of diamonds brushed the vegetation in all directions. Crags of foliage and blue skies reached out to her.

"What are you doing here?" Wesley asked, striding over to her as the officers left.

Even in the face of adversity, he was stunning.

"I'm sorry to show up unannounced. I tried to call. I hope I'm not imposing." She indicated the SUV leaving and saw that, even though there was no light bar up top, police insignia blazed the door.

Wesley turned and loped to his covered deck, opening the grill to check whatever was underneath. Her stomach gurgled at the scent of orange, ginger, and pepper.

Squatting, she picked up a handful of snow and crumbled it between her fingers. "Smells good, whatever you're cooking."

"Dinner," he snapped.

She shouldn't be here. She knew she shouldn't be here, and he obviously wasn't happy about it. She rose to her feet and strolled towards him, clutching a ball of snow in her hand, snow crunching under her feet and the melodious chatter of birds the only sound. No traffic, no sirens, no voices maiming every space. "Like I said, I tried to call several times," she continued, intending to make things better with an apology.

Wesley shrugged and flipped the meat. "Since you're here, you might as well stay for dinner. I'll grab another potato from the house."

He closed the grill and walked inside. Caitlyn dropped the ball of snow to the ground and wiped her hands on her jeans before following him inside.

"My house was finished this past week," he said. "I'm still working on moving in."

"It's beautiful."

She stepped across a snow-white tiled entry, bordered by a dark green area rug. Large picture windows highlighted the shattered rays of the sun.

"Beautiful," Caitlyn said. "Plants would love this area."

"I don't have time for plants."

Ignoring his attitude and determined to make the best of this situation, she followed him into the kitchen. Admired the vibrantly colored stone countertop as she deposited her purse on it. With the news she was about to give him, his attitude would worsen.

Windows loomed all around his home, creating a magnificent view of the world outside. The kitchen and dining area was bare save for a wooden dining table, two barstools at his kitchen island, and a few unpacked boxes set against the wall.

"How long have you been here?" she asked.

"Today's my first day. The house was only finished last week."

"Oh." Caitlyn retrieved the newspaper from her purse and handed it to him. Might as well get down to business. "I thought you might want to see this."

Wesley snatched the paper and paled as he read the headlines.

"I'm sorry," she continued. "I had nothing to do with that. I don't know how the media found out about the search."

Wesley tossed the paper on the counter and opened the refrigerator to fetch a potato and a bag of salad.

"What were those officers doing here?" Caitlyn asked. "Were they here to search your house like they did your RV?"

Wesley ignored her as he sprayed butter on the potato, pierced it with a fork, and wrapped it in foil to be placed on the grill. "Can you get the bag of salad?" he asked, grabbing a bowl. She followed him outside as he placed the potato on the grill and took the salad from her. He opened it and poured it into the bowl, never glancing at her once.

"Are you pissed at me?"

"I'm just really stressed right now." He snapped the lid on the bowl of salad and placed in on the outside table. She stood beside him as he stirred a fire in an outdoor fireplace.

Tension rose, radiating off him as he kept his attention anywhere but on her. His jaw clenched as he focused on mundane tasks.

Walking toward him, she fingered a wisp of his hair. Longing trolled through her belly and settled in her groin. "If you want to talk to me, you can. I promise I won't be a journalist."

When he turned to her, her pulse plummeted. Vivid green eyes captured her, thickening her blood. She dropped her hand. Her lips parted in an effort to breathe, and she caught the flicker of his eyes, the downward turn of his lips. The fire in the pit crackled, smoke billowing out of the smoke stack. They stood facing each other, watching each other, his gaze burned into hers, trailing fire across her skin. Caitlyn licked her lips. Wesley's eyes dipped to her mouth, lingered. Then, he turned and walked away.

Her neck tightened as she followed him inside. He had that effect on her. *Especially* when he wanted to kiss her. That was an expression she'd seen many times before. No mistaking it. She parked herself behind the kitchen bar, watching as he opened several cupboards and grabbed dishes and utensils before opening more cabinets, as if he couldn't remember where he placed everything.

"Yes, those officers were here to search my house," Wesley finally replied to her earlier question. "I guess it's like the newspaper said. I'm a suspect in Chad's murder."

Chapter Eight

WESLEY FINALLY FOUND a cooking pot and filled it with water.

"Why would you be a suspect?" Caitlyn asked.

"They found a file folder with my name in Chad's trailer. It was empty, save for a piece of paper with a drawing of my family tree."

"Why would he have something like that?"

"I thought maybe he just had info on all his competition." He set the pan on the stove and switched on the heat.

"Have you seen this family tree of yours?"

"No, just a picture. I've talked to the original detectives and they're going to send me a copy of what they found." He sat on the barstool next to Caitlyn. She straightened, studying him.

Wesley had a few weeks now to absorb the implications, Caitlyn only a few minutes. Her brows tightened, lips pressed together as she tugged on her ear. Was she pulling away from him? What was she thinking? Was she thinking he might in fact be a murderer? After all, he murdered his own mother, hadn't he?

That thought vanished as she fingered the side of his face and caressed his cheek. Smoothing his hair between her fingers, she cocked her head and skimmed the back of his neck in a light massage.

Her touch did nothing to soothe him. He closed his eyes, his skin cranked in response to her warmth. Tension tightened his shoulders. Her scent, a bouquet of spice and flowers, disarmed him.

It'd be so easy, *so easy*, to take her right now.

He snatched his eyes open and met her gaze. Her pupils were dilated, her gaze warm, open, trusting and wanting.

He shifted towards her, just an inch, and her lips parted. Soft, warm, ready and waiting.

Cradling her chin, he feathered his lips to hers, breathing deeply as fire stewed in his gut and burst into his loins. Her hand clenched the back of his neck and he deepened the kiss.

Her thighs slid open. He craved the touch that would bind them. She was like a magnet, and fighting to keep away from her was too painful. His hands cupped her face and his mouth remained on hers as he rose from the chair and stood between her thighs.

She closed her legs around his hips. He braced his hands against her lower back, pulling her close to grind his pelvis against hers. Exploring her mouth, tasting her, savoring.

He'd longed to sample her from the moment he'd seen her in his garage. Wondered if her taste had changed.

Fuck no. Nothing had changed. Her mouth was damned near perfection. And damned near torture. Deep longing idled in his body, ready to explode, cramping his jeans. His ears rang, a hollowness trying to be released. He felt himself sinking, sinking. He longed to sink with her.

Water hissed on the stove as it boiled over. He jumped and pulled away. She released her legs and he rushed to turn off the stove, looking anywhere but at her.

He snatched the pan from the stove and watched the steam bubble up around the pan, waiting for the fire in his own body to subside. He should've been glad for the distraction before he made a terrible mistake.

He wasn't.

He took his time searching for two cups. Emptied a packet of hot cocoa into them along with the steaming water and stirred. When he was sure his pulse had slowed and his limbs were once again steady, he carried the mugs to her.

"Thank you," she said.

He nodded. "I need to check the meat. We can sit on the deck and eat there."

She followed him, carrying both of their cups as he carried a platter and utensils. He was no longer hard, but his body still prickled with the longing to touch her.

Twilight fell, dagger-light, ironing orange flames along the horizon. The cold lanced his skin, made him forget about the heat that had consumed him.

He had to stay away from her. He couldn't make the mistake of kissing her again. She made things feel right, and things would never be right again.

"Aren't you going to ask me whether I killed him?" he asked as he brandished a knife, trying to lighten his mood and ease tension.

Caitlyn laughed. "I know better."

He lifted his lips in an attempt to grin, but weariness wore it down. He turned away to get the food and to hide from her discernment.

Chad's murderer still lingered over his head like a dark cloud. She didn't need to be involved with this.

Caitlyn was right. It wasn't hard to find information on him, considering his status. He hadn't changed his identity, only tried to erase the painful memories. Though his dad performed wonders to keep the details of that night out of the public, the possibility someone might talk always existed.

And now, with Caitlyn back in his life, trouble brewed again.

He couldn't forget. He would never forget. But damn, some things weren't worth forgetting.

***

Dusk settled over the mountain. Caitlyn worried about finding her way back to town, but she didn't want to leave. Wesley's shoulders relaxed, his smile softened. She didn't think leaving him alone to dwell on his problems was a good idea.

She curbed her fear. If the killer was, in fact, after Chad's information, maybe he would be after Wesley next. She wasn't sure how racecar drivers operated, but maybe Wesley had certain moves, certain secrets Chad kept a folder on.

Maybe his murder had nothing to do with racing. Maybe the file folder was just a coincidence. Maybe Chad had old enemies no one knew about.

Wesley, a suspect? No. No way. Was it possible his mother's death changed him? Made him vicious and uncaring and able to take the life of his opponent? No, she would never believe that about him.

They ate outside, sitting across from each other. The sun disappeared behind the mountain, casting a fiery hue across the peaks. A fire crackled in the pit but it was Wesley's heat that kept her warm, the scent of pork barbecue filling her nostrils.

She tried not to notice the way his muscles bunched under his shirt, the way night shadows lined his face and forearms.

"What are you going to do now?" Caitlyn risked asking after a bout of eating in silence.

"About what?"

"Clearing your name."

Wesley shrugged. The meat, although tasty, settled like ash in her throat.

"I've been in contact with an attorney, a friend from law school that I've kept close to. But right now, I'm just curious about this family tree. I mean, why would this be important? I have a lot of questions now." Wesley laid his fork on his plate and wiped his hands. "Things I ignored when I was a kid and didn't care enough to think about."

"What do you mean?"

"I mean, we lived here in North Carolina when I was a baby. My dad left when I was three years old, I don't remember it much, just pictures. He came back three years later and begged my mom to give him another chance. Claimed he wanted to be a husband, a father, and he missed his family. My dad had been gone for three years, and now I'm wondering what happened in that time. I hope I can trust you not to write about that," he said, as an afterthought.

"Most things about your past I already know. If you don't recall, I was very much a part of it at one time. I'm here to write about you, the here and now, and the things you tell me. I'm going to pretend I don't know you and only write what you tell me."

He picked up his fork again, and it clanked against his salad bowl. "I'm telling you this."

"You're telling me this with confidence as a friend."

"Maybe I need to research my dad's life. I don't know why I feel that way, but this family tree haunts me. He was adopted, you know."

"I remember," Caitlyn said.

Wesley nodded. "You ready to go inside?" he asked, and she wondered if he was trying to change the subject.

"I'm fine," she said, though the only thing keeping her warm when she stepped away from the dwindling fire was the memory of Wesley's mouth on hers.

"It's getting cold out. Besides, I need water." He stood and gathered dishes. Caitlyn took hers and followed him into the kitchen. They placed them in the sink and she washed them while Wesley fixed a glass of water for them both.

"You don't have anything stronger?" she asked, teasing.

Wesley's chuckle stirred her belly. "I'll be glad to fix you something. I don't have a full bar stocked yet but I might have some wine."

"No, no, water's fine." She took the glass from him and leaned against the counter, watching him as he sipped water from his own glass.

"Being a journalist has its advantages, you know," Caitlyn said.

Wesley's gaze flicked to hers. "Like what? Besides getting to hang out with cool people like me?"

"People like to talk. People like their fifteen minutes of fame. Maybe I can find out what the cops think they have on you. Maybe find something about this family tree of yours."

Wesley stepped forward and braced the side of her cheek, his thumb next to her ear. His green eyes smoldered into hers. "No. I don't want you to do that. I don't want you to put yourself in danger."

She opened her mouth to speak but he shifted his thumb

over her lips and shook his head.

"There's a high probability that someone in the racing circuit killed him. They could have planted evidence to frame me. Take the top two racers out. I don't want you endangering yourself."

Her tongue darted out to sample his thumb, his face inches from hers. His warm breath slithered along her skin, brows crinkling moments before he dropped his mouth to hers. His fingers skated feather light across her cheek. He swept his tongue along hers, sucking then plundering deep.

She ignored the warning in her head that this was a mistake. How could it be a mistake if they both felt it? She bottled her memories. They didn't matter now. The only thing that mattered was him, kissing her. Now.

Sex between them had been an explosion each and every time they made love. That was ten years ago and the feelings he evoked in her now were even more intense. They were both more mature, recognized the inconsistencies and unfairness of life. Understood that everything was fleeting and nothing should be taken for granted. What would sex be like between them now?

Judging by the way he kissed her, mind-blowing.

Caitlyn knew better than to take it further. Her heart would break again and she'd be left to pick up the pieces.

Again.

Chapter Nine

CAITLYN STRODE TO the car with her hands hugged around her waist, her head ducked against the wind. Wesley followed two steps behind, the crunch of his heavy boots in the snow deepening his gloom.

He didn't want her to leave. But she *had* to leave.

The scent of barbecue basted the air. Wesley caught a whiff of it in her hair as she turned back to face him, her hair flying in the breeze.

She gripped the door handle. Her lips trembled against the coldness, and all she wore was a stupid white sweater and a long-sleeved shirt to keep her warm. Lights blazed from the house, patio lights threaded across the rooftop. The cold was almost unbearable now that they didn't have the warmth of the fireplace on the porch.

"You aren't in Texas anymore," he stated.

Caitlyn opened the door and dipped her head inside to start the car. The windshield wipers skipped across the ice.

"You have to be prepared. You have to dress properly."

She straightened out of the car and leaned against the roof rail. "I know. I'm sorry."

"Always bring layers," he continued his lecture. "Flashlights. Extra water." What was he thinking letting her leave? "I can't let you go down that mountain."

"I've got to get back," she argued.

"What's the hurry?"

Shivering, she hugged her arms, shook out her hair so that it covered her ears, then released her arms to gather the ends of her sweater over her fingers.

"Dammit, Caitlyn." He ducked inside the car and shut off the engine then took her elbow, closed the door, and led her back to the house. "Nothing you have to get back to is worth your life. The mountain gets icy, it's dark. You're staying here tonight."

He wasn't about to let her leave. The roads were treacherous enough to drive on for the inexperienced, much less in the dark, on icy roads. The storm dumped more snow on the mountains than the weather had predicted, and the temperatures had dropped a good thirty degrees between now and their earlier meal.

Wesley led her to the living room, fetched a blanket, and wrapped it around her shoulders.

"I have a spare bedroom and bathroom. You can sleep there."

She nodded her head and clenched the blanket tighter, looking downright miserable. Well, okay, so she was ready to get back to where she needed to go. But it wasn't about to happen tonight. He wouldn't let her risk her life.

He showed her to the spare room, gave her some clothing, and bid her goodnight without even a kiss on her cheek. Best not to make things worse than they already were. The cold had numbed his body, but it didn't take long for his blood to restore the longing he'd spent years trying to hide.

He could never run from his past.

***

"I'm sorry." Caitlyn backed away from the doorway, not expecting to see a half-naked Wesley when she came down to say goodnight.

She'd showered, dressed in the boxers and shirt he loaned her, and came downstairs to say thank you.

She'd been numb earlier. Numb with the cold and numb with the confliction that she had no idea what to say, what to do next. Tried not to make things awkward between them. He'd accused her of coming back to start where they left off, and that had never been her attention. She didn't want him to think that was her intention.

And now here he was.

She hadn't expected to find him on the couch, playing a video game and cussing at the TV.

Wearing nothing but a towel.

She spun around, ready to bolt. Maybe he'd forgotten she was here or, most likely, hadn't expected her to come back down. It was his house and she was the one intruding.

"Wait!" He tossed the game controller. "Caitlyn?"

"What?" She whirled around to face him. Big mistake. He was standing now. Revealing a body carved from steel. She didn't know what to think of this stunt.

A towel?

A white towel that emphasized the natural darkness of his skin. The corners overlapped but offered a tease of what hid underneath.

"I'm sorry."

She gasped at the splay of muscles across his chest, which paved down his stomach and branched into the perfect six-pack. An almost imperceptible drop of water fell from his hair.

He reached for the towel around his waist and tugged it open. She opened her mouth and stepped back, not sure if she was ready to bolt up the stairs or run into his arms. Her face flamed, and he hooted his hysterics when he revealed his shorts underneath.

"The look on your face…" Wesley crouched over, clutching his sides in laughter.

Caitlyn planted one foot in front of the other to keep from falling. She attempted to shoot daggers at him, but her pulse went *thump-thump-thump*. She deepened the frown while inside her body reeled with pleasure and anticipation.

Wesley looked damn good laughing, even if he was laughing at her. It felt good to see him laugh, and she couldn't keep a smile from escaping.

She snagged the towel and slapped him with it. "Stop laughing."

"Ouch." He stepped aside to avoid the slap, a smile still covering his face.

"That was mean." Caitlyn drew in a breath. Every nerve hummed like a grandfather clock, just ticking, waiting for the hour to boom. Waiting for him to touch her, taste her. She did not want to make the first move. She couldn't make that first move. Once she did, no going back.

But *damn*. She wanted him to kiss her, more than anything in the world. She wanted to experience him, on her, inside her, as a part of her.

"I've shown you most of my house but the important part," Wesley said, interrupting her train of thought. For a moment, she was afraid he planned to take her to his bedroom and do all the things she'd fantasized. "Follow me."

"Where?"

"The garage so you can see my cars."

He turned, indicating she should follow. She admired his back, ripped in muscles, but didn't move. "Only after you put a shirt on," she said, stopping him in his tracks.

He turned to face her and held out his arms. "Do I offend you going shirtless?"

Damn his smile.

"Yes. I mean no. It's distracting, that's all."

"Sorry," he said, but he didn't look sorry. "I'll be right back, and meet you down here."

He turned away again, flexed his muscles, and chuckled as he disappeared up the stairs. It took him less than a minute to return, this time wearing a promo shirt with his picture plastered all over the front of it. Like seeing him in person wasn't enough.

"Nice shirt," she quipped. "You sleep with a picture of yourself?"

"You know I sleep in the nude."

Her eyes flickered, mouth tightening. He always did like to provoke her.

God, she wanted him. She wanted his hard, warm hands on her body and his warm, hardness inside her body. The lonesome night would prove to be intolerable.

She seriously doubted there'd be anything lonesome about tonight. Unless he had some admirable willpower or wasn't as turned on.

"Enough fun. Come on." Wesley took her elbow and steered her to his garage. She focused on putting one wobbly leg in front of the other but had to trudge through the shatters of nerves that escaped her.

They came to a garage. It wasn't merely a two or even a three-car garage that would protect his cars from the elements, but a shop full of necessary tools and his current project.

Wesley enjoyed working on cars, driving cars, and going as fast as possible. Caitlyn remembered several times working with him in his garage and getting grease all over them. Cleaning up was half the fun as they'd go down to his pond and scrub each other until they were clean. Never mind the fact a pool beckoned in the backyard.

A few acres away revealed a pond, flanked by large oak trees and cypress lounging in the water. Oak leaves left a trail, making it difficult to be sneaky, and one time they had heard the footsteps before his parents arrived, seized their clothing, and made the appearance they'd been swimming the entire time.

Her face flushed. His parents had to have known better, but up until they were teens and didn't know how amazing sex could be, there was no reason to worry. Once they found out, they did it everywhere.

"This is my current project," Wesley said, bringing her back to the present. "Well, it's practically finished."

"Nice," she purred, ogling the lime green classic car she couldn't name. "I need to get my phone for a picture. What is it?"

"Nineteen-seventy Plymouth Barracuda."

"Do you mind if I put that in my next article?" she asked.

"I don't mind," he said. "You going to write about your night spent with Wesley Webb, famous racecar driver?"

She laughed as he winked at her, and smacked his arm. "Some of this will be very interesting to the readers. What you do in your spare time, what your hobbies are. Videogames?"

"Relaxes me."

"Will you pose for a picture?"

"Wearing a promo shirt?"

"It's perfect. Reveals your vanity."

"Vanity," he scoffed, but posed anyway.

She snapped several pictures of him before he nodded her over, then he propped the side of his head on hers and let her shoot a few of them together.

He clasped her elbow. "Come on, let's go see my workout room."

His workout room was more impressive than most gyms and held all the contraptions a person needed to keep fit. The swimming room branched from the gym, holding a pool enclosed in glass, replicas of palm trees and even a sand bar. She followed him into the swim room and toed off her shoes.

She was proud of what he had become. He worked hard to be where he was, especially after the tragedy he faced. She admired him for taking care of himself, for following his dreams. Instead of milking off his family like a spoiled little rich kid.

"Your house is amazing." She dipped her toe into the pool water and discovered it heated.

"Thank you," he said. He swaggered to her and pretended like he planned to push her in. She sidestepped him. "You want to take a swim?" he asked.

"I don't have a swimsuit."

"Never stopped us before." His voice was like warm sugar, melting in a bowl of butter—gooey and soft—with a steaming heap of rum.

She wanted to throw out all her inhibitions and jump into the pool with him, naked.

He stood so close Caitlyn smelled the mix of his soap—like a country road—and the familiar musk she'd missed. Butterflies swarm deep inside her. Caitlyn made her mind up then and there.

She was going to have sex with him.

She parted her lips.

He leaned forward and cradled her neck with his hand, his warm hands siphoning her resolve to stay strong.

Head bowing toward her, his breath seduced her cheek as

he inched near and took his slow, sweet time. Her lashes fluttered closed and she moaned when his lips hovered closer, sweeping across hers before he captured her tongue in a sensual melody.

Shivers of heat swarm up the back of her legs and burst into her core. She swayed and planted her feet deeper into the floor as his mouth plundered.

The cell phone in his pocket rang. They both jumped away.

"Fuck," Wesley snarled as he grabbed his phone and studied the screen. "I got to answer this." Turning away, he clipped into the phone, "Yeah." His shoulders slumped and he paced away. "What? When?"

Caitlyn's belly cramped as Wesley turned toward her and continued pacing, his movements slowing, then came to a halt.

"No. No" His face scrunched, brows furrowed. He lowered his head in his hand. "What the hell happened?" She stood, motionless, watching him as he listened, nodded his head, rested forehead on a palm. "Okay, thank you." He hung up, cursed, and pinched the bridge of his nose.

"Is everything okay?"

He raised his head and looked at her, but the heat of his earlier gaze was now replaced with sorrow so deep, she stumbled.

"That was Adam. My crew member, Derrick, has been murdered."

***

The warm water stroked Wesley's skin as he dove into the pool. Instead of making him feel better, it made things a hell of a lot worse.

Derrick was dead. Murdered. With a knife, just like Chad.

Derrick had been a special part of his crew, always laughing and cutting up despite the fact he was undergoing hell at home. Wesley appreciated his jokes, the way he was always able to make people laugh. His invaluable insights and ideas made his car run better. Who in the hell would want to murder him?

His wife left him months ago and he had an eight-year-old daughter at home.

An eight-year old girl who would never see her daddy again.

No doubt the cops would be at his house tomorrow, questioning his whereabouts. Caitlyn was his alibi. Caitlyn, who was now asleep in his spare bedroom. He feared for her safety. A murderer was on the loose. The longer they followed innocent people like him, the longer it kept a murderer on the loose.

It was time for him to find out what the contents of that file folder meant. It was time to dig deeper and stop depending on the cops to solve this murder. They were too busy looking in the wrong direction.

His strokes became harder, deeper, faster, and he came up for air at the last minute when he thought his lungs would burst. He tried to deprive himself of at least the pleasure of breath for as long as he could stand it.

Derrick would never have the pleasure of breath again.

The warm water tore at his tears, but the ache in his throat was a tangible lump. He tried to push reality out of his mind, but all he pictured was Derrick. He'd been stabbed, and Adam said the cops guessed it was someone he'd known because there was no forced entry as in Chad's RV.

Wesley didn't believe in coincidence.

Chapter Ten

THE ONLY FINGERPRINTS found in Derrick's home were his own. He lived alone, was going through a divorce, and didn't have much company. With it being cold out, it wouldn't be abnormal for a visitor to wear gloves.

The racing community attended another funeral, but this one was smaller and more personal. Wesley liked it that way, though it was harder to disguise his grief in a smaller group. The media packed into the back and, like an insult to the man and his family, flashed their cameras.

Caitlyn stood among them. It was hard not to notice her, but he didn't offer her a seat. The article she'd written after Chad's death had been touching, and Wesley expected the same for Derrick. She'd already talked to a few of his crew members about Derrick and confiscated some pictures from them to share in the magazine, but he wouldn't share his grief or let her share it with his fans.

He just wasn't in the sharing mood.

He remembered another time, another funeral. The memory exacerbated today's grief. Caitlyn was in the hospital, crying because she couldn't pay her respects for his mom, but he didn't even have the strength to cry with her, to notice she was hurting just as badly, if not worse.

Tim had sat beside him then just as he was now, and the preacher spoke eloquently of another person he didn't know.

Guilt followed Wesley's life on a daily basis. He'd learned

to live with it, to almost look past it, but now it clobbered him, demanding his attention.

The cops released a statement in the newspaper about how they were investigating it to determine whether the two murders were related, but it was obvious to Wesley they were. They believed the 'person of interest' belonged in the racing circuit. They also stated they believed it was someone familiar to Derrick and Derrick had let him in his RV.

He sat as the rows emptied, studying people as they paraded by the casket to say their last goodbye. The media piled outside, waiting. He studied those he worked with closely and those he didn't know well but who were out on the track every week just like him, and wondered if the murderer was here, sitting and mourning with them. Cold rushed down his spine.

The dreaded moment came of walking by the casket and saying his good-bye. He wanted to run, to deny any of this ever happened, to hole himself in his home. But that wouldn't make any of this go away.

Why couldn't the media let them mourn in peace?

He walked by the casket, forcing his eyes to cooperate and his mind to shut off all emotion. He was used to closing himself off by now. Though his fans may love his tears, he wouldn't shed them.

The makeup artist covered the knife wound. You couldn't even tell he'd been...

God.

He swiped a hand over his face and studied the floor as he trudged away, managing to keep the tears from falling. Tim walked beside him, and the media fired their cameras as soon as they stepped out.

He cursed himself for forgetting his shades, leaving his tears and vulnerability exposed to the world.

Chin lowered, Wesley glanced up and his gaze collided with Caitlyn's. His breath shot out of him. She stood there, watching. No camera, no notebook or phone in her hands. Just her, watching him. Tears streamed down her cheeks. Time stopped a moment, save for a voltage planting a fine line between them. He wrenched away, severing their link. The media buzzed, thrusting microphones in his face, but Tim took over and performed a speech he'd prepared in advance. Wesley escaped, but turned when he felt a hand on his arm.

"Are you okay?" Caitlyn asked.

"Fine," he snapped, flinching away from her. He didn't want her here. He wanted to be alone to grieve.

She remained at his side as he lumbered to the truck, her steps staying even with his. Before he got to the truck, Caitlyn lengthened her strides and moved in front of him, shifting her body to face him. She leaned against the door, hugged her arms and locked her ankles, making herself comfortable.

His gut clenched. He considered shoving her out of the way but didn't. Instead, he let his eyes drink in her beauty, the dip of her cleavage and the way the hem of her dress grazed the top of her shapely calves. He clenched his jaw and ravished her with his eyes, doing his best to put her ill at ease.

"You'll let me know if there's anything I can do?"

"Yeah," he said, resenting her for saying anything, for giving him pity when he didn't want it. "But I already know there's nothing."

"Yo, Wes, get the truck ready," Tim shouted from a distance. He turned to see Tim hurrying their way, the media hot on his tail.

Wesley gripped Caitlyn's elbow. "Get in." He opened the door and nudged her inside.

Caitlyn shifted herself to the passenger side and locked the door. Smart woman. He cranked the truck and waited. He should have left Caitlyn outside to deal with the paparazzi, but a strong urge to protect her outweighed his need for privacy.

Tim's face flushed as he crawled into the back seat and slammed the door. "What's she doing here?"

"Couldn't leave her out there with those wolves," Wesley said as he drove the truck past the mob and onto the highway.

"Why not give her a taste of her own medicine?"

Caitlyn swallowed. Tim was being unfair, but she let him have his say.

"You couldn't have picked a worse time to be here," Tim

chastised Caitlyn. "Wesley's stressed enough as it is. He just lost a team member, a friend. He has to worry about proving his innocence and about what you might be writing in your damn magazine. He doesn't need your stress, too."

"I haven't written anything in my magazine—"

"Yeah, that bullshit about his RV being searched couldn't have come from you."

"Tim," Wesley warned.

Tim ignored him. "What happened that night screwed up his head," Tim said, referring to *that night*, ten years ago. It was a title now, and no one wanted to refer to it in any way except *that night*.

That night he killed his own mother.

Tim continued. "It's like, when he goes out to race he goes back to that night and tries to correct the mistakes he made by controlling his car. He does a damn good job of it, I might add, and he doesn't need you to screw it all up again. He's learned to live with his guilt and you bring it all back."

"He shouldn't have to learn to live with his guilt because he has nothing to feel guilty about," Caitlyn responded.

Wesley tightened his fingers on the steering wheel as he entered the interstate. He had no idea where it was going. He assumed Caitlyn's car was still at the funeral home and he wasn't about to go back there.

"He ran away from you before, why did you decide to follow now?"

Tim crossed the line. Wesley signaled off the interstate to find a safe place to park, choosing a gas station, and let the truck idle.

"You both need to calm down and talk about this like rational adults. Caitlyn, you're doing a story. We'll talk on a weekly basis if need be, I'll help you if you want to write about any of my crew, but it will not be that gossip shit other magazines print." Wouldn't that be the easiest way? Help her, get rid of her faster. "Tim, you need to accept that Caitlyn will be hanging around for a little while. You can show her the ropes. We'll all act like professional adults."

Yeah, professional, even if all he thought about was getting her in his bed.

"You know, I wonder if you casting blame isn't fucking him up worse." Everything he'd just said ignored, Caitlyn grabbed the door handle and shoved the door open. "You both need some serious counseling."

***

Caitlyn stepped outside with no thought of where she'd go. She'd call a taxi if need be but would not sit in that truck a second longer to be abused, verbally or otherwise.

"Caitlyn, wait." Wesley hopped out of the truck and clasped her elbow before she made her way into the gas station. "I'll drive you back to your car."

"No thanks." She broke away and dug in her purse for her phone.

"Look, I agreed to help you with your damn story. That doesn't entail you stalking me."

She whirled around. "I'm not stalking you."

"You were at Derrick's funeral."

"Covering a story."

"Pow-wowing with the paparazzi."

"God," she muttered, wheeling away and dialing a number, any number, in a cell phone that wasn't picking up shit.

"Get in the damn truck. I'll drive you back to your car."

She gulped, fought back tears, but did not move. So her cell phone wouldn't work. She'd use the station's phone or borrow a phone but refused to stand out here another minute with him. Her feet would not move. She was angry, *so angry* and afraid she was going to cry at any moment.

Caitlyn pivoted around to face him. "Tim is such an asshole." She swiped at a piece of hair falling into her tears. She hated herself right now for letting her emotions get the better of her.

"He doesn't mean to be," Wesley said. "He's always been a little over-protective of me."

"Yeah," Caitlyn scoffed. She doubted Wesley would ever defend her against his uncle. She wasn't important enough for that.

"Let me take you back to your car," Wesley said as he touched her elbow.

Her posture tensed. She glanced at the vehicle to see Tim with his head bowed, fiddling with his phone. A strong urgency to walk away overwhelmed her, but she didn't.

"No, thanks."

"Look, Tim can be a little intense," Wesley acknowledged. "He forgets you don't have the power to hurt me anymore."

Caitlyn's blood fired hot before draining to her feet. A sound escaped her and she wrinkled her nose and turned away.

"Caitlyn," he called. "Come on, I'll take you back"

As if she'd spend any more time with either of those men. She delivered a dismissive backward wave and responded, "No, thank you. I'll make my own arrangements."

Chapter Eleven

CAITLYN KNOCKED ON Blake's door, didn't wait for a reply, and entered, but hesitated when she noticed someone on the other side of his desk.

Blake shot up from his chair, looking guilty.

Should've knocked.

"Sorry," she said, ire burning her feet into the ground. "I didn't know you were with someone."

She lingered by the door and eyed a crooked picture, but didn't bother adjusting it. The visitor turned around and her world plummeted.

Johnson Webb.

Her body sagged against the door. She clasped the handle in an attempt to remain upright. Her mouth grew dry, palms sweaty as she gaped at the men.

Wesley's dad regarded her as if they were old friends and he was happy to see her.

"Johnson?" she croaked. What was *he* doing here?

"Caitlyn, how nice to see you." The room shrunk when Johnson rose. He strolled over to greet her, all casual-like as if their meeting was an ordinary occurrence.

She couldn't move, couldn't even accept his handshake. He took her sweaty palm anyway and covered his warm hand with hers. She was too numb to notice anything else.

Johnson dropped her hand and turned to Blake, who had his forearms planted against his desk to hold himself upright. "I got to run, but we'll catch up later."

"No. No." Caitlyn shrunk into the door, preparing to bolt. "You go ahead and finish." She was too shocked to say anything else.

"I can meet up with Blake later," Johnson said. "I have some things to do now. Good to see you." He thumped her on the top of the shoulder in an awkward hug, then moved her aside and opened the door, leaving just a memory of his presence.

He walked down the hall before she closed the door and propped against it.

"That was Wesley's dad," she whispered.

"You interrupted a very important meeting," Blake said. "Haven't I taught my employees to knock or buzz me before entering?"

"What was Wesley's dad doing here?"

Blake turned away from her and stared out the window, the horrid purple drapes pulled aside and tasseled by a thin twine.

She held up the papers she'd written last night, totaling close to fifty pages, and flapped them his direction. She'd gotten home last night to find a new assignment in her email and had stayed up all night to write two stories.

"Here's the article on Wesley. And the one on single life, which any person in this office could do. But why not choose me? It's not as if I don't have a billion other things on my plate."

"You know you're the best writer here and you've always been able to handle the work load before."

Caitlyn flung the papers to his desk and sat. The vinyl crackled as she tried to find comfort in a chair that seemed to be carved from stone before being sandblasted with plastic.

She pointed her thumb at the door. "Tell me why Johnson Webb was here. But first let me tell you that if I'm going to do this story on Wesley, then I refuse to do other assignments. And the next time you give me one, it's going to go undone. Period." She sliced her hands through the air for affect, but Blake didn't notice. His chest rose and fell, but everything else about him remained still.

"Now is where you tell me why Johnson was here."

Blake dropped the curtain and faced her. "He's not crazy about us doing a story on his son."

"And he came all the way here to tell you that?"

"Yes." Blake sat at his desk and grabbed the papers, shuffling them around before fumbling through his desk drawer in search of his antacids. Obviously not finding any, he slammed the drawer closed and tore a corner of the paper off, then stuck it in his mouth and chewed.

"That can't be good for you." Caitlyn hunted in her purse for a peppermint and pitched it at him. "I don't appreciate being left in the dark about this. You know this is the hardest assignment I've ever taken on, not only because the subject is a hard-ass when it comes to the media, but because it brings up my past. Not to mention, you've placed me in a dangerous situation. There is a murderer on the loose! Then, I find out you might have connections on the inside after you bring me his private cell number. *Then,* I walk into your office to see his dad sitting here."

She held up her hands in a *what-gives* gesture.

"I doubt you have any murderer to worry about."

"Really?" she mocked. "You think so?" Curling her fingers around the armrest, she scooted to the edge, her spine as straight as the pencil on Blake's desk. But she wasn't about to get up from this chair until he told her what she wanted to know about Johnson.

"That murder was personal."

"Well if you know so much, maybe we should let the cops in on it."

"Stopping being so dramatic, Cait."

"Tell. Me. About. Johnson," she commanded.

"Sit back. Relax a minute."

"I'm fine."

Blake nodded and tore another piece of paper, adding it to the one already in his mouth. "You know how I told you I started this business from the ground up, with barely any money in my pocket?"

Caitlyn nodded and glared as Blake spit the paper in the trash and fumbled to remove the candy wrapping of the peppermint. He plopped it in his mouth before he continued.

"I've actually known Johnson for a long time." He paused, expecting her to say something. But she would hear him out before she gave him a reaction. Even if she did want to kill him right now. "I needed some finances to get this business started and Johnson, being a friend of mine, was willing to be an investment partner. He didn't want control of the business and didn't want to have anything to do with it so he decided to be a silent partner. I could pay him back, but he doesn't want that, so to this day he continues to be a partner."

Her mind raced as she tried to absorb his confession. This is the last thing she would have expected to hear.

"You told me you started this business by yourself with a lot of hard work and barely any money."

"It did take a lot of hard work, and I did start with barely any money. It was my idea, something he was interested in, so it went from there. I'm sorry if you can't understand, but you wanted to know how I knew Johnson and that's how. He doesn't have any say in the going-ons of the company, so I thought it best if no one knew about him."

"Did you know about me and his son when you hired me?"

"I rarely speak to him anymore. He's left me and the business pretty much alone."

Caitlyn planted her palms on Blake's desk. "Did you know about me and Wesley when you hired me?"

The look on his face was the only answer she needed.

She shot out of the chair and paced, her movements short and jerky and self-contained. White-hot anger infused her, disbelief trailing a close second.

He'd lied to her.

He'd covered up his lies.

He'd used her.

What else did he know about Wesley?

"How long have you known Johnson?" she finally asked as she stopped pacing and clutched the back of a chair.

Blake adjusted his collar. "Since college. But we lost track of each other for a while."

"So you knew his wife?" she accused. Why not get to the point? Was he out for a story that would make his paper famous? Or maybe he was trying to blackmail Johnson into giving him complete control?

"No...no, I didn't know his wife," Blake said. "And I didn't know about you. Not at first. That's not why you got this job."

"Johnson doesn't want you to do a story on his son. Are you using me to get back at him for something? Maybe you want complete ownership of the company and he won't give it to you?"

"No, that's not it." Blake stood and went to his filing cabinet, removed a stack of paper. "You want to read more fan mail? This is why I'm doing a story on Wesley."

The letters landed with a whack on the desk.

"You didn't have those before we began this story."

"I have requests from all kinds of different people on stories, and sometimes I use those for my next idea. He's a good subject, and Johnson wouldn't shed any light on him. Mail and email have been pouring in ever since the first story. I printed each email."

"So I'm off the assignment now?" she asked, hoping and dreading of what his answer might be. "The big boss man doesn't want us to do a story on his son."

"He's not the big boss man," he groused. "And I'm not closing this out just yet. I won't disappoint the fans. That's what we were talking about. I showed him some of these letters and now he understands."

She collected the papers but remained standing, unable to react. He'd used her. No matter what he told her, he'd used her. Anger flamed down her arms as she leafed through the pages. The words swam in front of her.

Johnson, a private partner in the business, knew Blake for years now? Blake knew about her relationship with Johnson's son when he hired her? How could she ever trust him again?

Caitlyn ditched the papers on the desk. No point in trying to read them right now.

"What's going on?" There was more to the story than what he told her. The only reason Blake was in business, obviously, was because of Johnson Webb. Blake told Caitlyn he started the company by himself, with little money and lots of work. Years later, Blake wants to do a story on his partner's son, who hates the media, and Johnson comes here to tell Blake he isn't happy about it? "Are you trying to ruin Johnson?" she asked, her voice cracking. "Ruin Wesley?"

"Don't be so melodramatic. Not everything is as complicated as you make it out to be."

***

This wasn't going to be easy. Calling Wesley after she'd walked away from him. She'd hoped he would chase her this time. Lord knows he didn't last time.

But chasing would mean he cared, and he'd already made it obvious he didn't.

She had to tell him about his dad and her boss, so she called him, then sent him a message when he didn't answer. He called her ten minutes later, but his reaction surprised her when she'd told him. He wasn't too concerned, and she wondered if he had something else going on that he couldn't give her his undivided attention. He'd invited her back to Tim's Race Shop to watch him practice, and so now, here she was.

She watched as he spun his car around Tim's practice track. He and his car were beautiful, in perfect harmony.

She stood with her feet flush against the track, the closest she'd ever been. A low murmur echoed in her belly as the car whizzed around the track. She took pictures and wrote in her notebook with the intensity she felt. The sound of the engine as he drove by was almost orgasmic, but she probably shouldn't include that in her story.

That feeling faded when Tim approached.

"What are you writing?"

"Working on my assignment." She continued to write. She didn't expect him to like or be nice to her and she wasn't about to let him criticize her.

Wesley had lost contact with his dad over the years, and most of that was Wesley's doing. Caitlyn worried he'd have a new reason to distrust her.

"You want to drive it?"

Her pen froze on paper and she glanced at Tim, trying to determine if he deceived her.

"Good addition to your story," he replied. "Look, I owe you an apology but still stand by my feelings."

Licking her lips, she nodded but didn't reply to that statement. "You're right. Driving the car would be an awesome addition to my story."

Wesley stopped his car a few hundred feet away and slid out the window. "Woo-hoo," he yelled as he took off his helmet and handed it to someone. His crew slapped him on the back and gave him a high-five.

She could almost see the adrenaline coursing in and out of his body. He wore his uniform—looked damned good in it too—and lust engulfed her. Why, out of all the men here who were just as athletic and comparably dressed, was he the one her body gravitated to?

Wesley was never happier than when he was racing. She longed to experience why and Tim had just given her that opportunity.

"Caitlyn wants to drive," Tim shouted.

Wesley signaled her over. She strolled forward and set her bag on the ground. He nabbed her camera. "Got to get a picture of this," he said.

"What do I need to do?"

Wesley showed her the basics of the car, placed a helmet on her head, and helped her slide into the cockpit. She settled in, took a deep breath, and wrapped her fingers around the steering wheel. He gestured to her, mock flipped a switch in the air, and she followed suit. Suddenly, the roar of the engine was in the bottom of her stomach.

"Woah," she said before realizing nobody could hear her. The adrenaline she imagined in Wesley earlier now oozed through her. He stomped his foot on the track mimicking pushing the gas pedal and she did the same, only for real.

The car darted off and pushed her into the seat. Her heart was like the accelerator, stuck to the bottom of the floor. It felt like she was following the car instead of being in control. She breathed deeply and let off the gas as she focused her attention on controlling the car. She took it slowly around the curve, picked up speed on the straightaway, and let off the gas on the next curve until she finally got some sort of hang to it. She didn't take it nearly as fast as the racers did but got her speed up to eighty-five on the straightaway. That alone was horrifying, yet deliciously gratifying.

She came to a stop and just sat there, in awe, in complete surrender to what just happened. She couldn't move, could barely think. Wesley walked up to the car, stooped through the window and flipped the switch to turn off the ignition. He helped her climb out, his hands landing around her waist before he removed the helmet from her head.

"Oh my God." Her whole body shook and swayed as shock and pleasure exploded. Wesley clicked a picture and her smile grew wider. She noticed Adam and slapped him a high five. Wesley kept snapping pictures. "That was great."

It took a moment for sentiment to return and when it did, it was in a gush. "God, that was great!"

"Better than sex?" Adam asked.

Caitlyn laughed. "Almost."

***

"It's not exactly like that in a real race." Wesley handed Caitlyn her camera and, since he didn't have anything to clutch now, he gritted his teeth. Her smile expanded the width of Daytona Speedway and his heart beat about as fast as his car on race day. "It gets a lot hotter, especially in summer. There's no way you could run the car like that and wear that outfit."

"Oh." She glanced down and attempted to smooth out the wrinkles as if they were the problem.

"Don't worry about it," he growled. "It looks fine." An understatement. He longed to draw that skirt up around her hips and have her wrap her legs around his waist. The light lavender color of her shirt and short denim jacket brought out the depth of her eyes and the flush on her cheeks. The skirt billowed along shapely thighs and her shoes. How could mile-high shoes like that be legal?

He tore her away from the onlookers of men who probably thought the same thing he did, and led her to his private office.

Better than sex, Adam had asked.

Wesley had to fight the urge to punch Adam where he stood. Even now he had to clench his teeth together to keep from snapping at Caitlyn for laughing, like he had any control over what anybody did or said. What he ought to do is push her against the wall and kiss her. Make her forget any other man existed but him.

He'd lied last time he'd seen her. Told her she didn't have the power to hurt him, as if saying the words would make them true. He admired her grace, her self-assurance, and didn't want her to know she had more power over him than anyone should. So he tried to push her away with anger. But she remained unaffected.

This was a job to her. Merely a job. Get an exclusive and get out of his life. Maybe he should have given her one immediately so she'd be out of his life sooner. But that thought left him cold.

"Before I forget," Caitlyn said, interrupting his thoughts. She set on the chair opposite the desk and fiddled with the armrest. He'd never be able to look at the chair again and not see her. He'd never be able to sit in the chair again and not think of her. "I'm supposed to ask you about a couple of tickets to your upcoming race in Fort Worth."

Wesley scrubbed a hand over his face and propped himself against his desk. "You want to bring your boyfriend?" He cringed when his question popped out, but since the subject hadn't come up yet, might as well get that question out of the way now.

"No, no boyfriend. A good friend of mine, Rayma, wants to bring her boyfriend, who happens to be a big fan."

"Ah," Wesley said. "I can get you good seats. You can sit right behind the crewmembers."

"That would be awesome. I know they'll appreciate it."

It was like a versed event. An attempt to be normal and not awkward. But his hormones would never be normal again.

Wesley leaned against the desk in front of her. He didn't mean for it to be a power move, but oh well, he liked the view.

Grabbing his pencil holder, he rearranged the pens and markers. "I think you got a good story for your next article. You, the author, can now write about your experience and how it feels to drive a racecar. If Blake doesn't like that, he doesn't deserve his business."

"Thank you," Caitlyn said. "I really appreciate the opportunity you've given me." Caitlyn rose from the chair and shouldered her bag. "I should go get started on it. Good luck on Sunday."

He dropped the holder on the table and pushed away from the desk, feeling like an idiot. Him...nervous in front of a girl? Fuck, no. He seriously needed to get laid.

"You'll be there, right?" He wasn't sure he wanted the answer to be yes but even more unsure if he wanted it to be no.

"I'll see what Blake's plans are for me."

"Must be hard not to know from one day to the next what your day is going to bring. It's like Blake has you on puppet strings."

"Keeps things exciting." Caitlyn flicked away a piece of hair that had fallen into her face. "Don't you have that happen?"

"Making plans are impossible in this field, but I always know what I'm doing on what days. It's just what happens during that time that is a surprise. Will my car run, or will I have problems with it? Will we have to tear it all down and piece it back together? Will I even be able to finish a race?"

Caitlyn dropped her bag and grasped her infamous pink notebook. "Great quote," she said. "If you don't mind me using it."

"Of course not."

She leaned toward his desk and snatched a pen from the canister, holding it up. "Do you mind?"

"Of course not."

His lower body stirred as she licked her lips and scribbled on the pages with a pen he'd have to throw away if she didn't keep it. He shifted his feet, thanking the heavens he wore loose pants.

Better than sex. No, not in this lifetime and not with Caitlyn in your bed.

She snapped her notebook closed, stored it in her compartment, and shouldered the bag. How she lugged that thing around all the time was beyond him.

"Thanks again," Caitlyn said, handing him the pen.

"Keep it." He didn't want the damn thing after she touched it. He had a hard enough time getting her out of his head. "We need to talk about your boss and my dad."

Caitlyn brushed a strand of her out of her face with a finger, blowing the strays out of her eyes with puffed cheeks. "Yeah, I told you everything I know. I mean, I still don't know what to think about it all."

"How much do you trust your boss?"

"I've worked with him for years. I...he's a good man. So is your dad."

"Uh, huh." Wesley walked up and took her bag. She didn't give it to him, but didn't stop him from taking it either. She stood, chewing her lip, with one foot in front of the other.

She called two nights ago, upset and angry but managing to hold on to her cool, and told him about finding Johnson in her boss's office. He wasn't sure he could believe everything her boss had admitted. His claim that he didn't know about their relationship, that he wasn't doing this for any reason other than a story. Wesley didn't know what to think and he had no reason to distrust his dad. But he had no reason to trust Caitlyn's boss.

Wesley's dad might be a good man, but he preferred Johnson stay out of his life.

Chapter Twelve

"WHAT IN THE hell are you doing here?"

Keegan slathered mustard and ketchup on his hot dog with one hand while trying to hold it and a drink with his other. He hated the smell, he hated the crowd, and he hated being here just as much as that son-of-a-bitch Johnson hated him being here. Rayma was beginning to get suspicious of his motives for asking about Wesley. When he refused to go the first time she presented the tickets to him, he knew it would be his last time to see her if he said no again. One thing about the woman, she would cut herself off from any man she thought was distrustful.

"Rayma wanted me to come," Keegan said. "What the hell was I supposed to do?"

Johnson glowered at him, and Keegan couldn't help but notice the petite blondes and ample-busted brunettes ogling the fifty-something-year-old. The sonofabitch got more attention from the female gender than he did, and it pissed him off.

"If Wesley sees you–"

"Then Rayma will understand why I didn't want to come. I have it all planned. And what about you? What will you do if Wesley sees you?"

"I'm leaving. This is Fort Worth, close to my home. I wanted to see my son race."

"Yeah, close." Keegan, his hands full of junk food, turned to leave. "Four hours is close?"

Johnson disappeared on Keegan and, despite the gnawing

revulsion at sitting in the stands for hours on end, Keegan actually enjoyed himself. He was with two of the most beautiful women in the crowd, how could he not enjoy himself?

Caitlyn had grilled him with questions, but he had nothing to hide at this point. He wasn't sure he would even see Wesley because of his hectic schedule and, if he knew Rayma, she wouldn't be able to sit in the stands throughout the race, much less wait for Wesley to have time to meet them. Sitting still was not her strong suit.

It was unbelievably hot in April, but Texas weather was ever-changing. Tomorrow, a cold front was expected that might produce showers. Keegan was thankful he chose a short-sleeved shirt to wear with his long jeans, but he still had to pull the cotton away from time to time to keep the sweat from drenching him.

Knowing the schedule of a triumphant competitor, Keegan hoped Wesley would win first so his chance of seeing him would diminish. The confrontation was a long time in coming and had to happen sooner or later, but Keegan didn't look forward to it.

Apparently, he didn't know Rayma as well as he thought. She stayed throughout the race and lingered afterwards. Keegan yelled with the girls, urging Wesley on for different reasons. All hope was lost when Wesley pulled in second, milliseconds behind first-place.

Because of Caitlyn, they were able to talk to several of Wesley's team members while they waited for Wesley to emerge. If anyone noticed Keegan's growing agitation, nothing was said. He drummed his fingers against the metal handles of the steps, crisscrossed his feet while standing, then resorted to mini pacing. He wondered if Johnson left yet or if he planned on popping in for a surprise visit himself.

"Wesley, you did great out there."

Keegan braced himself, knowing his introduction was inevitable but not ready for it. He gave the ladies an 'I gotta piss' excuse and walked away.

Rayma called out for him but he pretended not to hear her. He heard her tell them he went to the restroom and would be right back.

He took his sweet time.

***

"What's taking him so long?" Rayma paced the grounds, admiring Caitlyn's patience. Rayma only thought she was being impatient until she glanced at her watch to see thirty minutes passed. Keegan still hadn't returned.

"Should we go check on him?" Caitlyn asked.

"Maybe I should. You wait here, I don't want him looking for us if he comes back and we're not here."

Before she was able to take more than a few steps, Keegan returned. "What took so long?" Rayma grilled.

Keegan clutched his stomach. "Something didn't sit well with me. Must have been the chili dog I ate. I think I should go back to the hotel."

"We have keys to Wesley's. You can rest there." Wesley had to take care of business with promises he'd get there as soon as possible and had given Caitlyn the keys so they could wait.

Keegan seemed almost pleased that Wesley wasn't around.

They sat on the couch in Wesley's impressive RV, too afraid to touch anything in his house. He was nice, nice looking, and didn't seem to mind handing the keys to Caitlyn. Rayma noticed the gleam in his eyes when he looked at Caitlyn and the flush on her face when she smiled back.

Just as she was having second thoughts about being here, Wesley walked in. This time, Keegan couldn't hide in the bathroom because Rayma clutched his hand in hers.

Caitlyn rose and thanked him for allowing them to wait for him in his trailer. Rayma said her hellos and was just about to stand and introduce Keegan when Wesley glanced at him. His face fell, mouth slackened, a pallor similar to Keegan's overrode his previous smile.

Something was wrong.

She let go of Keegan's hand and rested one knee on the couch to keep from falling.

"What in the hell are you doing here?" Wesley asked.

"You invited me."

"This is your boyfriend?" Wesley's heated glare pierced Rayma before turning back to Keegan.

"Apparently you already know him." And apparently, as before, she trusted a man she shouldn't have.

"He's my stepbrother."

"What?" Rayma lost her balance and had to stand upright. That proved difficult as reality imploded within her. She glanced at Caitlyn for reinforcement, but her friend was just as shocked.

"Sorry." Keegan grinned sheepishly and remained seated. Rayma wondered how sorry he truly was about lying to her. He'd been infatuated with Wesley, said he was a huge fan, and never once did he mention they were even remotely related. He'd had ample opportunity. "I should have told you sooner."

"Why didn't you?" Rayma didn't have to ask. Wesley did it for her.

"I didn't think I'd ever see you again," Keegan informed Wesley, finally standing as if sitting was dwarfing him. It probably was. Even standing, Wesley was taller. "We met a couple of times when Johnson married my mom but didn't get along that well." Keegan turned to Rayma. "And I hated Johnson. Didn't think he was worth mentioning."

Was the world that small? Was Keegan using her to get close to his stepbrother?

No, the idea was ludicrous. How could she even think that? How would he know she was the best friend of Wesley's ex? Even still, Wesley and Caitlyn hadn't spoken in ten years. Rayma wasn't sure what to think. Coldness surrounded her.

Caitlyn converged behind her and planted a warm hand on her shoulder.

"We never got a chance to know each other," Keegan continued, speaking to Wesley. "I didn't want Johnson or the way you feel about him to prevent us from liking each other."

"So you show up all of the sudden, when all this other shit is going on in my life?"

Keegan shrugged. "I'm sorry. I wasn't aware of anything going on in your life. I know I should have called but do you know how impossible it is to get in touch with a celebrity? When Rayma presented me tickets to see you with the chance of meeting you through her friend, I jumped at the opportunity."

"I bet you did," Rayma said. "Using me to get to him."

"Why would I do that?" Keegan gawked at her. His face was long but finally held color, as if the stress of seeing his stepbrother had finally been confronted and it was okay to breathe again. It made Rayma feel somewhat small, wrong in assuming this situation was strange.

"You just said it was impossible to contact him," Rayma accused.

"It is, but I had no idea you happened to be a friend that happened to go to school with Wesley and just happens to be working on a story on him at the time. Pure luck on my part." He cradled her chin. She kept her expression blank. "I'm truly sorry. It was an awkward situation and I handled it poorly. I didn't know how to handle it."

Rayma wrenched away. Caitlyn grasped her hand and led her to the bathroom where only then, in the sanctuary of her best friend's embrace, did she cry.

"I don't know how I feel about this guy," Rayma hiccupped through her tears. "Things have been happening so fast. But just once, I want the truth told to me."

"Maybe he is telling the truth."

"Does it sound like it?" Rayma pulled herself off of Caitlyn's shoulders and nabbed a tissue.

"Rayma." Caitlyn gripped Rayma's shoulders with her hands and gave her a slight shake. "You wouldn't believe it even if it was the truth."

"Am I that bad?" she asked as she blew her nose.

***

"You have to believe me."

Keegan appeared downright browbeaten. Wesley didn't know Keegan well enough to know what to think, but if he didn't have the balls to tell Rayma, did that mean he was hiding something?

No. Wesley knew all too well the reasons for secrets and continued to keep them today.

Keegan and Wesley's relationship had basically been nil. Johnson married Keegan's mother too soon—in Wesley's opinion—after his own mother was killed. They'd met after Wesley graduated from law school and decided to give it up for racing. This time professionally. Keegan had been in law school at the time and Johnson was proud of him. He'd always wanted his son to follow in his footsteps but Wesley hadn't been that son. Johnson again tried to lecture Wesley on racing, making those memories of the night his mother died more potent than ever. His dad didn't support him and told him of how Keegan was doing the right thing and Wesley should learn from him. He'd cut himself off from any relationship with his dad.

It'd been over six years. He hadn't seen or spoken to Johnson in that long. Now he finds out Caitlyn's boss is a business partner with his dad and Caitlyn's friend is Wesley's stepbrother's girlfriend.

It made Wesley sick to his stomach. He didn't believe in this many coincidences.

"I really love this girl," Keegan said. "She's so damned suspicious of everything. I don't know what the last man in her life did to her, but I'm the one paying for it. She keeps secrets, too."

Chapter Thirteen

WHEN CAITLYN AND Rayma stepped out of the bathroom, Wesley and Keegan were drinking beer and playing cards.

"Care to join us?" Wesley asked, shooting slow shivers down Caitlyn's legs. He had to be exhausted after today and the last thing he should be doing is entertaining her friends, even if one of them was his long-lost stepbrother. "There's beer in the fridge and wine in the cabinet. If anyone is hungry I can fix us something to eat."

"You've been working all day," Keegan said. "The last thing you should be doing is worrying about feeding guests."

"I've been racing all day. That's hardly work."

"You really love it, don't you?" Keegan asked as he exchanged one card for another.

"Absolutely. Driving fast cars all day? What's not to love?"

"That type of concentration seems like it would get exhausting."

"Sure, it is exhausting."

"If we're intruding—"

"You're not intruding," Wesley assured Keegan.

Caitlyn's gaze roamed over Wesley, drinking in his relaxed posture and tousled hair. Her fingers tightened at her sides as she repressed the need to drum them together. She'd rather drum them across his chest, slide into the seat next to him and rake her nails over his body.

God, she was the one exhausted. Daydreaming about things

that would never happen. Could never happen. She wasn't here to pick things up where they left off. She was here for a story, nothing else. Except a purging of emotions. And having sex with Wesley wasn't going to do that.

And Keegan? Yes, this whole situation was strange, but she tried to give him the benefit of the doubt. He kept clearing his throat and rearranging his cards as his gaze darted between Wesley, his cards, and Rayma, who stood stock-still beside Caitlyn with her arms crossed.

She didn't know that he was on the up and up about everything, but found it hard to believe that he would date Rayma just because he wanted a chance to see Wesley. Maybe fate had opened this door for him, not that she believed in fate but if she did, she could believe that's what happened.

Wesley's acceptance of the situation swelled her pride. He was so calm, so accepting after his initial outburst. Tears burned her lids. No wonder she'd never stopped loving him.

Keegan laid down his cards. "Looks like you win another hand."

Rayma's forehead bunched and lips tightened when Keegan rose and strode toward her, but she didn't push him away when he wrapped his arms around her. Settling his chin on her head, he muttered low in her ear.

"Excuse us a moment," Keegan said as he led Rayma outside.

Once they were outside, Caitlyn exhaled loudly and sat at the table across from Wesley. "I'm so sorry about that."

Wesley shrugged and shuffled the cards. "No worries."

"I know you must be exhausted."

"I wouldn't be able to sleep. This is good downtime."

"Playing cards with a stepbrother you never liked and dealing with my friend's drama is good downtime?"

Wesley's mouth lifted in a mock smile and he glanced at her and winked before dealing the cards. "It's not that I didn't like him. We just didn't have an opportunity to like each other. Not really. Bad timing and all that."

"I see." Caitlyn didn't see. Not really. Wesley was downplaying his emotions, but now wasn't the time to push. She had no right to push.

"It is a little awkward," Wesley admitted as he glanced at the cards he'd dealt himself and frowned.

Caitlyn picked up the hand he'd dealt her and stifled her grin when she spotted two aces and three tens. "That's an understatement."

Wesley nodded and studied his cards.

Might as well make the best of this situation. "What are we playing for?" she asked.

"I still want that Janis Joplin record your mom gave you when you were fifteen."

"And I want that Cuda you've got parked in your garage."

"That's a hard bargain."

Caitlyn shrugged. She'd never take his vehicle over a winning hand, no matter how tempting. "Maybe just a drive then."

"Fair enough."

Caitlyn laid down her cards. Full house.

"Damn woman. You're not even going to give me a chance?"

"Nope. I want that ride."

Wesley dropped his cards. A jack, eight, nine, three and an ace. Caitlyn laughed as he whisked them away and shuffled again.

"Two out of three," he said.

She picked up another hand and her two tens won over his hand of nothing.

"Guess we better plan on a time when I can take that drive. Oh, and don't forget, I will be the one driving."

"What game are we exactly playing here, anyway?"

Caitlyn shrugged. They'd grown up playing this game together. "I dunno. I thought you made this game up."

"The one I made up is the one where I always won."

"Hah. That's because you always cheated."

Wesley's eyes narrowed. "Me? Never. I just wanted to see you naked."

Caitlyn let out a throaty laugh as heat slithered under her skin.

"Are you hungry?" Wesley stood, as if what he'd just said had done nothing to affect him.

She wiggled in her seat and pressed her knees together. She'd never be able to eat. "Not right now. You?"

"Maybe a little." He opened the fridge and rummaged around, pulling out food.

"Ha-ha. You're just afraid of losing again."

Wesley snorted as he pulled out a tray and sliced fruit. Her gaze was drawn to him, his broad shoulders, ropy forearms, and the way he moved so comfortably in the tight space of his RV.

She breathed deeply, silently, attempting to let go of the awkwardness and doubt and desire that clobbered her.

Wesley could have kicked them out ages ago. She didn't want to overstay their welcome, but had no idea what he was thinking because he'd never say. Should she be the one to say thanks, but we need to leave?

God, she didn't want to go. Not yet. And besides, Keegan and Rayma needed to talk alone. Not that they couldn't do that once they got back to the hotel.

Or maybe she should go to him and wrap her arms around him, press up against his back and rub his shoulders to ease his tension. He'd never been able to deny her before. Would he be able to now?

Her phone buzzed. She groaned at the message from Blake.

"What's wrong?" Wesley asked, his back facing her as he prepped food. She admired his back, his butt, his long legs, the way his shoulders flexed as he diced up fruit. It'd be so easy to pretend things were normal between them. That they had no history and their past didn't matter. If they could just keep playing games, drinking beer, and talking about old record collections, maybe reality wouldn't be so harsh.

He moved swiftly in the kitchen, and she wondered if she could say something about his cooking in her next article.

The article Blake was already pressing her for.

"Blake wants to know if I got a good story for him."

"Have you told him about my burning desire for your record collection?"

Grinning, Caitlyn shook her head. Wesley glanced at her, threw a strawberry in his mouth, winked, then returned his attention to the food.

"I'm assuming you still have it."

"Oh, yes. It grows every year." Caitlyn had inherited most of her records from her grandmother, and her mom had continued to give her one has a gift on her birthday. Wesley had always anticipated her birthdays to see which record she'd get. They'd spend hours playing them together, dancing together. Caitlyn had teased him about only wanting to marry her for her record collection. "I lost a few after moving one year. Probably was stolen by the movers, but I could never prove it. But I have more than enough. I often beg my mom to stop or I'll need an entire room to store them."

"I'm sure they're all labeled and organized."

Caitlyn pressed her elbow into the table and relaxed her chin in her hand. "How else could I keep track of them?"

Wesley slid a plate of cheese, fruit, and bite-sized sandwiches across the table. "Should I go check on Rayma and Keegan?"

"I can send her a text."

"So that I don't interrupt anything?" Wesley's smile twitched, eyes twinkled he sat in the seat across from her and grabbed a sandwich. "Probably a good idea."

"And what about Blake?"

"What about him?" he asked then bit into his sandwich.

"What should I tell him?"

Wesley's jaw tightened before he glanced away. He finished chewing before speaking. "What does he want to know about me? What does anyone want to know about me? I have a car collection almost as big as your record collection. I'm a huge fan of zombie movies, and I don't believe in ghosts."

Caitlyn picked up a sandwich, but it knotted in her throat as she chewed. "That's random."

He held up a finger. "But interesting."

Every nerve ending in her body tingled. She didn't want to press for an interview, and she'd be able to think of a story no matter how late she had to stay up to write it, but finding one that wasn't too personal but personal enough for Blake was difficult.

The last thing she wanted to dig up in the article was ghosts.

"Blake is hoping for an exclusive," she said, her voice soft. She didn't want to press this. She wasn't ready for the interview because once that was done, she'd be pulled from the assignment. She wasn't ready for the assignment to be over. If it ended now, things would only be worse.

"I don't do exclusives. This will have to be enough."

Rayma and Keegan knocked lightly on the door before walking back inside, holding hands. Caitlyn rubbed the back of her neck as dread rolled in her stomach. She wasn't ready to leave, wasn't ready for this night to end, but the expression on Rayma's face said it was time to leave.

Don't crave more than what was possible at the moment.

Make him miss me.

Keegan strode forward and held out his hand. "Wesley, thank you for everything."

He stood, shaking his hand in return. "No problem. It was good to see you."

"Are you about ready?" Rayma asked Caitlyn.

She shot her gaze toward Wesley before landing on Rayma and nodding. Snatching a strawberry from the plate, she stood. Heat charged her but she bottled her longing. They were her ride. Unless Wesley offered a ride back to the hotel.

He didn't. And he shouldn't. God no, he shouldn't.

"Everything okay?" Wesley asked his stepbrother. If a man was worthy of falling in love with by the way he treated a girl's friends, he would be that man. Not that she didn't have plenty of reasons to fall for him all over again. But he'd been so accepting, so caring.

Was it all a show?

This assignment was supposed to purge him out of her system, not flood her with longing. Things were going to be worse, so much worse on her when this assignment was over.

***

She was a reporter, after an exclusive. Nothing else. He had to remember that.

Many journalists had vied for an exclusive, but Caitlyn's history with him could give fans insight no one else could.

She wasn't a friend, she wasn't even a fan. She'd hated racing when they were growing up, had never understood his devotion to the sport on Sunday afternoons. She'd never known how important it was to him, how much he longed to get behind a car, how much fun he had visiting his uncle when he was allowed to get behind the car and race along the track with Tim's friends.

It was hard to believe that the only reason she was here now was for a story. Although he had to give her credit for playing it cool and not pressuring him, for writing decent accounts of his racing so far, for acting like she was having a good time. He had to remember she was a high-minded career girl who walked along a path he couldn't respect.

She needed money to pay her increasing rent. He had to remember that.

But damn, she hadn't written anything about his past, or even his crazy present. A step-brother returns, a step-brother he had resented, and now they were playing cards together.

Maybe he should give her what she wanted. Give her an interview and get her out of his life so he could move on with his. *Again.*

He didn't want to. If he did, she'd be done with her assignment and out of his life. He wasn't ready for that.

"Everything okay?" he asked.

"Everything's great," Keegan said in reply to his question. He shook his thoughts aside and focused on his company.

Doubts about Keegan crept in. He wanted to believe it was coincidence and that Caitlyn had no idea about their relationship, but life was handing him too many coincidences lately and he didn't like it.

He shook Keegan's hand and hugged Rayma, then stationed his hand on Caitlyn's lower back and escorted her to the door.

He clenched his jaw, ignoring the tug of possessiveness he felt. *She doesn't belong to you. She's never belonged to you. Let her go.*

"Be careful," he said. The temptation to ask her to stay thickened his blood, but she was already bounding down the steps with her friend's arm hooked through hers.

"I'll take care of them," Keegan said.

Chapter Fourteen

I'LL TAKE CARE of them.

Bullshit. It wasn't Keegan's job to take care of Caitlyn and it'd be over Wesley's dead body.

He called the next morning and offered her a ride home, ignoring the warnings in his mind that he should stay away. Let her go, don't follow.

Just like he hadn't followed her last time. He'd tucked tail and run, punishing himself with a sentence worse than prison. Until he'd started racing. So why was he chasing her now?

He'd loved Caitlyn at one time and wasn't ready to love again anytime soon. But if he did, it shouldn't drill pain behind his skull or make him sullen and consumed. God, but he did right now. He felt like nothing else mattered, and he wanted her to be with him.

Stupid. He had to get back on the track. He had to win, let the engine rumble in his gut and the racetrack spin these thoughts of his mind. Forget everything else.

"That'd be great," Caitlyn said when he asked her if she'd like him to take her home. "If you're sure. Keegan wanted to take a side trip and take Rayma to meet his mom."

He met her at her hotel, and a quick ride in Tim's private jet didn't allow long conversation. He questioned his motives over and over and over again. Maybe he should just take her to bed one last time, get her out of his system. What the hell did she expect from him, anyway?

Before long, they were in a taxi headed to her apartment.

The sun descended in a fiery ball, clouds blanketing the inferno, muting to a stream of orange and gold along the horizon.

They didn't speak at all throughout the taxi ride, but her thigh grazed his in a whisper-soft caress. His body tingled, his ribcage tightening with the need to touch her. Taste her. Feel her. Experience every breadth of her and make her forget the past ten years of her life were spent without him.

When they made it to her apartment, he paid the tab before Caitlyn had a chance to object. Wesley didn't play the gentleman and let Caitlyn enter first. He opened the apartment and went in, inspecting the rooms.

"What are you doing?" she asked.

"Checking things out."

"Making sure no one is hiding in any corners?" she teased, her smile weary.

"Something like that."

"Just as I left it," she said and placed her purse on the table. She opened the blinds to let in the weak sunshine, almost gone by now. "Blake has been calling and texting all day. Guess I better give him a call. Can I get you something to drink?"

"No, thank you." Wesley roamed her apartment while she called Blake. He admired her nicely sized kitchen. Pinkish gray and white granite countertops with cabinets the same rich wood as the floor bespoke elegance and comfort, and the floor plan opened into the living room, which revealed the same stunning hard wood overlaid with a blue printed hearth rug.

Wesley scanned the photographs hanging on her wall. Antique barn wood and glossy black framed most of the photos, which consisted of nature, people, unusual buildings and vibrant scenes. A picture she had obviously taken during one of his races hung among others he assumed were taken from previous assignments.

"Nice pictures," he said when she approached. He brushed one of the black frames with his finger and found it glassy to the touch, smooth and cool.

Kind of like the vise gripping his heart.

"Thank you. I took most of these photos."

"Really?" he asked, though not surprised.

"I love taking pictures."

"Yes, I remember. I didn't think you would ever be this good."

"Thanks a lot," she said and lightly smacked him on the shoulder.

He turned towards her but kept the space between them. "I didn't mean it like that."

"I need to dig out my old pictures. I have so many of you with your old cars, fixing them up. Your fans would love them."

"Mmm, maybe. What did your boss want?"

"To let me know when my next assignment is due. I reminded him of his promise not to give me any more assignments as long as I'm working on this one, but he informed me I'm off of this one now. It isn't working out for him. First, he wants me to do it no matter what, then he says never mind. I don't get him."

"Did you tell him I've granted you an interview?" Wesley wasn't sure why the words poured out, but hearing her boss was pulling her from the assignment was like hearing the harsh squeak of tires against asphalt. Charging his gut with dread.

Caitlyn's lashes flickered. "No. I didn't know I should tell him that."

He wasn't ready to accept the assignment might be over when it had barely begun. He couldn't accept he might never see her after this.

It was inevitable she would leave eventually, go back to her life. They were different people now with different goals in life.

Being in lust, having chemistry, being old friends just wasn't enough to make something last.

The only thing he needed to last was his racing career, but he owed her at least an interview. And if he was ever going to agree to an exclusive, it might as well be with her.

"I'll sit down with you and give you an in-depth interview, Caitlyn, I promise." He took hold of her hand and squeezed. His blood pressure dropped.

He wanted to take her to bed. Make her forget everything.

Make *him* forget everything. But he couldn't. Not yet. Not ever. That would only make things awkward now that he had agreed to an interview. So he'd play it cool for now. He'd learned patience, but his patience was quickly wearing thin.

His ribcage tripped as she worried her lip with her tongue.

"You'll give me an interview?" she asked. Her voice taunted the fear in his body. If he let down his guard, he'd never get over her. Not twice.

Wesley held up his hands. "Yep. An exclusive. Friday, after I qualify. He'll have to let you off to watch and you can see what happens during qualification. We'll talk afterward and if you still want to do a biography, I'd appreciate if you let me read it of course, but I can't stop you."

Now why in the hell did he say that? A biography would mean revealing all kinds of things to his fans that he would never want revealed. He wasn't ready for that. He'd never be ready for that.

He wasn't sure why he didn't just agree to let her interview him now, get it over with, and go back to his life. Racing would plug the hole in his heart. Maybe, just maybe after he let her interview her, he'd take her to bed. Then get on with his life. The sooner the better.

Wesley swallowed a moan at the sight of Caitlyn's quivering chin. Taking her to bed would only make things worse.

She smiled. "Thank you, Wesley. Thank you so much."

He wasn't ready to let her go. That's why he tilted up her chin, put a chaste kiss on her cheek, and said his goodbye.

"See you next week."

***

"I'm giving Caitlyn a formal interview." Wesley placed the barbell back in its cradle on the bench, sat up, and grabbed a towel.

"I don't know about that, man," Adam replied.

Wesley got up and let Adam take his seat. They'd been workout partners for years, and worked out every morning either in a local gym or with the equipment Wesley kept in his RV.

"What's not to know?" Wesley asked as he spotted Adam on his chest press.

Adam let out a ragged breath and sucked in another before replying. "You've never granted a formal, in-depth interview with anyone. Why her?" He sat up. "Why not a television interview or something?"

"Because I trust Caitlyn."

"And if you do a television interview, they can't fuck up what you said because it's right there on TV for everyone to see."

"Yeah, unless they change it around and put it out of context."

"Live TV," Adam stated.

"What do you have against Caitlyn?" Wesley asked, lifting dumbbells to perform bicep curls. Adam lowered to the floor to do pushups. "You're the one who let her in the garage in the first place."

"I don't have anything against her," Adam said, rising from the floor. "She's gorgeous. Maybe that's why I don't trust her."

"She's a woman. That's why you don't trust her."

"You should follow my example," Adam said.

Wesley winked and reversed positions so Adam did his bicep curls while Wesley did pushups.

"So there's a relationship here?" Adam asked.

"Mutual friendship, that's all."

That was true, it had to be true. If they could live in the present tense as Caitlyn said, and not dwell on the past, friends were all they could be.

Yet Caitlyn's body played havoc with his restraint. Her words, her looks, her personality. Damn, the sexual energy inside him was about to combust. If only he could find a girl, just any girl, to ease his desire. But that wasn't about to happen.

Not until whatever surged between him and Caitlyn came to a head.

"Look," Adam said when they finished their next set, "I haven't told you yet that my wife left me."

"What?"

"I'm never home," Adam said, giving a good impersonation

of a nagging wife. "She doesn't know me anymore. She needs more out of life."

"Do you need to take some time off to go see her?"

"Hell no." Adam grabbed a towel and did arm stretches.

"Damn, I'm sorry," Wesley said as he did the same.

"You want to go out tonight?" Adam asked.

"It's Friday. I have to qualify today and Caitlyn is coming over."

Adam wiggled his brows. "Ah," he said.

"Hey, you'll be plenty busy tonight getting ready for Sunday's race."

"So should you," Adam said.

"Don't worry about me. I'll be ready."

***

Even after all these years of racing, butterflies still swarmed Wesley's gut on qualifying days. It was more dangerous than race day, because he hit top speed and ran risks in order to make the best position possible. No other cars hindered his progress, just his own jumbled nerves. When he climbed into his racecar, any current problems in his life remained at the pit stop, parked at a standstill. Despite the dangers, it was the ultimate way to live stress free, in Wesley's opinion. Plus, it gave him a rush.

When he passed the sensor indicating he was finished with his lap, he slowed his car to a crawl then stopped. His team cheered. He felt good about his time, but being locked in the cockpit, it was hard to know for sure how well he did until he talked to his team.

"I think we'll stand," they decided after talking it over.

Caitlyn was flushed, smiling, and resembled a true fan when she came up to him.

"What does that mean?" she asked, her pink notebook in hand.

"It means I won't qualify again, we'll stand on my time and hope it'll be good enough to make the race so I don't have to watch it on TV." He couldn't remove his gaze from her, despite the work still needing to be done. She was exquisite, with her piercing blue eyes and face beaming. Her excitement filled him with pride.

"You did great out there," she said. "I was so scared when you went around those curves that fast, but it was awesome. I think I got some great pictures."

Caitlyn hung around and talked to some of his crew members as he performed more practice laps. Occasionally, she caught hold of Adam's arm and laughed at something he said. When Wesley could take no more, he pulled his car into the garage and said he was done for the day.

His frown was heavy when he approached Caitlyn and Adam. She wore a denim skirt with black boots and a white lacy top that spliced in the middle. It was hard for a man's eyes not to linger on the necklace dangling between the dip in her breasts. A camera hung around her neck and the bag she always carried around with her, a somewhat lighter load without the laptop, sat at her feet.

"I have some great stories to put in my next article," Caitlyn told Wesley, holding up her spiral notebook. Apparently, Adam fed her stories. Adam backed away at Wesley's frown.

"How's your wife?" Wesley asked Adam, his fingers twitching.

"Still gone," Adam replied.

Of course she was. Wesley pinned Adam with a hard *keep away* glare before he turned to Caitlyn and grabbed her bag. The least he could be was a gentleman and carry the damn thing.

"You ready to go?" Not waiting for a reply, he nodded to Adam then turned and walked away. Caitlyn followed.

"I'll meet you at your hotel in an hour or so," Wesley told her as he ushered her to the rental car. He needed to get some last minute things accomplished and he didn't want to be sidetracked by her.

Wesley hated the sting of possessiveness and had to distance himself in order to regain his equilibrium. Jealously had never been a factor in their relationship. Damn, now he was referring to it as a 'relationship'. They hadn't had one of those in so long. What in the hell was wrong with him?

Before they'd had sex, he'd been Caitlyn's protector, her

best friend. That protective instinct now consumed him.

Before this was all over, he was going to take her to bed. Where was his protective instinct now?

Seeing Caitlyn again brought back memories. *Too* many memories. She was very much alive and very much a person he'd loved. He grew up, slept with other women, but never had he fallen in love or felt what he felt with her. He thought, given time, he'd find a woman to spend the rest of his life with. He just wasn't ready.

Caitlyn made him ready.

And that pissed him off.

Chapter Fifteen

CAITLYN PREENED IN front of the mirror and refreshed her makeup. Wesley was on his way. She wanted to look good for him, wanted to knock his socks off. Why now? She didn't know.

Of course she knew. She wanted Wesley to desire her, to beg for her body. Wanted to feel him, to be close to him, and desperately wanted to do crazy stupid things with him.

Going to bed with him would be crazy and stupid. But didn't mean she couldn't at least tempt him by looking good.

Wesley preferred to be interviewed here, in the dingy last-minute-before-the race motel. It would be near impossible to grant an interview in public without fans racing up to him. She figured he didn't want to hold it in his trailer so he could leave whenever he was ready.

Her plan to expunge Wesley from her memory had gone seriously awry and she wondered what her life was going to be like when this was all over. She was falling for him all over again. Hard. Would she ever be the same after tonight?

A knock sounded at the door and she glanced in the mirror one last time. Her pulse somersaulted as she opened the door, even if she had just seen him an hour earlier.

He'd changed into something more comfortable but no less appealing. He wore a tight black shirt and a pair of dark jeans. He removed his cap and ran his finger through his already mussed hair before stepping through the door. He smelled clean but musky.

He hadn't shaved, and she fought the urge to touch the dark

stubble lining his face.

Sexy personified.

Caitlyn tried not to notice as they settled at the table. She clutched her notebook, forgetting all the words she rehearsed in her mind earlier and the questions she wanted to ask him. She inhaled a deep breath, trying to put herself into the persona she adopted when she interviewed people and trying to forget she was once in love with this man.

Once? Had she ever stopped loving him?

She stared at the page. She wouldn't look at him, wouldn't breathe him in.

"Adam thinks I should do a televised interview," Wesley said.

Caitlyn glanced up. "Do you want to? I'm sure Blake would love to televise an internet broadcast."

"I'd rather not."

Caitlyn nodded and glanced down, drawing circles on her page before she caught herself. She preferred pen and paper over a laptop because it offered a deeper connection to her subject and her words, but she couldn't allow the page to sidetrack her.

Wesley's charisma was enough of a sidetrack.

"Do you want to tell me a little about the race, things you do to get ready for one?"

"Drivers don't just jump in the car and drive. There's so much more to it than that. Our days are filled with activity. We must be resourceful and multi-talented to deal with the day-to-day happenings."

"Do you have a game plan before the big day?"

"Impossible. Nothing is planned. You have to focus on the here and now and expect the unexpected." Wesley's lips curled as he spoke. His eyes beamed as he rested his palms on the table, face up. Enthusiasm poured from him, and Caitlyn tried to portray it on the page so readers would understand how much Wesley loved to race.

She tried to maintain the steadiness of her hands as she wrote in her notebook. The steadiness of her heart was another story. She'd lost that a long time ago.

"What about wrecks?"

"What about them?"

"Well, I mean, I've always thought racing was so dangerous."

"No more dangerous than anything else."

"Going two hundred miles per hour isn't more dangerous than anything else?" She hadn't meant to bring this up, it was an interview after all, but the chance of an accident had always been her biggest fear for him.

"The cars are built for safety." He folded his palms in, big sign that she was overstepping her bounds.

She bit back her retort, and kept going. This wasn't about her. It wasn't about her concerns for his safety.

And it damn sure wasn't about her telling him that she'd love to see where their relationship could go, if they'd just try.

"Why do you race?" she asked.

He shrugged. "Why does anyone do it? Adrenaline, competition, thrills. Fans, winning, victory lane. There's no way to describe how and why you do something you love."

And there's no explaining why you pursue someone you love who just didn't love you back, but she wasn't going to say that.

She took a deep breath. Usually her interviews became more personal. She wasn't sure how personal to get with him. She knew a lot about him—at least she used to—but she was scared of asking him the wrong thing. She didn't want to set him off.

"What's your favorite color?" Caitlyn held a pen in her hand, poised to write, trying to concentrate on the task at hand. Her focus, though, was Wesley's deep green eyes. Eyes able to pierce her and reach a part of her no one had ever been able to touch before. Something about the way he looked at her, like he saw only *her*, deep down, clear to her soul.

A hint of danger lurked in his eyes, a predator-like stance that made her sense he was ready to devour her, sexually and otherwise. A vulnerability that made Caitlyn yearn to take him in her arms, to be as close to him as possible. His gaze held no arrogance, no indifference, and no deceit.

Her throat felt parched. His eyes devoured every morsel of her power and well-being.

She couldn't think of a decent thing to say. Thank God it was his turn to talk.

"My favorite color," he said as he leaned across the table, closer to Caitlyn, "is the capricious color of your eyes."

His lips were only inches from hers so that his breath licked against her skin. His eyes possessed her.

She clutched her pen in midair, frozen in space for a mere second. He touched her hand.

The pen fell.

"Blueberry," he said as he trailed a light kiss across her knuckle, his eyes still magnetizing hers. Her heart stopped in her throat. "Dark and wounded. Cornflower blue, tantalizing with banter and witticism." He kissed the tip of her pinkie and went on to taste each finger, slowly taking his time with each one. "Sea blue, bright and sparkling like the waves catching a sunset, when you're happy."

Caitlyn, entranced with his words, was amazed he even noticed her eyes and more amazed he practically recited poetry. Where had he come up with this?

"Storm clouds," he continued as he stroked the inside of her palm. "Brewing with a passion and desire you're too afraid to feel. Sometimes periwinkle, sometimes almost lavender and sometimes a sultry gray. Right now though, they are definitely–"

She pulled her hand away and scooted back in her chair. Thoroughly aroused, she squeezed her thighs tighter in an attempt to bury the spark.

"You're full of it," she said. "My eyes don't change colors that much and even if they did, you wouldn't notice."

"What makes you say that?" He leaned back in his chair, taking the two back legs to its haunches, something they both used to get in trouble for when they were kids.

She shook her head and didn't answer. The touch of his warm mouth on her fingers still burned in her core.

"I always notice your eyes."

Caitlyn ducked under the table in search of her pen, a good attempt to conceal her red face. Her whole body burned. She spotted her pen and reached, feeling like an idiot. But at least it took her mind off everything else.

She straightened and smoothed her skirt, which she now regretted wearing. Ignoring him, she returned to her seat and adjusted her low-cut top.

"So," she said as she scribbled *favorite color* on the tablet. "Your favorite color is blue?"

"Come on, Caitlyn, what's with the interview? I thought you knew everything there was to know about me?"

"It's been ten years," she reminded him, this time finally looking at him as she straightened her rumpled hair and made an attempt to discount the object of her passion. "I thought your favorite color was black."

"Why?"

"The old sports car you drove when we were teenagers, the one you used to keep nice and shiny, was black. Almost all of your fixer uppers were eventually painted black. And you wear the color a lot."

"I look damn good in black." He grinned and winked.

Caitlyn agreed, but then again, he looked damn good in anything.

"What's *your* favorite color?" he asked.

"Green," she said and immediately regretted it.

His smile spread wider, more roguish, if that were possible. He shot the chair back down on all fours and folded his hands on the table.

"Oh? Any particular shade?"

She wasn't going to be baited by him. She could describe the color of his eyes as immaculately as he had described hers. The way they changed from light to dark and every shade in between, from delight to anger, aloofness to desire, tantalizing to satiating. Deep, dark emerald green in passion, olive green when he became perturbed and a light, apple green, like now, when he teased.

"We're not here to interview me." She adjusted her body to fit the contours of the seat more comfortably. "What's your favorite food?" Surely food would be a safe subject.

"You know I'm a meat man. Steak and potatoes mostly. Builds big muscles." To prove it, he demonstrated by flexing a well-toned bicep.

She grinned and rolled her eyes. "Favorite fruit?"

He lowered his arm and looked into her eyes again. "Blueberries. Definitely blueberries. Or strawberries," he added as his gaze trailed to her lips.

She shied away, writing in her notebook. Wesley reached up and touched her lips softly with his fingertip. Her gaze flew to his and she tossed her pen. It bounded off the table to the floor, again.

"Wesley!" She gripped his hand, was tempted to squeeze him toward her, but pushed it away instead. "Please! What are you trying to do? Do you want to just strip naked right now and do it on the table, to hell with the consequences?"

"I'd like to," he said and laughed.

Caitlyn loved the way his body moved as he laughed and his eyes crinkled—that was new—when he smiled.

"I'm sorry," he said, all laughter ceased. "I'll answer seriously now."

"Why did you think that was funny?"

"What, the getting on the table and doing the wild thing?" She nodded.

"It wasn't your words so much," he answered. "It was your look. Like you were afraid I might actually take you up on that offer. Not that I wouldn't want to," he added.

She huffed and glanced away all the while thinking he was wrong in that respect. She did want him to take her up on her offer. Very badly.

But for some reason, whenever either of them got too close, the other pushed away. He'd done it at her house. She'd done it when he dropped her off at her hotel. It was an ongoing cycle, them pushing each other away, and it should have been a clue.

Don't have sex. Don't touch each other. Don't even look at each other. Hell, don't even associate with other.

"Shall we get on with it?" she asked. He nodded and she cleared her throat. "What's your favorite drink?"

"Water and milk. Builds bigger muscles." This time he used his other arm to demonstrate, but Caitlyn didn't smile at his fun.

He coughed and sat up in his chair. "Sorry," he said with a sheepish grin.

"You know, this interview would take half the time or less if you would give up on your antics."

"Good thing we decided not to record it then, huh? I can't believe someone would want to know what my favorite book is. Come on, ask me something interesting."

"Tell me what got you into racing."

"My Uncle Tim."

"Ah, so I was right," Caitlyn said.

"No, he helped me with a passion I already had."

Caitlyn wanted to ask him why anyone wasn't aware of that passion, but she didn't. And as far as asking him something interesting, she didn't know what to ask him. Most questions she would ask people were off limits. Too personal. He didn't want to talk about that. She could tell.

"I'm tired of sitting here at this table and getting antsy," Wesley said. "Can't we go out and get some sunshine?"

"We haven't been here long."

"Yes, we have." He pulled his long legs out from underneath the table and stood up. "Let's do something. I can't sit still much longer."

She stood along with him. "How do you sit in a racecar for hours on end?"

"That's different, but I think it's also why I can't sit very still when I'm not racing."

"That's good," she said as she leaned over to write his comment, a personal aspect of Wesley he wasn't ashamed of.

***

As Caitlyn leaned over to write, her shirt, which was only slightly low cut, hung lower. Wesley saw the unmistakable sign of pink underneath the tee. His breath whooshed out of him at the thought of what hid underneath that concoction: dusky pink tips, full and poised in perfect unison. He longed to brace her with his hands and cup her perfect breasts.

She continued to write, stopping to think before writing again and clucking her tongue a couple of times, in tune with the words flowing on paper. A pang of lust shot through him and he stiffened. His entire body hardened.

She didn't notice. Did she?

Finally straightening, she picked up her tablet of paper and pen and sauntered away. "Be right back."

He watched the sway of her backside and practically drooled. He knew exactly what would be covering that perfect ass of hers: panties, lacy and silky and pink. Pink panties to match her pink bra. She always wore a matching bra and panties, telling him once that it made her feel sexier, like a woman should feel. Would it be a bikini, a thong, or those sexy boyshorts?

Wondering made things worse, made him want to lift up her skirt, wrap his hands around her firm ass, and find out. That thought lingered on his mind when she emerged from the bathroom.

"Wesley?" She sashayed over to him and stopped within an arm's length, her eyes level with his torso. When he didn't reply, she snapped her fingers in front of his face. "Are you okay?"

He saw her, every inch of her, even the parts covered. And if he hadn't been able to see her, her scent gave her away. He breathed in and closed his eyes a mere second.

Summoning his willpower, he turned away from her and headed for the door. "I gotta get out of here."

***

The tap-tap of the keyboard as Caitlyn typed mimicked the sound of her heartbeat. Chattering, stopping to think then pounding away again. When a thunderous knock crashed at her door, she jumped. She'd been deep in concentration, focusing on the words she typed.

After Wesley left, she moped around for at least an hour and then finally fired up her laptop. Her written words soothed her, and it wasn't even the assignment she was supposed to be working on. Journaling calmed her

Saving her work, Caitlyn closed the laptop and clumped to the door. Her body, still on edge after being startled so abruptly, weakened when she spotted Wesley.

Caitlyn couldn't handle anymore. She just couldn't keep doing this.

She opened the door and was overtaken with a stunning bouquet of flowers.

"What's this?" She placed a hand on her hip and frowned. The flowers were beautiful, but he'd left her in the middle of an interview. She resented that he thought flowers would fix everything.

"I noticed when I was here earlier your room is dreary. Thought you might appreciate a splash of color."

"Oh." She wasn't sure what to think, but she had to remember this was not a game. It wasn't a relationship. It wasn't anything.

It was her job.

And his job.

Nothing else.

She accepted the spray, stepped aside for him to enter, and set the flowers on the middle of the drab table. He was right. The bouquet, full of purple and orange and yellow, did brighten the room. "Nice vase. Thank you, I do appreciate it."

An awkward silence followed as they faced each other. She wasn't sure what to do, what he expected her to do, or if he was about to leave.

Wesley ran his fingers through his hair. "Sorry for being a little shit."

Caitlyn was taken aback by his apology. "Okay." She pressed on the knot forming in her neck, compliments of stress and the long hours she spent hunched over as she wrote.

"I hate being interviewed and asked personal questions. I hate feeling like I'm being put in a spotlight. And I hate that with you it's different, because you know so much about me. Things that hurt."

He stepped forward and replaced the hand on her neck with his. She palmed his face, tracing the stubble on his jaw, unmindful of the pain she would suffer when this was all over. She'd gladly face them for one night of passion in his arms. She wouldn't let him go without a fight.

"Who am I kidding?" Wesley murmured, his low rasp igniting fire across her skin. He swept a strand of hair out of her eyes. "I ran because I want you. I fucking want you bad. And I knew that if I didn't leave, I was not going to be able to stop."

Her lids fluttered, mouth parting, as he continued to stroke her face. "Then why did you come back?"

"Because I fucking want you bad," he growled before his mouth came down on hers.

He offered no softness in his kiss. This was all give and take, hungry and gratifying. They kissed as if it was their first kiss, their last kiss. His hands ran down the length of her, swooping under her rear to pull her closer, to crush her pelvis with his. The bulge in his jeans intensified her liquid ache.

She gripped his shoulders, reveling in the curve of muscle, the swell of his bicep. He groaned inside her mouth, his tongue reaching deep. They stopped kissing long enough for her to rip his shirt over his head then their mouths joined again as if that's where they belonged—locked in synchronous time.

Her hands explored the grooves of his chest, arms, torso, neckline. She could touch him forever and never grow tired. His hands, course and raw and rugged, slid under her shirt to touch her breasts, then down to lift her. She wrapped her legs around him the few steps to the bed and he lowered her, gently. Heat and cold consumed her as she watched him remove his shoes, his jeans.

Eyes locked with hers, his fingers skated under her skirt, dipped inside her thighs, through her lacy thong to where she burned. He pushed up her skirt, his fingers grazing her inner thighs without touching where she really needed his touch. She was wet. God she was so wet and ready for him.

He remained just within her reach and took time exploring her body. Kissed her neck then stripped her of her shirt and bra to suckle each breast. Made his way down her body to remove her skirt and panties, then opened her legs and lowered his face into her.

She cried out at the initial contact. The way his warm tongue darted in and out, in and out, sweeping over her skin, licking her heat. He instinctively knew where to touch, where to taste to make her quiver for more. She arched back, gripped his hair, and cried out when she finally exploded.

He rolled away and grabbed a condom from his wallet, tore it from the package. His body shook as he rolled it over his length.

"Are you sure..." he asked, but she grasped his shoulders and brought him to her.

"Yes," she cried, arching to meet him.

He thrust into her, and she spread her legs for him to go deeper. He filled her. Oh, how he filled her.

"God yes," she cried again.

Their bodies moved together, their senses heightened, hands exploring, ears attentive to every moan.

Nothing in her life had ever felt more right. Wesley was the person she should be with, the part of her missing for so long. They moved together, in a natural rhythm, until they came in a maelstrom of emotion too deep for anything but a declaration of ecstasy.

***

Wesley couldn't help but wonder what Caitlyn's reaction would be after that breathtaking event. He'd never experienced anything quite like it. Since Caitlyn, other women left him longing for something more...emotional. He couldn't explain it, hated the reality of it, but only Caitlyn could complete him.

In the past, he'd always been ready to leave immediately after sex. With Caitlyn, forever etched his heart.

In the past, he'd attributed it to being a horny teenager. Now, he knew better.

His body, satisfied, yet, he wanted more of her.

Taking her had been his exact intention when he'd come back to the hotel. He'd even stopped at the store to purchase condoms.

They couldn't keep pushing each other away like this. The

stress, the tension, the longing for soul-binding sex would break them. Hopefully, she wouldn't blame him for taking advantage of her. Would she be upset? Full of regret?

His fears were set aside when the brush of her fingers feathered down his side. A light tickle played on his skin. Wesley pushed himself up on his palms and studied her. He clutched her hand and held it against the bed.

"Hey," he said. "That tickles."

She inched her free hand around to his other side and tickled him there, remembering just where to touch to irritate him. Wesley seized her other hand and pinned her beneath him.

"I said," he growled, but with a smile on his face, "that tickles."

He gripped both her hands in one of his and held them above her head. He used his free hand to tickle her along her sides and across her stomach. She screamed, laughed, and thrashed around.

His body stirred. *Damn this woman.* His energy had just been exhausted, but he was ready again.

He freed her hands and moved aside, so they were lying on their sides facing each other. She stroked her fingers across his chest. "Your body is absolutely gorgeous." She rested her head in her free hand and traced his stomach with her eyes and then her hands.

He let out a shuddering breath. "So is yours. You. Everything about you is absolutely breathtakingly beautiful."

"And that's not a bad six pack you've got going there," she said and playfully smacked his stomach.

"So it's just my body you like, then?" he teased.

"God, yes!" She grinned, gleaming as she touched his face, his cheeks, and the corners of his eyes. "Your eyes are pretty darn spectacular. I don't think I've ever seen any quite like them."

"What makes you say that?"

"They're so green and intense. You look at someone and you make them think they are the only ones on the planet with you. I mean, they're so attentive, or something. They're a beautiful color, but the intensity coming out of them is amazing."

"No," he said. "They're intense because *you* are intense, and you have my undivided attention when you're in the room."

She laughed and playfully swatted him. He seized her hand and pulled her over, rolling so that she straddled him.

"You ready?" he asked.

She wiggled against him. "So soon?"

"Hope we have enough condoms."

***

"What am I going to do?" Wesley poked his head out of the shower and held up one of Caitlyn's old razors. "I don't have a razor. I don't have a toothbrush."

Caitlyn, clad in a long satin robe, snatched the razor he held and rummaged through her suitcase until she found a new blade. "You can use my razor. I have new blades."

He touched the fuzz on his face. "A *woman's* razor?" he exclaimed.

"What's wrong with that? It's a new blade." She changed the blade and he turned off the shower. He stepped out, dried himself, and wrapped the towel around his waist.

Caitlyn gave the razor back to him. "You going to let me borrow your toothbrush, too?" he teased.

"You could always opt not to shave." Caitlyn swept her finger over his face and down his chin. "I think your stubble is pretty damn sexy."

She grinned, snatched the towel from around his waist and stepped back, popping him with it. Anticipating her movement, he shifted his foot and grabbed her arm, bringing her against his very naked body. He touched her, trailing his hands under her robe and across her warm body.

She stepped back. "You're going to be late."

Today would be a busy day, starting with a meeting he had with his crew members, practice sessions he had to run through before tomorrow's race, and an hour long gathering with his fans. "Unless you really do want to borrow my toothbrush, you'll need to get back to your RV," she said.

"Yeah, I'll be late but I have a great excuse." He wrenched her even closer and moved his hips against her. "I have the pleasure of a beautiful woman's company. Surely they'll understand."

"I don't want to get you into trouble," she said.

"Darling, I'm already in trouble."

Chapter Sixteen

IN TROUBLE?

Well, it didn't appear that way to Caitlyn. Not after two weeks and only talking to him a few times since.

Caitlyn, still clad in her workout gear with a matching featherweight jacket, sat her groceries on the counter. Her gaze ping-ponged between the bottle of wine she'd bought at the grocery store and herbal tea. The tea would be the better choice.

But today was cause for celebration, even if she did have to celebrate alone. The story on Wesley had published and she'd gotten plenty of other calls from the media, though she'd ignored them all. She hadn't even seen the article yet or checked social media.

Screw it. She'd drink alone. Rayma was with Keegan and Wesley obviously wasn't going to return her call. She opened the bottle and poured, savoring the taste of tobacco and chocolate.

Tension knotted her neck, and she moved it from side to side. Blake had enjoyed her story but already had her running off to new assignments. Her worst fear that she'd never see Wesley again was coming true. He had his busy career, and she'd go back to hers.

That had been the original plan. But the original plan included purging him from her system. Getting over him and moving on her with life. Not having sex with him and certainly not falling in love with him all over again.

She slurped the wine and topped off the glass, deciding

she'd work out harder tomorrow. Social media's reaction to her article could wait. Everything could wait. She bent over to stretch, reaching the glass toward her toes. At least it was something.

Caitlyn begged Blake to let her continue her work with Wesley and reminded him of all the fan mail they received and continued to receive. He told her it was complete and had nothing more to write about.

When she turned in her vacation request, Blake refused and told her it was bad timing.

She couldn't just up and leave her job, up and quit. Blake gave her the promised raise, but that wasn't enough to cover flying to Wesley's races on Sunday only to come back home that very night to start work again the next day. There would be no time to drive either.

And Wesley hadn't asked her to, hadn't offered.

She straightened and took another sip before setting the glass on the counter. Clutching the bar for balance, she extended her leg and circled one ankle, then the other.

Deep down, she knew they didn't stand a chance. They had too much history, too many things going on in their lives, and were both married to their jobs. Wesley traveled extensively for his and hers was too demanding.

A knock sounded on her door and she jogged toward it. Might as well make the most of the exercise, right? She hoped Rayma had changed her mind and had come to spend Friday night with her. Caitlyn might even be in the mood to shower and go out.

Even better, Wesley stood on the other side of the door.

"What a pleasant surprise," she said, going with an easy welcome instead of jumping in his arms. That would be pathetic.

Brow furrowed, Wesley pushed past her and strode to the middle of the room before turning to face her. Her pulse tripped at his stiff jaw and the look of...utter hatred on his face.

Oh God, something horrible had happened. She closed the door and braced herself against it. Had there been news about the murders?

Or something worse? Maybe more murders?

"Is everything okay?"

When she stepped toward him, he shook the magazine in her direction. "I can't believe you did this."

"What?" She recognized the magazine. His picture graced the cover as he stood beside his stock car, his team in the background. She hadn't had time to read it, but she'd written it and nothing would be changed without her authority. "I thought it was good."

"Good? I can't believe I trusted you!" He wheeled around and hurled the magazine across the room. It slapped against the bar and hit her glass and the bottle of wine. They all shattered to the floor. The resonance of the glass striking the tile augmented the tension in the room. Dark purple liquid spread over the tile, staining.

Caitlyn's breath froze. She stumbled back a step.

Why was he so angry?

His nostrils flared as he glowered at her. She opened her mouth, licking her lips as she wondered what in the world she would say. What could she say? She had no idea why he was so upset.

"I...I haven't read it yet," she stammered. Maybe this was all a big joke on his part.

"You wrote it," he interrupted, his voice sounding calm but holding an edge. "You know what it says."

"I didn't mean to—"

"You didn't mean to what?" He took a step forward and stopped. She shrank into the door, her fingers curling into the frame. "Didn't mean to destroy me?"

Her lungs constricted and she opened her mouth again but couldn't force out any words. His steps ate up the distance between them and he stopped inches from her. A vein throbbed in his neck as his face hovered near hers.

"I can't believe I trusted you." This time his voice was calm. Steady. Low. Deep. Her nerves retaliated with a tremor. "I only hope no one reads that trash of yours."

He pushed her out of his way and stormed out, making sure the door crashed behind him.

She stood there a moment, staring at the door and hoping

it would open back up and he would waltz in, laughing at her. "I was just joking," he would claim, and wrap her in his arms.

But that wasn't going to happen. She went over in her mind what might have upset him but couldn't think of a plausible answer.

Her thighs trembled as she sidestepped shards of glass and bent to retrieve the magazine from the floor.

Caitlyn attempted to sop up the wine with a towel, flicking shards of glass away. Pieces nicked her, but she didn't care. Her soul had already been nicked.

Why would Wesley come all this way in such anger? She hadn't mentioned his past. Favorite colors, hobbies, and how important racing was to him were the only personal things mentioned. She'd given no indication of his family at all. As far as the story was concerned, he could have been brought by a stork.

Hands trembling, Caitlyn finally got up the nerve to open the magazine. She thumbed through the pages and found the article. The beverage she craved earlier now an ingredient of the pages. She sank to the floor and curled into a ball, the words she read revolting her stomach.

No wonder Wesley was furious.

No wonder he hated her.

***

Caitlyn stood at Blake's door, pacing, waiting for him to arrive. She gripped the paper, stained by wine.

She hadn't slept at all last night. Her eyes were red and puffy but she didn't care. She'd relentlessly called Blake last night, but he never answered the phone. No doubt he hoped to avoid her.

The words within these pages were not hers.

Wesley's past, his mother's death, the pain of everything he'd experienced and things only and she Wesley and Johnson had known were written on those pages. How could Wesley possibly believe that she hadn't written it?

And yet, it was harsh and demeaning, based on propaganda. The same propaganda he had accused of the media.

And it held her byline.

How could Blake do this to her?

The picture inside was one she'd taken at his house when he wore his shirt. He leaned against his hobby car, arms wrapped around his chest, displaying an arrogant smirk. Blake was not allowed to use any of her photos without permission, and this one made Wesley look like an arrogant ass. Sure, he could be at times, but this photo had all been taken in fun.

Her hair was pulled back in a ponytail and coworkers watched her with worry. When one approached, Caitlyn scowled and waved her away. No one else came close, but she could hear their whispers. They had to know, they had to have seen the story.

She worried Blake might not come in today. He may choose to hide, let her cool off for a while.

But no, he arrived mid-morning. She glared as he approached his door.

"Are you so stupid to think I wouldn't see this or it wouldn't bother me?" She shook the magazine still covered in purple and hopefully still littered with glass. She hoped it'd jab Blake when she threw it at him.

She aimed for his chest and he caught it, scowled and captured her elbow. People ogled them, but she didn't care. Let them see. They deserved to know what kind of man they worked for.

He unlocked his office, escorted her inside then slammed the door behind them. One of his precious wall photos crashed to the floor. He turned on her, his face red. "How dare you confront me in front of my employees!"

"How dare you take my story and completely falsify it," she countered.

"What is written in there isn't false."

"It has my name on it. I didn't write that! It's false. I should sue—"

"That must have been a mistake." He leafed through the pages until he came to the one in question. "We'll be sure to correct that in the next issue."

She clutched her throat and kept her fingers on her chest.

"You'll...you'll be sure to correct it?" Did he think that would fix everything? That he could just correct her byline and this would all go away? Hot anger crashed over her. Disappointment that he could do this and wave it off like nothing. Like things would go back to normal and they'd go back to a good working relationship.

Never.

How could you do this to me?"

"I'll correct the author byline right now on social media. Then I'll make a formal correction in next month's magazine. I'm sorry."

Sorry? Oh, he was going to be sorry. She wanted to slice him apart right after she quit.

Only now, she couldn't pursue her new goal if she quit. She planned to find out what his vendetta was. Why he had given her this assignment, and why he was out to get Wesley and his dad.

Without saying a word, she walked out of his office and into hers. But not before knocking another photo from his wall and hearing it crash to the floor behind her.

***

Caitlyn slinked through Blake's office, determined to clear her name with Wesley. But the evidence she found wasn't what she expected.

Wesley might not believe she had nothing to do with that article, but he would have to believe something was not quite right when she gave him this information.

Blake's two-drawer file cabinet was full of information about Wesley's family.

She glanced around the office, afraid Blake would waltz in at any second and not sure what to do if he did. She didn't belong in his office, especially in the middle of the night, and it hadn't been easy to break in. Once she managed to get into his office, she rummaged through drawers in search of a key to the file cabinets.

It hadn't been easy, but then it had been a lot easier than she'd anticipated.

Her muscles twitched and she jumped when something

scraped across the floor.

A mouse? God, please no.

Her flashlight thudded to the ground and rolled, stopping at the box she'd put together for the documents. She kept expecting a hand to reach out at any moment and grab her, so she sat with her back flush against the wall, allowing her a view to the entryway.

She reached over and grabbed the flashlight. The handheld attracted more shadows than it cut, and she wasn't sure what was worse. The small beam of the light, or no light at all. She shut it off but decided shadowy light was better than nothing. Especially if a mouse roamed.

It was past two in the morning. She was known to put in plenty of late nights, but no one was allowed in Blake's office. She'd worked open the latch with a small pocket knife and would have no explanation if she was caught.

The wind scratched against the window. She jumped and huddled into her flashlight. Was that the wind? She couldn't be sure and didn't want to stand and find out.

She wasn't sure about anything anymore.

She found an extensive amount of information on someone named Jack Forrester, but none of it made sense piece by piece. It was like a puzzle, and she made copies of what she could to take with her and patch together to try to make sense of it. She took other things, information she hoped Blake wouldn't notice. Information on Johnson Webb.

Newspaper advertisements from over twenty-five years ago, character sketches of Samantha and her family, a picture of Wesley when he was in grade school. And birth certificates of people she'd never heard of.

Cold rushed down her spine when she found a copy of Wesley's family tree.

Johnson played a part in Blake's business, but something didn't make sense. People didn't keep information about their business partner's families unless they had ill intentions. And information the cops had found in the deceased home?

Why was Blake infatuated with this family? Was there something about Wesley and his family she didn't know? Her imagination thumped into overdrive and she wondered if they were in the witness protection program. Wesley was adamant no one know about his past. Was there more to his past than she knew?

Caitlyn was cautious to put everything back where she found it, so it wouldn't look like anyone disturbed Blake's paperwork. She placed the key in his desk drawer and wondered why it would be in such an obvious spot in the first place. She wondered if this was the information Chad was killed over and if so, why hadn't Blake hidden the key more carefully? Did he want someone to find it?

Oh God, was Blake involved in Chad's murder?

She took as much as she could in one box. Her keychain, which held a small can of mace and her pocket knife, was looped through a finger as she carried the box of copies with her. Her purse slapped against her thigh, and she had to sit the box down in order to lock the door behind her.

Wiping her hands down her pants leg, she stopped over to pick up the box. But that didn't help her clammy hands as she hurried to her car.

Even during a perfectly normal night, she'd feel wary. And this was no normal night.

Once inside the car and driving home, she kept one eye peeled to the rearview mirror to make sure no one followed.

Chad had been murdered. She had no idea what information he had, but Blake had a file cabinet full of information about Wesley and his family.

She wished Wesley was here with her. Maybe he could offer insight. But how did she know he wasn't capable of murder? Maybe his mother's death had done more to him than she realized. How did she know he wouldn't murder to hide his past? The old Wesley, no, did she really know him? A lot could change.

Once home, she brewed a cup of coffee and studied the documents. By seven, she sent Blake a quick text to tell him she was sick. She didn't want to give him any reason to be suspicious of her, but no way would she go to work today. Maybe he would think she was still trying to get over her anger.

She worked up the nerve to call Wesley, but of course he didn't answer. She sent a text.

Wesley? We need to talk.

She paced the floor for an hour before sending another message.

It's important. I found something you need to know about.

He's reply was short and succinct: *Nothing to discuss.*

She dialed him again. Voicemail picked up, and she called again, three times in a row before he finally answered.

"What?" His animosity stretched over the phone line.

Her voice shook, not at his anger, but at her growing fear. Should she take this to the police? If Wesley didn't want to talk to her, maybe the police should see this information to compare the information they pulled from Chad's RV.

"I said, we need to talk."

Silence.

She didn't know how much to reveal to him, especially over the phone, but he would never forgive her enough to listen to anything she said unless she came right out and told him what it was about.

She wondered if he'd hung up, but his breath over the phone line pulled at her throat.

"Look, Wesley, I know how pissed you are. I'm pissed, too. Blake admitted to replacing my article but not my byline. I found some information in his office, information concerning Chad and the file folder he had on you. I don't want to go into details over the phone, but you need to see this."

***

Tim lent his plane, and Wesley met Caitlyn at a small airstrip outside of Austin.

He didn't know who to trust anymore. Caitlyn's article prompted a lot of wavering in the racing community and fans, but he'd received more support than he'd expected.

And yet, none of that mattered to him. Caitlyn had betrayed him. He'd never known for her to be a liar, but a lot of things had changed. She had changed.

Wesley hauled a Banker's box into the plane as she carried a small suitcase. Indifference had taken the place of hurt and anger, and now he'd like to see what explanation she offered.

The only reason he'd agreed to this was curiosity

Once inside the plane, he dropped the box on the floor and opened the lid. "Is this what you insist is important?"

"There's a lot of stuff in there. I don't know what went missing from Chad's trailer, but I found a family tree. Or at least, parts of a family tree. I didn't have time to pour over all of it."

Wesley nodded and replaced the lid. She had been there the night Chad was murdered. He hadn't known it at the time, but she had watched the race. How did he know she didn't already know Chad? How did he know she didn't take this from Chad? Maybe she had waited ten years to destroy his reputation.

"So you think I should believe that Blake killed Chad?"

"No. Blake wasn't there that night. And what was his motive? But the fact he had the same information Chad did is suspicious."

"Maybe it wasn't the same information. It was taken, so we have no way to know."

"Maybe your dad—"

"My dad is no murderer," he snapped. He might not trust his dad, but he'd never believe his dad would take a life.

Caitlyn's long breath cut knives under his skin. His jaw tightened and he lowered his gaze. He had nothing left to say.

"You have to believe me that I didn't write that article, Wesley."

He gave her a blank expression. He had suffered tremendous pain and now there was nothing left.

"I confronted Blake and he agreed to correct the byline."

"If you didn't write it, then who did?"

"He didn't tell me."

"There were things in there no one could have known but you. If you didn't write it, you at least told Blake stuff he didn't need to know."

"I didn't tell him shit. Your dad knew. Your dad is his business partner. Maybe he told him a long time ago. Maybe Blake knew."

Wesley shook his head and glanced out the window, not that there was anything to see where he sat except blue sky. His dad had worked too hard at covering it up. He'd even managed to make the police believe Samantha was the one driving. Even when Wesley became semi-famous, none of the officers there at that time revealed anything they might have known about what happened that night. Why now?

He needed to contact his dad, ask him about Blake. Ask him about a lot of things he'd chosen to ignore over the past ten years.

He wanted to believe Caitlyn, but her name on the article was too damning. Many journalists had contacted him over the years and fluttered their heavy-lidded lashes, expecting him to give them dirty details of his day-to-day or offer an adventure they wouldn't find in their normal life.

Tim had been involved with a reporter for almost a year before realizing she was a journalist who merely wanted to get inside the racing community, and she'd been screwing at least one rival's team member. Maybe more. Not to find secrets, necessarily, and certainly not to uncover Wesley's, but because she was a groupie who got her kicks off being indirectly involved in the sport. Tim had almost married her before realizing she was using a pseudonym and posting status updates, pictures, and blogging about sticky topics. Nothing too libelous and nothing to cause damage, so Tim hadn't seen the need to pursue legal action. But he'd suffered a broken heart. Was still suffering. Some people even loved her for it, and she published a book about being the girlfriend of a racecar driver that quickly nosedived.

Last time they'd checked, the woman had moved on to hockey and was publishing short stories while working for a small newspaper. But it had changed Tim's life forever. Wesley's, too. And it had taught them to trust no one.

***

"Want something to drink?"

Caitlyn glanced up from the stack of paperwork covering

the floor. "More water would be great." She pushed the documents aside and lolled on the floor while Wesley stepped around the piles. It was like maneuvering a maze to get to the kitchen.

He brought back a bottle of aspirin and water. She declined the aspirin but gratefully took the water and sat up to take a drink. She screwed the top back on the plastic bottle and placed it beside the couch, then rested her back flat against the floor in a Yoga corpse pose. The floor offered no comfort for her aching neck.

"I've been sitting on this floor too long." She held up her hands, "and I have ink all over me."

"Sit on the couch a minute," Wesley said. "Take a break."

"I did that once. Ended up falling asleep." She moved her head from side to side to stretch her neck before sitting up again, then took another swig of water and grabbed the last document she'd been studying. It was a partnership contract between Blake and Johnson and the business. Something anyone would keep, just not in this pile of mess. "You might want to look at this one," she said, handing the contract to him. "You have a law degree, you can make more sense out of it than I can."

She and Wesley had combed through the information all night. It was already mid-afternoon the next day. She explained the conversation she had with Blake to Wesley and showed him the original article meant to be printed. She didn't know if he believed her, but the fact he let her stay spoke volumes.

"What else did Blake have in this cabinet you weren't able to get copies of?"

"Folders full of documents," she said. "Large manila folders and envelopes stuffed with things. I grabbed a few out of each one, made copies of some and then just took others. I didn't actually take a whole envelope with me. I thought it'd be too noticeable."

"I'd love to go through it," Wesley said. "What if we took it all to your house to study it then brought it back before he ever noticed it was missing?"

"That would be risky."

"And what you did wasn't?"

Caitlyn shrugged but had no reply. Yeah it had been risky. Being alone in the office at two AM wasn't the smartest thing she'd ever done. But she had to do something and she didn't regret what she'd done.

"Maybe there's more to this than even you're telling me," she said as she wriggled her butt up and rested her back against the couch.

"Like what?"

"I don't know. Maybe you're part of the witness protection program." Wesley wrinkled his forehead at her, then shook his head. "Why not? Your parents were both attorneys. Maybe your dad defended a mob boss or was working on a big case and lost, and maybe his life and that of his family was threatened."

"You *should* write a novel," Wesley interjected. "You have an overactive imagination. How could a famous racecar driver be in the witness protection program and get away with it?"

***

"Maybe Blake is just a freak," Wesley said, which he was more inclined to believe. If her boss used her to do a story on him, then completely changed her story and tried to harm Wesley's career by printing about the horrible wreck in such gory detail, *and* lied to her about starting the magazine on his own, what kind of person was he?

What else had he lied to her about?

"How do we know Blake didn't kill Chad?"

"How would he have gotten into his RV?" Caitlyn asked. "Isn't the security pretty tight? I didn't think just anyone could get back there."

Wesley shrugged and snatched the copy of his family tree— possibly the same family tree Chad had in his possession before he was killed—and studied it. Nothing made sense together or apart. There were too many gaps. Some birth certificates, things anybody would save, yet Blake had them on a family that wasn't his and on people Wesley never heard of.

"We have to find out who this Jack Forrester is," Wesley said, ignoring her statement. He had nothing further to discuss with her and even if he did believe she had nothing to do with that article, he'd still carry doubts.

"I can get Rayma to look in to it. She has connections."

"And why did Chad have this shit?"

"We don't know this is what he had."

Oh he knew all right. Somehow, her boss was involved with Chad and if that were true, Caitlyn's life could be in danger. Both of their lives could be.

Why this information would be worth killing over was beyond him. Maybe it wasn't. All they had found in Chad's trailer was a family tree and a large file folder with his name on it. It could be just coincidence.

Yeah right.

He thought his life was fairly simple, he thought he knew his parents' life story.

But what if he didn't?

"We have to go back and look through this information," Wesley said. "But I don't want you to go by yourself."

A knock at the door startled them. He'd called Adam earlier and told him he wouldn't be available and didn't want to be disturbed. He should be running practice laps, working on his car, greeting fans. He had canceled his plans and holed himself in his RV, this new information consuming him. The curtains were closed tightly against the sun but it still shined through the cracks.

They hurriedly stuffed the papers back into the box, losing the order they had spent hours placing them in. The knock grew more forceful.

"Just a minute," Wesley yelled as Caitlyn took the case and scurried to his bedroom. He wasn't sure why there were worried about hiding it, but all he needed was some cop to search his home again and find it, then naturally think he had taken it out of Chad's trailer.

There was his motive.

"Damn," he said as the thought struck him. If Chad had this information, and now Wesley had it that could create an assumption of guilt. The headlines reeled through his head.

Wesley Webb kills Chad to protect his identity.

He peeped out the spyhole. The ground dropped out from

under him.

Dad?

He opened the door and scowled. "What are you doing here?"

Chapter Seventeen

THE SOUND OF Wesley's voice proved he wasn't pleased with whoever knocked on the door. Caitlyn only heard low voices and not enough to figure out who it was, but her heart pounded furiously nonetheless. She hid the box full of documents in the back of his closet, and finally sat on his bed to take a deep breath.

As an invited guest, she had no reason to be scared. No reason to hide.

But the box...she was concerned about the box and the information in it.

She hadn't slept much last night. Wesley had taken a nap on the floor and she stretched out on the couch, but nightmares had plagued her.

She'd dreamed she was in a tightly closed room, surrounded by stacks of papers on walls, stuck to corners and along the ceiling. As she removed the papers in an attempt to escape, they grew into larger stacks. The only way to get out was by figuring out how the pieces fit together. Only, every time she took one piece apart to fit it to something, another room opened revealing more of the same things, sinking her further into a hole.

Coffee and data buzzed through her veins, and though her body was tired, her mind wouldn't rest.

Wesley opened the door and his normally healthy complexion was mixed with the weariness already present, and a new pallor. One not there before. She just stared, waiting for his next move. Waiting for him to say something.

"What's wrong?"

"My father," he said. She sprang from the bed, quickly going to him. She thought something happened to his dad but before she said anything, he corrected her. "He's here. He wants to see you."

"Me?" she asked, taking a step back. "Why? Did he say?"

Wesley nodded.

She stepped through the doorway, limbs heavy. What was he doing here? Why did he want to see her?

Johnson regarded her, grimaced, and tried to cover his pained expression. He failed. She'd been pulled uphill on an emotional roller coaster for the past few days. Seeing his face gave life to her fears. The roller coaster lost control and plunged, only she forgot to scream.

"I'm afraid I have bad news," Johnson told her, confirming her fears that whatever the reason for his visit wasn't good. "Blake has been in an accident."

"Blake?" She placed a hand over her chest to steady herself. It didn't work. She had expected bad news but never expected it'd have anything to do with Blake. "Is he..."

"He's in ICU."

Caitlyn's legs buckled. Wesley's arms snaked around the back of her and held her upright. Didn't he know she didn't want to stand? She just wanted to sink to the floor and let it consume her.

She clutched her throat. "What happened?"

"Car accident. The Jaws of Life had to get him out. He's alive, but we're not sure if he'll make it. We've been trying to find you. I'm not sure if he told you, but I'm a partner in the business, so I rushed over as soon as I heard. I'm going to be taking care of things for a while."

Blake. She hated him sometimes, was furious with him now and their last encounter hadn't gone well. She would never trust him again but he'd been her mentor. Gave her a start in this business. She'd worked for him so long she didn't have a choice but to develop some type of relationship with him. She never wanted him hurt. Not seriously anyway.

"How..." she began, "how did he wreck?"

"Nobody really knows," Johnson replied. "It was a one car collision. He seemed to go off the road, maybe hit the ditch, and flipped several times. It was early in the morning so we're assuming he was going to work. Maybe he swerved to miss an animal. Maybe he was still tired and fell asleep. It's all speculation right now."

She wrenched herself from Wesley's supportive embrace and slumped to the couch. Maybe without those strong arms around her she could actually think.

Blake was alive, but might not make it. He had information, possibly the same Chad was killed over, and now he could lose his life, too.

Or maybe somebody had tried to kill him. Maybe someone tried to run him off the road. She didn't voice her opinion aloud but wished she could trust Johnson and tell him what they found. Why would information about Johnson's life be involved in all of this?

"Are you okay?" Wesley rubbed his knuckles on the back of his neck as he sat beside her on the couch.

No she wasn't okay. Someone tried to kill Blake, she suspected, and over information that was, at this moment, hiding in Wesley's closet.

"We need to talk about some things," Johnson said. "I'll be running the office for a while, so I'm your boss right now."

"Why'd you come all the way here?" Wesley asked, the tone of his voice clearly stating he didn't like it. Caitlyn wondered if he suspected his dad of something.

"We couldn't locate Caitlyn and I knew she was doing a story on you. I finally found out she came here. It's not really something I wanted a complete stranger to tell her, and it's not something I wanted to tell her over the phone, so I flew down. Besides, you're my son and I haven't talked to you in ages."

"There's a reason for that."

***

Caitlyn hated hospitals.

She'd spent a few days in one when she'd been hurt in the wreck involving Samantha's death. That recollection only intensified her distress as she walked down the hallway to Blake's room, her shoes squeaky against the puke-colored floor.

He'd been moved from ICU and was now allowed visitors.

She knocked on his door before entering, but received no response. She poked her head in to see he appeared asleep.

Tiptoeing in, she closed the door and set a vase of flowers on the table. He looked so helpless, not like the man she was accustomed to fighting with. Tubes were attached to his chest and a monitor kept a steady beep. His prognosis was good and she hoped he would be out soon. Maybe then she could find some answers she needed.

Not ready to disturb him yet, she turned to leave, but he called out to her. She faced him to find him watching her. He tried to offer a full-fledged smile but only managed a contortion. She'd take what she could get. At least it meant he was still breathing.

His finger signaled her to come near. She walked to him and clasped his hand. "How are you?"

"How do I look?" he asked.

Bandages covered parts of his body. Deep scratches lined his face. His paleness overcome by yellow bruising. "You're lucky to be alive. Lucky to be conscious right now."

Blake struggled to sit up and grimaced. Caitlyn pressed a hand on his chest, urging him to stay put.

"I'm sorry this happened," she said.

"It wasn't your fault."

Caitlyn scooted a chair closer and sat, not at all sure what to talk about now. She wanted answers. She wanted to know why he printed that article with her name on it besides ratings. She wanted to know how Blake knew about it and why he made Wesley sound like a cold-hearted jerk.

And she wanted to know why he had Wesley's family tree.

"Is everything okay between us?" Blake asked, attempting to tear a piece of paper from the napkin on his bedside.

"Not really, but I hate that this happened to you."

Blake stuck the napkin in his mouth and chewed on it like

bubble gum. "I'm sorry about everything."

"Sorry about the article printed in your magazine containing my byline?" Blake averted his eyes. "I should sue you," she continued. "Wesley should sue you."

"Nothing in there is false."

"How do you know? You told me you didn't know anything about him. Come to find out, you do. Even if it isn't false to an extent, it makes him sound inhumane. I can tell you he isn't."

"It sounds like you really care about him."

"I've known him since I was six years old. I thought I was going to marry him once. Of course I care about him. He's like family."

"I've never had a close family," Blake admitted, the first insight into his personal life that she remembered. She only realized now how little she knew about him but knowing how important keeping the past a part of the past was, she never brought it up. "You're about the only family I have."

"Families don't do what you did to me."

Blake sighed, tried to move, and winced. He was tired and she should let him rest, but the mixture of sympathy and anger kept her grounded to the chair.

"There are a few things you should know," he said. "I guess it wouldn't hurt for you to know them."

"What?"

Blake hesitated. Whatever he had to say obviously wasn't easy, and for a moment she felt guilty. At this point in her life, Caitlyn was ready to walk away. Now with Johnson supposedly running the magazine, she didn't want to work there anymore. She'd lost her ambition, her trust in Blake and in her job, and it was time for her to look elsewhere.

But the stacks of paperwork still hidden in his office kept her hanging on. If she left now, she would have no connection to the information, which might be vital. Until she and Wesley solved this mystery, she had no intention of going anywhere.

"My son..." he trailed off, "was recently killed."

Surprise shot through her. Blake had been married? And he had a child?

"I'm...sorry for your loss." What else could she say? His loss didn't give him an excuse to ruin her life, her name. She was waiting for that explanation.

"I got married when I was young but it didn't last long. She left me. I didn't know I had a son until he was half-grown. She was already remarried and he knew that man as his father. I wouldn't let up until she told him about me and we had a chance to get to know each other."

"What was his name?"

The roaring AC drowned out the silence, but it was their conversation that brought chills to her arms. Blake hesitated too long.

The nurse returned to check on him. After she left, Caitlyn rose from her chair and paced.

"Blake? What was his name?"

He huffed out a breath. "Chad Armstrong."

"What?" She stumbled back as cold rushed into her core. Her mouth opened, going dry. Blake shifted his weight to sit up higher.

"Can you put this pillow behind my back?" he asked.

She obliged, then sat and stared at him, demanding to know more.

He closed his eyes and, even without bandages, he'd be impossible to read. She wasn't sure he was well enough to be having this conversation, yet she'd selfishly draw everything out of him she could.

"What a coincidence he was into racing, also, and one of Wesley's prime opponents," she accused, finally finding her voice.

"I've always enjoyed racing. I kept up with Wesley's accomplishments. Chad met Johnson, unaware his relationship with his son was strained. That made him want to try out racing and he succeeded. He always looked up to Wesley. There were reasons why he shouldn't let Wesley know he knew his dad and he understood. But he loved racing. And did it for no other reason."

"And why is that?" she asked.

"Why is what?" His eyes opened. They were red, dry, and tired.

Where was her sympathy?

"Why shouldn't Chad let Wesley know he knew his dad?"

"Oh come on, Caitlyn. You know the reasons. Chad and Wesley's relationship was already difficult. Why should he add to that?"

"Then why did you send me to do a story on Wesley?"

"Reasons I already told you. I found out you knew him and hoped you could use that advantage to get a story on him. Our magazine has been falling behind lately."

"Apparently, you already knew the story on him," she said, on the verge of admitting what she found in his office. "You printed it. I want to know what's going on. I want to know why you printed that story."

"Because I thought it would get a better reception than your heartfelt hero's story," he said. "As I told you, our magazine is flagging and I needed something worthwhile to be printed."

"Or maybe because you blame him for your son's death."

"No," Blake said, but it didn't convince her.

"I don't believe you." Caitlyn rose from the chair and turned away lest she pummel his already beaten body. She had to get out of here but before she left, she turned to him, holding on to the doorknob for support. "Something's going on. Your son's been murdered and I can't help but wonder if it's the same reason that put you in this hospital. You print this story in your magazine and expect me to accept it and Johnson is the reason this magazine exists in the first place. Believe me, I will find out what's going on."

"Drop it, Caitlyn. Please."

"Why?"

When Blake didn't answer, she opened the door. "Bye Blake. I'll be praying for you."

"Caitlyn," he croaked. She paused, waiting to see if he'd changed his mind and was now willing to tell her something. Anything.

"Watch your back."

***

"Cut."

The ringing of Wesley's cell phone interrupted the commercial he was filming, and the scowl on the director's face relayed his annoyance. Wesley normally didn't do commercials, but this was for his sponsor's new and improved oil.

Unfortunately for the camera people, Wesley's car and crew members were in a slight crisis hundreds of miles away and needed to call him regularly. This was the third time in less than two hours. And, also unfortunate for the director and his crew, Wesley's problem was a lot more important than a damned commercial.

But this time it wasn't Adam. "Hello, Wesley."

"Rayma?"

"Yes, I've been trying to reach Caitlyn, but she hasn't answered her cell."

"She went to see Blake in the hospital," Wesley said, somewhat irritated. How had Rayma gotten his cell phone number? "She's not here."

"I'm sorry to be calling your cell phone. Caitlyn said absolutely do not use it unless it's an emergency, and I thought this might constitute one."

"What is it?" Wesley ambled away from the onlookers and waved his hand, indicating he'd get back with them in a minute.

"I really need to find Caitlyn."

Wesley's blood ran cold. "Is she in danger?"

"She could be. I just found out Chad was Blake's son."

"You're kidding?" Wesley clamped a hand to his chest and glanced around, scanning the crowd for his father.

Caitlyn had gone to see Blake, but Johnson decided to stay and visit with his son. Wesley, determined not to let his dad's presence bother him, went on about his business, showing his dad just how busy he was. They didn't have time to talk, much less sit down and visit, which was fine with him. Wesley couldn't figure why Johnson chose to stick around, why he chose to watch the filming. Other than the excuse his dad had used that he wanted to pursue a relationship with his son. But that out was out the question. Wesley had no desire to get to know his dad now. Not after everything.

Instead of seeing his dad, he saw two officers speaking to the director, who pointed Wesley's direction.

"Oh fuck," he muttered. "Rayma, I've got to go. Please find Caitlyn, make sure she's okay."

"Wesley Webb?" One officer asked as they approached.

"Yeah," he huffed, ending the call.

"You're under arrest for the murder of Chad Armstrong."

***

"I've filed a writ to hear before the judge to see if we can get you out of here."

"I didn't ask you to do that. I have my own attorney." As a matter of fact, Wesley had already been in contact with him.

"You've been charged with murder. You need all the help you can get."

"You're not licensed to practice law in North Carolina. Only Texas."

"Actually, I have a license in both states." Johnson sat back in his seat and adjusted his tie.

"You've got to be kidding me." Wesley scrubbed a hand over his face.

"Good thing, huh?"

"Yeah," Wesley muttered. "A big fucking celebration."

"No need to be so pissy about it."

"I'm being charged with murder, and my dad wants to be my attorney. My dad, who also has a license to practice law in the state Chad was killed in."

Johnson shrugged. "Sorry. Don't forget we lived here before we moved to Texas."

"Oh, I haven't forgotten."

"They found your fingerprints in Chad's RV. Easily explained." Johnson held up his hand to silence his son's forthcoming outburst. "You worked with the victim. You probably visited his trailer on more than one occasion."

The statement proved his dad was accustomed to the

defense side of an equation. No matter his client's guilt or innocence. Wesley wasn't guilty, and it pissed him off to be here, in this tiny room, talking with the man who'd appointed himself Wesley's legal counsel. It pissed him off to be here, locked in jail with actual felons, all of who eyeballed him like he'd be their next tasty meal. Lucky for him, the jailer was a racing fan and had given Wesley his own cell. For now.

Wesley would miss Sunday's race, and possibly the next few races, losing valuable points in the long haul.

And he was the only suspect. Were the cops giving up their investigation and going on the only information they found? It was crazy. The only thing they had to go on was fingerprints and a family tree. Fingerprints might be probable cause to arrest, but not to keep him there indefinitely, without bail?

"Tell me how you know Blake."

"What has that got to do with any of this?" Johnson asked.

"Blake is Caitlyn's boss. Come to find out, you're his silent partner. He sends her to do a story on me the same day Chad is killed. Chad, as you know, is Blake's son. And let's not forget Keegan is dating Caitlyn's best friend. It's like one big fucking family reunion."

***

Rayma knocked on Caitlyn's door after Caitlyn stewed, mulled, and attempted to call Wesley several times. They left the information she'd found in his trailer so she didn't have that to study, and nothing else would hold her attention. She was tempted to return to Blake's office and search some more but heeded Wesley's warning.

Blake was hiding something. But he'd refused to tell her anything else.

Rayma waltzed through the door and helped herself to Caitlyn's wine. "Here, have a drink."

Reminded Caitlyn of the last time she had opened a bottle and where it ended up, now part of the pages of the magazine she kept as a reminder of many things. For one, why she needed to stay with her job a little longer.

"Everything okay?" Caitlyn leaned her elbow on the counter and watched her friend drain her drink and pace across the living room.

She was nervous herself. She'd been looking over her shoulder since she left the hospital after Blake's threatening words. He'd assured her he was only concerned about her wellbeing and just wanted her to be cautious.

Yeah, right.

"You're making me nervous, Rayma. Would you sit down and stop fidgeting?"

"I talked to Wesley today. I've been trying to call you."

"You talked to Wesley?"

Rayma set down her empty glass and flexed her fingers, turning away from Caitlyn to pace again. "Yeah, I was trying to find you. Wanted to let you know what I found out about Blake."

"Blake told me about Chad."

Rayma's head snapped around. Thank God she had finally stopped pacing.

Caitlyn sighed, sagged on the couch, and Rayma joined her. "He admitted that Chad was his son. Said he was married for a short while—"

"No," Rayma interrupted.

"No?"

"No. He wasn't married. He had an affair. *She* was married."

Caitlyn's heart sank. Another lie. "That's not what he told me."

Caitlyn curled her feet up under her as Rayma grabbed her laptop from the table and fired it up.

"When did you talk to Wesley?" Caitlyn asked as she studied her friend's stilted movements. "I've been trying to call him all evening."

"Earlier, on the phone. I couldn't get in touch with you so I called him. What's your password?"

"Webb87."

Rayma's lashes flickered. "Webb?"

"Yes, plus eight-seven."

Rayma nodded and keyed in the password.

Caitlyn chuckled. "Do you have a problem with my password?"

"No, it's just no wonder you couldn't get over your first love when you surround yourself with reminders of him."

"He wasn't just my first love," Caitlyn whispered. Her friend didn't understand, and she wasn't in the mood to explain it right now. Besides, Rayma was in a tizzy about something anyway.

Rayma shoved the laptop to her. "I don't know how to tell you this, so I think I'll just let the news tell you."

Her stomach rolled. "What is it?"

Rayma tapped the screen. "Watch."

Footage of Wesley being placed in cuffs and ushered into the back of a police car flashed across the screen.

"Wesley Joel Webb was arrested today for the murder of his rival, Chad Armstrong, known as 'Strong Arm' to many of his fans."

"What!" Caitlyn shot up. Rayma managed to catch the laptop before it plummeted to the floor, but Caitlyn could care less about the laptop. Her whole world had plummeted.

The newscaster appeared to have no concern in the world, as if her news hadn't exploded Caitlyn's already shattered world.

Her nose clogged, chest heavy as tears stabbed at her. She rubbed her eyes, trying to eliminate the fog overtaking her mind.

"You okay?" Rayma stood beside her and jostled her shoulder.

"He didn't do it." She folded her hands and pressed them against her chin, fighting back tears "He didn't do it," she said again, this time with more force. She wheeled to Rayma and clutched her friend, desperate to find hope. "I have to go." She dropped Rayma's hand and whirled away, her thighs shaky.

"Where?" Rayma asked, following Caitlyn into her room.

"To see Wesley." She stopped, shoulders hunching as she looked at the floor. "Tell me he bailed out."

"They haven't set bail," Rayma said.

"Oh God."

She wanted to rant and rave. Wanted to call every cop in

the world and tell them Wesley did not kill Chad. He didn't. How could this happen? How could they accuse him of murder?

She rubbed her neck and blindly went to her closet, her footsteps scuffing against the floor as each forward motion seemed to push her backward. She steadied herself on the doorframe, her body limp, and skimmed her closet but saw nothing.

She couldn't just stay here and wait. She sensed Rayma's presence behind her but everything around her was dark and muted.

A knock sounded at her door. She bolted into action, sprinting to the door all the while praying it was news about Wesley.

"Keegan," Rayma said when Caitlyn just stood there. "Come in." Rayma grabbed Keegan, eyed Caitlyn, and pulled him inside.

Caitlyn ignored him and returned to the bedroom, pulled clothes from her closet and stuffed them into a suitcase. No thought of what she grabbed or if she'd be able to wear any of it.

Emptiness crushed her as she pictured Wesley, in a cold dark jail cell and with his name in ruins. First the article, now his arrest. Had she inadvertently caused this? Was Blake involved?

Yes Blake was involved. He wrote that article and forged her byline. To destroy Wesley. But how did Chad's murder relate?

Chad. Blake's son. Maybe Blake suspected Wesley of murdering his son and set out to destroy him with that story. Was it a coincidence Chad had been killed the same night Blake assigned Caitlyn to do the story?

Doubt knotted her stomach.

Rayma snatched the clothes out of the suitcase that Caitlyn haphazardly threw in. "What are you doing?" Caitlyn asked.

"Preventing you from making a horrendous mistake," Rayma said. "You won't be able to see Wesley anyway."

"I can stand outside with the rest of the crowd and support him."

"Yeah that shows a lot of support," Rayma said as she hung a shirt in the closet.

"I can be near, so when he gets out..."

"Do you really want to be a part of the media mob?" Rayma

asked. "You're staying here. Keegan needs to talk to you."

"I have nothing to say to him." Caitlyn pulled clothes out again. It was a chain, her pulling clothes from her closet, Rayma stuffing them back in, but was finally broken when Keegan gently tugged Caitlyn aside.

"Johnson wanted me to tell you a few things," Keegan said. She observed him, wondering who this man was and if she and her friend should truly trust him.

"You're right, I shouldn't go tonight and stand in that crowd," she said, replying to Rayma's remark of earlier and ignoring Keegan's hands on her shoulders. "I should find out from Blake what the hell is going on, *then* I should go."

"You shouldn't go see Blake," Keegan said, "because you shouldn't trust him. He's the cause of all of this. He's trying to sabotage Wesley's career to get to Johnson because they had a major falling out. He hates Johnson."

"Enough for him to kill his own son?"

Keegan shrugged. "There's no love lost between them."

"I've worked for Blake a long time," Caitlyn said, trying to digest this information. "There's no way this could be true. I don't even know you." She wrenched away from Keegan, crinkled her nose at Rayma, and marched into her living room.

"You said you hated Johnson. Was that a lie?"

"Please listen," Keegan said, following her. "You may think you know Blake—"

"I think you should leave," she said, interrupting his spiel. Didn't matter that he was right. Blake *couldn't* be trusted. But she had worked for him far too long to believe he was capable of murdering his own son or framing an innocent man. Even if she hadn't known he had a son. "I need to get this straightened out on my own."

"Cait." Rayma caught her elbow. "Blake keeps lying to you. He lied to you about being married. He's lied to you for years about his business. You can't trust him. What else do you think he's lied to you about? He sent you on this assignment, then put his own story in the magazine with your byline. He's using you, and you're going to get hurt."

"I'm not going to see Blake. I'm going to see Wesley."

Chapter Eighteen

THE CROWD SURROUNDING the county jail was a mixture of people who supported Wesley, those who wanted to see him hanged, and those who wanted to catch a story. Why they would wait around on the verge of mauling each other was beyond Caitlyn, but she was doing the same thing.

She tried to keep her professionalism when a news cameraman panned right over her, but realized anyone who spotted her—including Wesley—would think she was only here for a story.

A story didn't matter to her anymore.

She acted like a needy woman who, after the most memorable weekend of her life, now thought her future was to include the man who gave it to her. Their lovemaking didn't mean they had a relationship. It didn't even mean he wanted her back in his life. Yet here she was. And she planned to stay a while.

"What are you doing here?" Someone captured her arm and she whipped around, ready to defend herself.

"Tim?" Relief washed over her when she recognized Wesley's uncle through his hazy disguise, although relief probably wasn't something she normally experienced when she saw Tim.

"What are you doing here?" he asked again as he pulled her through a throng of people. She never realized Wesley was *this* umm...popular, and cringed to see some people holding signs reading 'execute him.'

Caitlyn had to slow down and let go of Tim's hand when

she couldn't keep up. She carried a bag small enough to utilize as a carry-on for the airplane. It held bare necessities: her phone, pens, a notepad, a tablet and camera, but she'd left her coveted laptop at home. The bag was still awkward to carry. She bumped into several people and when they glared at her or pushed her around, she had to take it slower. Tim looked back, grabbed her bag and her hand, and pulled her away again.

She had no idea where he was taking her, or why she was following him.

"I came to give Wesley my support," she said once she was actually able to hear herself think.

He tipped his head toward the crowd. "In a mob like that? Most of them will be staying overnight, sleeping on the ground. No telling what could happen."

News vans were perched in the parking lot, cameras rolling, newscasters talking and showing viewers what was happening outside the jail.

"I've been known to do that myself," Caitlyn muttered, none too proud.

"How will Wesley even know you're here for support?"

"How did you know?" she countered.

"Saw you on the news." Tim stepped up into a motorhome, much smaller than Wesley's RV, and ushered her in.

She spotted a television, Wesley's picture splayed all over the news. Tears burned her eyes, carving a hole in her chest. She couldn't believe he was in jail.

Tim cranked the motorhome and drove off. Caitlyn didn't protest. He could've had something to do with Chad's murder. She wasn't sure she could trust Tim but if he was taking her to her death, she didn't have the strength to fight.

He drove to Wesley's RV, situated inside the RV camp set up for the racers and their families.

"You can stay here for now," Tim told her. She followed him to the door and waited while he unlocked it.

She wasn't sure how to feel about staying in Wesley's RV, alone. Not that she wasn't fine being alone, used to being alone. But Chad had been murdered in his RV.

Alone.

She shuddered and ran into Tim's back when he halted at the door.

A scream formed at the edge of her throat.

Wesley's trailer had been ransacked. Broken dishes left trails of a madman. The couches were gutted, tables overturned, and cabinet doors left open. Even the refrigerator door was open, its contents spilling to the floor.

It appeared the intruder had been searching for something in a hurry, and didn't take the time to be nice about it.

Tim laid a hand on her shoulder before she could run to the bedroom to check on the contents of the suitcase.

If it was gone...

What did this mean?

"Stay here while I make sure whoever did this is no longer here."

He grabbed his phone and skirted the rubbish on the floors, picking his way through so he wouldn't step on anything. Caitlyn assumed he was dialing 911 when she heard the three number cadences on the phone.

She didn't stay put. She waited until he was deeply concentrating, then she ran into the bedroom, opened the closet and prayed the case would still be there.

It was gone.

***

"You have a visitor."

Wesley was accustomed to those words now and expected to see his dad. But when he saw Caitlyn instead, his steps faltered.

Happiness, fear, dread. *Relief.* God, how could he face her?

His eyes roamed over her as he sunk into the chair and took the phone.

"Are you okay?" Caitlyn touched the smeared glass and curled her fingers against it. Her eyes were puffy and red, her face swollen. She looked like she hadn't had much sleep.

Damn, she was beautiful. Even with her face all pale and

puffy and swollen.

Wesley nodded and steeled himself against his rising grief.

"Tim was going to let me stay at your RV...but, we found it ransacked."

He tightened his grip on the phone and brought his free hand to the glass. He wouldn't react. Wouldn't reveal a reaction. Not because he didn't trust her, but because he didn't want her to worry.

If someone had ransacked his RV, that someone was probably the murderer, and that murderer was still on the loose.

"I don't want you staying there," he said, more forcefully than he intended. At her frown, he continued. "Whoever broke in could be back. You don't need to be there when they do."

"The box is gone." Her words were weak and shaky. It took him a moment to realize she was talking about the paperwork hidden in the box. The paperwork that might hold the key to his innocence, if only he could figure it out.

"I have it," he said. Her saucy eyes implored his, and he continued. "It's at my house."

"Oh," she said, frowning. "I should go look it over."

"No. Not without me."

Her fingers folded in as if she reached for him through the glass. He imagined she was squeezing his hand.

He shifted in his seat. "Whoever went to my RV could go to my house next. I don't want you there alone."

"I could take Tim."

For some reason, that left a sour taste in his mouth.

Tim didn't think much of Caitlyn. He had access to Wesley's RV and was always welcome, even though it was strictly Wesley's. Letting Caitlyn stay the night in his RV, without asking Wesley, was a step in Caitlyn's favor, even if it was only to keep an eye on her.

Or something worse. God, no. He swiped his hand over his face in an attempt to swipe the doubt from his mind.

He focused on Caitlyn. For the first time since his confinement, he feared he'd never make it out of here. Never be able to touch Caitlyn again.

"Wait for me?" He yearned to take his hands and wipe away

the worry line creasing Caitlyn's brows. He wanted to touch her face. Feel her soft skin beneath the roughness of his fingers. But that wasn't possible.

Why hadn't he touched her more when he had the chance? He should've. Every damned chance he had, he should've.

As soon as he got out of this place, he would touch every crevice of her body. He'd make up the past few days, the past few years. And she would know, without delay, how he felt about her. The words he couldn't say.

For now, he was left with touching her hand through the glass separating them.

"Of course I'll wait for you," Caitlyn said. "And I'll do what I can to get you out of here."

***

"I want to know what's going on," Wesley demanded the moment Johnson entered the room in the jail's meeting room.

Johnson was immaculately dressed in a gray pinstriped suit. He took his time shedding his jacket and placed it on the chair behind him.

Contempt rang hollow in Wesley's ears. His dad was always good at melodrama.

"Blake is after me," Johnson admitted after a lengthy silence. Wesley wondered if it was to give his dad an opportunity to think about what to say or if he already had it planned. "He's been trying to take over the company for years and I have learned recently he will stop at nothing to do it. He's trying to destroy my career, my family's career."

"And how is Caitlyn involved?"

"I don't know if you should trust her," Johnson said. "She works for Blake, probably has a grudge against you. He's trying to sabotage my entire life and that of my family. He'll bring you down to bring me down and he's using her to do it. Just look at that article in the magazine. It had Caitlyn's name all over it."

"She said it wasn't her. Maybe Blake did it."

"How did he know all that stuff if she didn't tell him?"

"You, maybe."

"Now why would I do that after everything I did to cover it up?"

"Anyone could find out if they wanted to. News is news, and with the internet these days, it isn't hard to come across shit like that."

"It was buried well back then," Johnson said.

It was true. Wesley had no idea how his dad did it, but it was almost like that night had never happened. He often wondered if that attributed to his guilt. Maybe he should have owned up to it instead of running away from the people who loved him. Johnson claimed he loved Samantha but wasn't willing to let his son suffer for her needless death.

Johnson took a sip of the coffee from the Styrofoam cup. How could he drink that shit? A million other things tasted better than jail coffee. No telling what all was in that stuff.

"Tell me about Chad," Wesley said.

"Haven't we already discussed this?"

"I want to know everything."

"How is it going to prove your innocence?"

"If we can piece it together, we can find out who in the hell is doing it and they can take my place in jail."

"And if it's Caitlyn?"

"Why don't you sell your part of the business to Blake?" Wesley probed, ignoring Johnson's accusation.

"That's a long and complicated subject, son. I probably would have if he hadn't threatened me."

"Is that why you killed his son?"

Johnson almost choked on his coffee before it spilled all over the place. He fumbled for a napkin to wipe some from his shirt. No one milled around the small meeting room, and Johnson had to use his suit jacket to swab the spill from his clothes and from the desk, which drenched some of his paperwork. "Dammit, this was my good suit."

"You don't have any others?"

Johnson rubbed at the stain on his shirt with his hands in an attempt to prevent it from soaking into the fabric. "I can't believe you'd even think that I could be involved in what happened to Chad in any way."

"There's more to this than you're telling me. Would you go so far as to kill to cover up my past?"

"No," Johnson said, his attention still on the stain. "Why would I take those chances?"

Wesley shrugged. "Maybe you don't want to risk being charged with tampering."

Johnson scoffed. "They couldn't pin that on me. The statute of limitations has run."

Bile rose in Wesley's throat. How far would his dad go to cover up his past?

Probably not near as far as Tim.

Wesley shook that thought aside. Tim had nothing to do with this. Wesley would bet his life on it. And his life might be all he had left.

Chapter Nineteen

"WE'VE GOT TO get him out of there."

"And just how do you propose I do that?"

"Find someone to take the fall. He'll be compensated."

"No one will be willing to admit to murder."

"For enough money they will."

"No way. You don't have enough money to motivate someone to confess to murder."

"Find someone. Make sure he understands we'll get him out."

***

"Wesley Webb." Wesley turned to see his dad and an officer. The officer unlocked the door. "You've been released."

What?

His dad nodded at him and turned to walk away. The officer glared, tapping his toe against the concrete as Wesley just stood there.

He was being released?

It took him all of two seconds to follow his dad out and catch up to him.

"What's going on?"

"They've had a confession." Johnson parked his arm behind Wesley in an almost hug as they made their way to retrieve Wesley's belongings.

Though they had never seen eye to eye, his dad deserved a

big thanks, so he returned the awkward hug.

"What happened? Who was it?"

"Some friend of Chad's admitted to having a falling out with him."

Johnson opened the door to reveal a sun Wesley never thought to see again.

"What about Derrick?"

"Ongoing investigation."

Gratitude filled Wesley when Johnson handed him his cap and sunglasses. They swam their way through a pool of media and Wesley wondered if it had been that way every day, or if news about his release had already gotten out.

He was impressed with the way his dad handled them. "There's been a confession to Chad's murder and now they have the correct person in custody. We're glad Wesley's been released and we appreciate his fans' support. You'll need to contact law enforcement for the details of the defendant's arrest."

The media stuffed microphones into Wesley's face and fired questions one after the other.

"I'm glad to be released," Wesley said. "And like my attorney said, I appreciate everyone's support."

The heat choked him. Damn, his lungs felt like he'd run a marathon. It hadn't been this hot two weeks ago. Had he missed that much of summer already?

"What will you do now?" someone asked him.

"Race."

Johnson pulled him away and they ignored the rest of the questions. He dropped Wesley off at a Tim's RV.

"Why don't you come in for a while?" Wesley asked. Even if he didn't like his dad, he'd helped tremendously in making a bad situation a little better.

"No." Johnson eyed his wristwatch. "I have some things to take care of." Wesley wondered if he avoided coming in so he wouldn't have to see Tim, but he didn't question it further.

"Send me a bill for your services," Wesley said.

"No," Johnson replied. "I won't send you a bill for my services. You're my son."

Wesley outstretched his hand. "I owe you a thank you."

Johnson ignored the hand and gave him a hug instead. "You still have a lot to do to get your life back together," he said. "Let me know if I can help."

"I'll probably need representation to get my butt back in racing."

"I'll be in touch."

***

As Wesley showered, scrubbing himself of the filth permeating his body after his jail time, he prayed this nightmare was finally over. Being cooped in a small cell had almost killed him. He longed to get out on the track and experience freedom. He longed to race.

He didn't know the man who had confessed, but Wesley was glad the spotlight was off him.

He'd missed two weeks of racing, but his rankings were high and he still had a chance to win the championship. He was bound and determined to win and now that his goal was first and foremost in his mind, especially after spending time in a jail cell.

Someone had confessed to Chad's murder. There was nothing more Wesley could do. Nothing more he wanted to do but win the championship.

And spend every night in Caitlyn's arms. He'd missed her.

With the news running rampant on his life, the information already printed, and fans hungry to know more about him—especially now—it would be the perfect time for a biography of his life. So why shouldn't he agree? Let her write the biography, let her be a part of his life every day.

He was falling for her again. It'd be easy to get used to her presence. To have her stay with him, watching and supporting him. To make love to her every day. Other racers kept a family, why couldn't he?

He'd called her, asked her to meet him at his home, so he could spend the next few days with her as he waited for the decision on when he could return to work.

***

Wesley and Caitlyn spent the next three days in bed. By the third day, he decided eating finger foods and champagne was getting old, so he slapped some steaks on the grill and went to find Caitlyn, who had gone outside to snap pictures of the landscape after a light rain.

He missed racing, and tomorrow was qualifying day. He'd have to get up early and fly to Pocono to get to the track. Although Caitlyn hadn't said anything, he could tell by the downward curl of her lips that she agreed with Tim. He should take more time off.

Wasn't going to happen. He'd already taken enough time off and he had to get back out there. But he wanted her with him.

She hadn't quit her job yet. He wasn't happy about that, but he understood her reasons. She wanted to find out more about Blake's and Johnson's partnership and she was afraid she couldn't do that if she left. But her boss had agreed to give her time off.

His dad had confessed to telling Blake about their past and explained that Blake had been the one to write the article and used Caitlyn's name to protect himself. Wesley couldn't really complain anymore. His popularity had soared.

He found Caitlyn underneath a large shade tree. Sunlight crumbled through the rain clouds. The air had cooled and the rain was just enough to stir up dust.

She turned and smiled when he walked up, waving the dirt-soaked daisies she'd picked. "Hope you don't mind."

Locking his fingers behind her neck, he pulled her forward and supported his forehead on hers. "Do you know how much I missed you?" he muttered, his lips hovering over hers, drinking in her breath.

"You've been gone less than twenty minutes."

"That's twenty minutes too long."

Her lashes skipped across his cheek as he pulled up her t-shirt and thumbed her breasts. Her head arched backward, exposing her neck, and his tongue explored every crevice.

She dropped the flowers and swayed. He wrapped his fingers around her ass and kept her steady. Not that he would stay steady much longer.

Thunder rumbled.

"Wesley." She pushed against his chest as he continued kissing her neck. "Wesley."

"Hmm."

"It's going to rain."

"Mmm hmm."

"We're going to get wet."

"I hope you're already wet," he growled as he trailed kisses along her neck and pushed her to rest against the tree.

"Soaked," she breathed.

Her hands explored his body as the light rain arrived in cold drops, the tree lending sparse protection as the rain fell harder. She shrieked, then laughed.

He lifted her. She locked her legs around his waist as he carried her to the house.

The smell of steak curled through the air. He deposited her on the covered porch and she hugged her arms under her breasts. His eyes trailed to her soaked shirt, admiring the way it defined her nipples. Water dripped from her coiled hair.

"I've got to check the steaks."

She watched him as he flipped the steaks, and he regretted his decision to cook anything that required drawing his attention away from Caitlyn.

"A few more minutes," he said as he cantered forward and reached out his arms.

She slapped his ass and turned away, smiling. "I've got to shower before dinner."

He tugged on her wrist. "No way, woman. You'll wait for me. I'll get the steaks off now." He never wanted to take a shower again without her in it.

He had many regrets, many things to make up to her. And probably would have many more considering the state of his intensity when it came to race day. But tonight, the only intensity she'd find in him was his exploration of her body.

He wanted to give her the performance of a lifetime tonight. And Sunday, he wanted to show her the race of a lifetime, to show her how much it meant to him to have her there, supporting his race.

***

Caitlyn gripped her seat as Wesley's car zoomed around the track.

Racing was a high octane sport, dealing with exuberant energy and incredible athletes. At almost two hundred mile per hour turns, racers held fast to the curves and onto their lives, knowing one wrong move could cause an accident and take their life or that of their colleagues.

She wondered if Tim was right. Maybe that's why Wesley loved it so much. Not able to control what happened that night ten years ago, was he now trying to correct the mistakes of the past with the control of his racing?

He could have used another week of rest, at least, but he was determined to get back on the track and win and Caitlyn wouldn't dare risk an argument. It wasn't up to her and sex didn't give her the right to convince him otherwise. Though he was tired—it was written all over his face—and stressed—probably compounded by the fact she and Johnson were here and Tim didn't like it—the race would pump him in ways no amount of rest ever could.

She also worried that she hadn't given him enough rest the past few days.

Energy poured from the crowd and Caitlyn let it feed her. Her hands tapped against her knees. She'd never relax completely and was sandwiched between Johnson and Tim, who hadn't said one word to each other.

Johnson brought Caitlyn a cold drink and she shot him a grateful smile. At least he was trying. It was hot outside and the cola tasted good. Tim was being too hard on him. Tim was being too hard on both of them, in Caitlyn's opinion.

She'd spent the last few days with Wesley and was excited when he'd agreed to let her do a biography. Judging by the colorful signs from the stands, the article hadn't destroyed him or his devotees. If anything, it increased his appeal, backed by the one Caitlyn sold to the New York Times. Fans were supportive, wanted to know more, and loved how he had come out in the spotlight. He'd promised an interview with The Today Show in the future, but right now his focus was on the race.

The crowd roared when Wesley's car bumped close to the wall. Caitlyn cringed, but he got it under control. Every turn, every moment, skewed her adrenaline. Her senses heightened, tingling, fearing. She held her breath, wondering how much longer she could maintain her sense of calm.

Calm? Who was she kidding? She hadn't felt any sense of calm since the moment Wesley came back into her life. And each whoosh around the racetrack heightened her concern.

It wasn't the first time to see him race, but it was the first time she hadn't gotten up to walk around. Her butt hurt, her legs hurt, her back hurt. And the frenzy in the crowd was stronger since Wesley's jail release.

She snapped pictures. That fed her frenzy for something to do. Kept her from hyperventilating with worry.

Suddenly, a car slammed into Wesley, bringing all her worries to fruition. He skidded across the pavement. She jumped up, screeching as she watched an oncoming car, barreling toward his stationary one. It struck him in the side. Metal shrieked at the point of contact and tires squealed across the pavement.

Her drink crashed to the ground. Her camera clattered, hitting her toe. The car continued to flip, over and over, over and over.

His car finally stopped in the middle of the field. Fire ruptured from the back end. It was upside down, in a crumpled heat.

People in the stands stood transfixed in silence as they waited for Wesley to emerge.

She remembered another time this happened. The first time she'd seen him race. She'd only seen the tail end of that one because she'd been mingling in the crowd. He'd gotten out. That wreck hadn't been this bad. That time, they weren't in a relationship. He hadn't even known she was watching. They hadn't been sleeping together. That time, she wanted to go to him but didn't have that right. This time, she did. At least, she thought she did.

She tried to jump over the pit wall but someone grabbed her arm and wouldn't let go.

"Let me go, let me go." She flailed out her hands, fighting to no avail. She needed to make sure Wesley was okay for own self. Watching from the pit wall drove her insane.

"Stop, Caitlyn." Tim shook her. "They'll take care of it, there's nothing you can do."

"No! No! I have to get to him, see if he's okay!" She struggled to get out of his grip but he clenched his arms around her waist even tighter.

"Dammit, Caitlyn, stop." Tim's voice held an edge she couldn't comply with right now.

"He's still in that car," she said in despair as she stopped moving. Weakness, along with the arms still around her waist, made her immobile so she couldn't run even if Tim let her go. She'd have fallen if Tim hadn't been holding her up. "It's burning. He hasn't come out yet."

"They're working on it. You'll only be in the way."

***

Tim didn't speak to Caitlyn on the way to the hospital, which was fine with her. She was too upset to speak to him anyway, and she could tell he wasn't happy she and Johnson tagged along.

Well, too bad. Tim would have to accept the fact Caitlyn was a part of Wesley's life, albeit briefly. And Johnson was Wesley's dad. He worried about him just as much as Tim did.

Her steps slowed when they walked into the hospital, feet moving forward one sluggish step after the other. The doors whooshed open, closed, and at one point Johnson stopped and glanced back to see if she followed.

Wesley was alive. He *had* to be and as long as no one confirmed otherwise, she'd continue believing it.

Her worst nightmare had just come true. One of the reasons she never wanted to support Wesley in his racing career. One of the reasons his mom didn't like the career he chose. And one of the reasons Johnson fought so extensively with Wesley for not following in his footsteps.

They waited an eternity. Visitors flocked in to see if he was okay, but no one was allowed to see him and most people left, leaving prayers and cards, flowers and sentiments.

Tim finally told her he'd drive her back to her motel to rest, but she wasn't about to leave. She didn't tell him she no longer had a motel room, she was staying with Wesley. How would he take that news?

No doubt she was getting on Tim's and the nurses' nerves. She fretted anxiously, walking up to them every half hour and asking if there was any news on Wesley. When they told her no and the doctor would let her know whenever they had any news, she sighed heavily and walked away, all the while knowing if Tim and Johnson hadn't been there, she wouldn't have been entitled to anything.

They were both remarkable men, both demanding respect in the way they carried themselves, formidable if one should get on their bad side. The female nurses fluttered around them, trying to make sure they were comfortable while waiting, letting them know of the cafeteria they had available should they need to eat. Caitlyn wanted to gag. The women got perturbed with her when she wanted something, but Johnson and Tim couldn't ask for enough. She wondered what they would act like with Wesley. A younger version of both men. They had all been blessed with good looks.

Caitlyn walked outside to call her mother from her cell, needing to talk to somebody who cared about her. She was composed when she dialed the number, but as soon as she heard her mom's voice she started crying, comforted by a familiar voice but not sure what to say after all.

"Caitlyn, is that you?"

"It's Wesley," she croaked. Her mom knew she had been doing a story on him, but she didn't know the extent of their circumstances and what had transpired between them.

"What's wrong?" her mother asked.

"He's been in a wreck. I'm at the hospital now."

"Do I need to come down there?"

"No. No." Caitlyn cried into the phone as she told her mom what happened. Just hearing her mom on the phone was sufficient enough for Caitlyn. She had no idea what was going on, how serious it was. No one came to tell them anything. If this was it, if he died, she would only be a grieving friend, stuck at the back of the row, not entitled to any heartfelt wishes or condolences. Not that she was seeking any, but she wanted to be more important to Wesley and his family than just a bystander.

She hung up the phone and sat on the asphalt curb, trying to shield her eyes from a sun that descended and cast a tremendous color around the earth. It conflicted with her mood. Set brilliantly against an azure sky, birds sang their contentment with it.

She needed to see Wesley again. Needed to know he was going to be okay. She longed to tell him so many things.

"Caitlyn?"

She wrenched her head around at her name being called and stood when she noticed Tim. She waited. Had he come in hope or despair? Did she really want to know?

If he said the words, that would make them true. As long as there was silence, there was still hope.

"He's awake and doing fine. The doctor says we can go see him."

"Oh!" She nearly collapsed where she stood, then ran into Tim's arms in an effort to share her emotion with someone close to Wesley. He stood there, not pulling away and not urging her closer.

She released her hold, stepped back, and rubbed her hands along her arms.

Awkward.

Together, they walked into Wesley's room, where he was eating ice cubes. Johnson sat in a chair across the room, looking grim but relieved.

Caitlyn wrung her hands together and darted her gaze between the men as she kept her distance.

"You had us worried there for a while," Tim said.

Wesley's face crinkled between a smile and an 'I'm-sorry-I-didn't-mean-to-do-it' chagrin. His mouth barely opened when he said the word, "Sorry".

He eyed Caitlyn. She remained silent, afraid she'd cry if she said anything. What was she supposed to do? Run up and hug him? Would he appreciate that or push her away?

"You okay?" he asked.

Caitlyn nodded, her heart in her throat. "I am now."

"Come here," he said, waving her over. She went willingly, keeping her steps slow so as not to appear desperate, then she buried her face the crevice of Wesley's neck.

Wesley explained to her at one time how the cars were built to protect the men in them, how they could sustain a lot of damage in the event of wreck. He tried to ease her anxiety, but Caitlyn knew better.

The doctor would keep him overnight and run more tests in the morning, but so far a CT scan and MRI revealed a slight concussion and compressed vertebra the extent of his injuries. A few minor scrapes and burns. Nothing life threatening.

She gulped in relief.

"He wants to keep me from racing for six weeks, minimum," Wesley spat. "There's no way that's going to happen."

"You'll do what the doctor says," Tim said as Caitlyn sat near the bed, helpless. Wesley held both her hands in one of his and traced patterns on hers with his fingertips.

"I'm racing next weekend if I have to use crutches or wear a brace or whatever. I don't care, I'm racing, and no doctor is going to tell me otherwise."

"Bullshit, Wes. You are in no shape," Tim argued as he paced across the room. "I shouldn't have let you race this time."

Wesley's eyes flashed then darkened. "You shouldn't have?"

"No. You should have taken more time off."

"I already had plenty of days off while I almost wasted away in jail for a crime I didn't commit. And the racing officials gave their permission."

Tim sat in the chair nearest the door and leaned back, all relaxed, legs open and hands splayed on his thighs. Tension crackled the room. Even Johnson, who leaned with crossed arms against the wall, seemed to shrink.

"Don't forget that's my car, my team. I can refuse." Tim's threat shocked Caitlyn. She was glad he chose his nephew over the sport. And why wouldn't he have?

"Then I'll find another team."

"You'll do no such thing."

Caitlyn pulled her hands out of Wesley's tightening grip and scooted the chair away from the bed so he would have a clearer view of his uncle. Wesley didn't seem to notice.

Even if they were married, she would have no right to keep him from doing what he loved.

"Okay, Tim, whatever you say," Wesley hissed.

"We'll talk about it later." *As in, now isn't the time to discuss this.*

Wesley laid his head back on the pillow and studied the ceiling.

After a few moments of silence, Tim stood. "Okay, we're heading out. You need to rest. Call me if you need anything."

Wesley winced as he held up his head and glanced at Caitlyn. "Will you stay?"

Chapter Twenty

THE HOSPITAL ROOM filled with cards and flowers. They had made arrangements for only family to visit him so Wesley's fans wouldn't disturb his recovery. Caitlyn was allowed to stay long after visiting hours only if she agreed to let Wesley rest, and she knew that was only because of Johnson and Tim. It was a step in her favor if Tim thought she'd be good for his nephew's recovery.

When Johnson and Tim left, Caitlyn wondered what was going to happen between the two men now that no one else was around. Unless Johnson caught a taxi, Tim would have to take him back to his rental car left at the track. It might be good for them.

Wesley slept, Caitlyn in the chair by his side. The ache in her neck forked into her lower back, but no way would she leave.

She checked social media and assured the world Wesley was alive and well. At one point, Wesley even allowed her to take a picture of them together and share it. The response was overwhelming.

Wesley would wake, they'd talk a little, and he would go back to sleep. He urged her to return to his RV and rest, but she had no intention of leaving his side.

When the breakfast cart was wheeled in the next morning, Wesley woke, claiming his hunger, and asked when the doctor would be in to release him.

"He's making his rounds," the nurse assured him.

"Are you hungry?" Wesley asked, his gaze sparkling over Caitlyn as he waved his spoon to present his clumpy oatmeal.

"Ma'am, there's a cafeteria on the second floor," the nurse explained.

"I'm fine, thank you."

"You sure?" Wesley asked once the nurse was gone. He made a show of chewing on his oatmeal, squeezing his eyes shut as he swallowed. Grabbing his fork, he shoveled scrambled egg into his mouth. "The egg isn't so bad."

Caitlyn laughed. "I'm fine." No way could she eat anyway. She was still nauseous from the terror of last night's accident.

"You should go. Get some rest. The doctor will probably be releasing me this morning after he checks me over. Tim called and said he'd be here in a bit."

"I don't have a vehicle anyway, so I'll just wait on Tim."

Wesley finished his breakfast, pushed the cart away, and swiped his mouth. "God, I need a shower. And some pain pills."

"They just gave you pain pills."

"Yeah, well I need more. I hurt a lot more today than I did yesterday."

Caitlyn didn't dare tell him Tim was right and there was no way he should race next week. She wondered how much control he and the doctor actually had over the situation.

"What is it about us and hospitals, huh?" Caitlyn teased, but judging by Wesley's disappearing glint, she should've never brought up that subject.

"No kidding," he muttered. He moved aside and patted the bed for her to sit.

She sat and rubbed his chest. His neck and back were braced into some sort of contraption, and she didn't want to hurt him.

She considered the conversation she'd like to have, the one that had plagued her for ten years. Now, with Wesley confined to a bed, was her best chance to tell him what she was feeling, tell him of her past mistakes, and know how much he was willing to take another chance on their relationship when all they seemed to be met with was tragedy.

"You hurt me when you left without an explanation," she mumbled as she circled patterns on his torso.

"I hurt me, too." His words surprised her. So far, so good. He coiled a piece of her hair around his finger. "And if you don't stop doing that, you're going to hurt me a hell of a lot worse."

Her lips curled as she snatched her hand away. "I assume you're still working down there, then."

"Hell yeah, woman. If I was eighteen again, I'd tell you to go lock that door so I can show you just how well I am working."

"Why did you do it?" She laid her head on his chest and assured herself his heartbeat was still there. "Why did you leave when you knew I never meant it? I would have moved heaven and earth to be with you."

Wesley let out an audible sigh. "Did I? How could I have known for sure?"

"You never even said goodbye."

"I told you goodbye. I told you I was leaving, and I left."

Yes, he had left without a backward glance, and she figured he'd do it again, now, if he could. He didn't want to talk about this, he never wanted to talk about it, and she shouldn't push him.

But she needed to talk about it. Their relationship could never go any further if they continued to ignore the reasons they hadn't been together the past ten years. And she would always worry if he'd do it again: leave her without a backward glance.

"Why was it so easy for you to leave me?" she asked, hating the way her voice rasped over the words.

"The accident, Caitlyn. I couldn't live with myself anymore. How could I expect you to live with me?"

She arched her head up and stared into his tortured eyes. The flame in his green depths pained her. This is why they needed to have this conversation. This is why Wesley would always have a wall around him if he didn't chisel the guilt away. "You did not kill your mother."

"Yes. I did." He blinked, the rise and fall of his chest heavy.

"Wesley, you did not." She sat up, using an abusive tone with him so he'd get her point. "I doubted myself for a very long time. I thought I did something wrong. I thought you blamed me for what happened. We were all fighting the night of the wreck because they weren't happy with your news either. I was upset, crying. If she hadn't unbuckled her seatbelt to move closer to me, to comfort *me*, she would still be alive."

"We've already been over this."

"I wasn't good enough for you. I knew you were in pain, but I tried to help in the best way I knew how. I tried to give you space, but that wasn't good enough for you."

He pulled on her hair as he unwound it from his finger. "You tried to make me change into someone I wasn't."

"I never tried to make you change. You never gave me a chance to accept your dream."

"I didn't mean to hurt you," he croaked. "But you hurt me, too."

"How could I hurt you? Like you said, you have to have feelings for someone for them to be able to hurt you."

"I did have feelings for you!"

"Did?" she asked softly.

He tried to sit up in bed but she pushed on him to keep him down. "You don't need to get up right now."

"Yes, I do."

"You are so stubborn! Let me raise the bed if you want to sit up. You're going to cause your stitches to come out and who knows about that contraption around you. Do you want to start all over?"

A grin tugged on his lip and he grasped her wrist. "You're feisty."

"I'm worried about you. And I think you're just trying to change the subject."

"Why would I do that?"

She pulled her hand away. "If it was up to you, you would avoid this subject as long as you lived." He turned his head away and clenched his jaw. She caressed him and ran her fingers through his silky brown hair, feeling large bumps caused from his wreck. There were bald splotches where they had to shave his head, but his hair would grow back in no time.

Patches of dark stubble intensified his sex appeal and even with him in the hospital bed, she couldn't stop thinking about doing exactly as he had suggested and lock that door.

Wesley pulled his head away from her touch. "Women need to talk about things to get over them. Men don't. What women don't understand is that they worry so much because they dwell on that shit. Why can't we just move forward?"

"I...I don't know if I can," Caitlyn whispered.

There, she'd said it. She didn't know if she could watch his races every weekend and wonder if that would be his last. Didn't know if she could stand by his side while he put his life in danger every weekend. Didn't know if she wanted this life for herself and didn't know if she could watch him be killed the way she'd watched his mom die.

Her worst fear had come to fruition and now all he cared about was getting back on the track.

He hadn't professed his love but even if he had, she couldn't give him an ultimatum. And even if she could, his choice was obvious. Racing would always be his first love.

His only love.

Could she live with that?

"Well, darling. That's your choice."

Was it? Was it her choice? He'd never asked her to stay. Never asked her to try to live with his choice. Never professed his love to her.

Maybe it would be different if he did.

"You want to talk about it?" Wesley sat up straighter and clenched his jaw. "Fine, let's talk about it. You're giving me an ultimatum."

"I'm not," she said, her pulse a hard mass of nerves. "I didn't give you one then. I'm not giving you one now."

"You don't know if you can do this. You don't know if you can move forward—"

"I don't know that I can watch you put your life in danger every weekend."

"Racing isn't dangerous."

"Oh!" she scoffed. "That's why you're in this hospital bed right now."

"It's no more dangerous than your writing."

"Writing isn't dangerous. I don't risk my life every week to do it."

"It could. What if you got some jungle assignment, or had to go to some war? What if you caught a disease while in a foreign country?"

"I don't do that kind of writing."

"What if you got run over by a racecar when you were there to do a story?"

"Don't be ridiculous!"

"I'm not being any more ridiculous than you are," Wesley growled.

"This–" Caitlyn said, spreading out her hands to indicate the hospital room, the machines attached to him. "This is exactly why your mother died. So you wouldn't. This is why we all fought that night, because they didn't want you to do something so dangerous."

Wesley visibly tensed, and she regretted the words as soon as she'd said them.

"Get the hell out of here." Wesley pointed to the door, his voice deadly calm. "And out of my life."

***

Wesley watched her leave, closing his eyes against the agonizing pain.

She'd made her choice, and he made his.

Blowing out a breath, he wrapped a hand around the remote and resisted the urge to throw it against the wall. Throw something, anything, just to expel his anger. His hurt, his frustration.

I don't know if I can.

He didn't know if he could ever get over his guilt, and she didn't know if she could live with his racing.

During his time in jail, two thoughts had consumed him. Racing, and having Caitlyn in his arms. He never wanted to let go, of either. But now he was pushing her away, and he had no idea why.

Of course he knew why. This could never work. No point in

delaying the inevitable.

I don't know if I can.

He wasn't about to call out to her. Damn if he called out to her and begged her to come back.

His mouth soured. Not because of the hospital, his lack of water, his lack of hope. But because he didn't know what to do next, didn't know how to apologize to Caitlyn. Didn't know how to tell her none of this mattered. It was his life, but none of it mattered without her in it.

It had to matter. He wouldn't give up racing. Not for her. Not now, not ever. Not for anyone.

But he wanted her to love him, love the sport as much as he did, wanted her to support him, fight for him, believe in him.

Forgive him.

If she didn't, none of this mattered.

Racing would allow him to run from his past for the rest of his life and it wouldn't appear he was running. But he didn't want to run.

He didn't know how he felt about Caitlyn, not anymore, only that he'd never felt anything stronger, more confusing. Shouldn't love be more obvious? More intuitive?

It'd be in his best interest to let her leave, no matter how painful it was to watch her go. His pulse thrummed low at the knowledge. Was that true, or was it only his fear?

The truth slammed into him, hard. He didn't want to outrun his past. He wanted to own up to it, embrace it, and stop making excuses.

Excuses of why he couldn't love again. He'd never love anyone, ever. Not like he loved Caitlyn. He'd tried. No woman had ever had ever made him this damn crazy. Guilty. Stupid.

And heroic.

None of this was about his past. He'd like to convince himself it was. Like to convince himself that the way he felt about Caitlyn was only the memories. He'd loved her once, but he'd walked away. He'd do it again if he had to. If it was to punish himself, so be it. He could punish himself for the rest of his life and be just fine with it. But this was the here and now. Take away everything else and the only thing left was crazy, stupid, and heroic.

He wanted Caitlyn in his life. He wanted to love her forever.

***

Caitlyn tore the sheets and pillow casings from her bed, fighting back tears as she balled them in a pile and stuffed them in a trash bag.

Did she deserve to be unhappy? Was that why everything in her life was falling apart?

So Wesley didn't want to talk about it? That was fine with her. It was *all* fine with her. He didn't want her to be a part of her life?

Fine.

Her breath heaved as she whisked the new fitted sheet and tightened them on the corners of her bed. The smell of downy-soft cotton and rain-scented fabric softener gave her a headache and did not make her fresh and clean.

God, why had she even said anything to him? Why hadn't she learned the first time not to open her mouth?

She might be suffering a mental breakdown, but she would be fine with it. She had known the consequences but decided to punish herself anyway. She was stupid, hoping maybe this time it would be different. Maybe this time he would *want* to talk. Maybe this time he'd tell her that he loved her.

She tossed the bottle of cologne in with the bag of sheets and hauled them to the Dumpster outside. She should donate them but didn't want the bag lingering in her house a minute longer. Didn't want them to exist anymore.

Why she sprayed her bed with his smell for the past ten years was a question she didn't have an answer to. She tried throwing it out before and found she couldn't sleep. This time, she had no choice if she wanted to get over him. She would never resort to spraying that scent on her bed again. She'd grow used to the smell of cotton and if nothing else, she'd spray lavender or some woman scent on her bed.

Once back inside, she fluffed the new comforter on the bed

and admired her new pillows. Bright orange with red roses lent a feminine appeal. She was tired of masculine. Tired of purple, seeing as how Blake's entire office was sheathed in purple. She needed color. Lots of color.

Wesley was the one who didn't want to work a relationship out, the one who couldn't talk about the problems, the one who didn't want to find happiness because he didn't think he deserved it.

She sunk to the bed and grabbed a pillow, hugging it into her stomach. As much as she tried to convince herself of no fault, guilt consumed her once again.

She should have left well enough alone.

He'd continue to race. That's what he loved, and eventually he'd find a woman to marry, maybe even have kids together. With his scars, the relationship probably wouldn't be as deep as a woman would like, but maybe he'd get lucky and find a woman who wasn't looking for deep.

She curled into a ball, fighting back tears. She hoped he'd never find a woman to share what they once had. She'd never find a man, but why shouldn't that be okay with her? After all, many people would never experience even once what she experienced, so if she had to settle for a mediocre relationship for the rest of her life, so be it.

As long as she never saw Wesley again. Forget the biography, forget the past. Maybe she'd write a fiction story or something. She would stop talking, stop questioning men and their motives, and just be alone for the rest of her life.

She'd start by quitting her job. She couldn't work for Johnson Webb. And definitely not with Blake, the man who'd lied to her.

But she had one thing to do first.

Chapter Twenty-One

"I NEED TO talk about my parents."

Wesley opened Tim's refrigerator and took out a beer, popped the top and guzzled a quarter of it, before turning on his heel and shutting the door with his foot. He sat at the barstool and took another drink as he watched Tim chop vegetables.

After being released from the hospital two days ago, he agreed that he should take time off from racing. And yet, racing was the last thing on his mind. All he could think about was Caitlyn. He missed her.

Garlic, oregano, and tomato laced the air as Tim created his world famous spaghetti. He dropped veggies into the skillet and turned to peruse Wesley.

"What do you want to talk about?" he asked.

"Everything. How they met. What happened to them when I was three years old and he left for three years. Things like that."

"I have pictures." Tim placed a lid on his sauce to let it simmer and removed the noodles from the heat. "I even have a journal of your mom's."

"You do?"

"Yeah. When she died, I went over to the house and took some things without Johnson knowing. I hoped eventually, when you started a family of your own, you would want those pictures. I was afraid Johnson would get rid of them, or keep them and you'd never get to see them." Tim strained the water out of the noodles and placed them on the counter, checked his sauce again, then grabbed a beer and sat beside Wesley.

"Well where are they?"

Tim nodded and rose to fetch the pictures, while Wesley stole a piece of tomato from the salad in the fridge.

"Hey," Tim said when he walked in and caught Wesley.

"I'm hungry. Don't tell me I'm gonna spoil my appetite."

"It's damn good spaghetti. Try not to spoil it." Tim handed him a suede-covered, well preserved book. "Here are the pictures. Her journal."

He accepted the journal and sat at the table, afraid to open the pages. Had it even been opened since her death?

"And I almost forgot about this."

"What is it?" Wesley asked as he took it, but realized what it was. His baby book. He and his mom had mused over it together several times.

"Does my dad know you have this?"

"I don't even know if he knew it existed," Tim replied. "And if so, who the hell cares. It's yours, not his."

Wesley fingered the book, not quite ready to open it. It was like opening another chapter of his life and if he did, would he ever be able to go back?

Did he want to go back?

He couldn't mend the chapters he'd already damaged so why not just write another one? Starting with confronting his fears.

His fear of losing. Again. His fear of never being able to get over his pain, his past. His fear of having Caitlyn back in his life only to lose her again.

Loving meant losing, and he never wanted to experience that pain again.

He thumped his chest and opened the book, but almost snapped it closed when sadness seized him. The words waved in front of him, but he couldn't cry. He wasn't sure he even knew how to cry.

What if Caitlyn was right? Maybe he did need to talk about things, get them out in the open, before he could get on with his life.

Oh, if only things were that easy.

He scanned the book and reminisced about the things his mother wrote, the pictures she stored, the memories they wrote together. Many pictures of him and Caitlyn.

She'd loved Caitlyn. Did she have some kind of motherly instinct to know Caitlyn was the one for him? The only woman he'd ever love? Or was it wishful thinking on her part?

Samantha, despite her being a hard working woman and a mother, found time to write things, little tidbits of information about him growing up, little notes to him she hoped he would see when he was older. Things she hoped to share with her grandchildren. Grandchildren she would never know.

"She loved you," Tim said, breaking into his thoughts. "She would never blame you for what happened. She only wanted the best for you."

"I know." He blinked, his gummy eyelids burning. The pressure in his throat was almost too much and he jumped from the table to grab another beer. "She wasn't ready to die. She wanted grandkids. She wanted..."

"No one's *ready* to die," Tim said. "It's a part of life. You can't blame yourself. Wesley, that guilt is eating at you and it'll eat at you for the rest of your life if you allow it."

"Caitlyn tried to tell me that," Wesley said. "I brushed her off."

"And that's why you brushed her off. Because you'll continue to let it eat at you for the rest of your life. You'll continue to take chances with your own life because you don't feel like you deserve to live."

"Caitlyn tried to force me to talk about it."

"Women think talking about things help. Sometimes they do. And sometimes you just have to let them talk. Maybe it doesn't make you feel better, but it makes her feel better."

"I told her to get the hell out of my life."

Tim shoved his fingers in his hair. "Why in the hell did you do that?"

"I shouldn't trust her."

"Says who?"

"My father."

"Oh come on, *he's* the one you shouldn't trust."

"You used to agree with him."

***

Caitlyn slapped the envelope against the heel of her palm and eyed Blake's door. She'd like to waltz in there and throw her resignation on his desk. It would be a nice little surprise for him to find tomorrow, but that wouldn't do. He still kept the door locked and he'd wonder how she got in. He'd also wonder how, considering she'd left before him and she didn't want to explain why she'd returned after hours.

So instead, she stuck the notice in his inbox. It was full enough he wasn't likely to know she'd added it at close to midnight.

The notice was for two weeks. She'd been offered an opportunity as the press coordinator for an event circuit in Austin, and she couldn't wait to get out of here. She no longer trusted Blake and wasn't happy with her job. It was time to move on.

Blake wasn't fully healed from his wreck. Today was his first day back, and he shouldn't have even come in. His closed office taunted her, the shadows lining the wall in a dare. She might not have another opportunity in the next two weeks.

It shouldn't matter to her anymore. Wesley told her to get out of his life. He hadn't called to apologize, and she didn't hold high expectations for an apology.

She wouldn't apologize either. Not that it would do any good. But this could be her last chance to discover what else Blake had in his office concerning Wesley and his family. And why Blake was hell bent on destroying them. In all her regrets, she didn't want to leave and regret not rifling through Blake's office.

She rubbed her arms and glanced around. Why was she so worried? Nobody would come to the office this close to midnight. She kept the hallway light and the one in her office on. If anyone were to ask, she'd tell them she was putting in a late night to finish up her assigned stories so she could leave earlier than expected.

After finagling with the lock, she slipped into Blake's office and made copies. She didn't have time to go through everything. It'd take hours to figure out what was important or what was just junk.

More than likely, it was all junk. But she'd make that call later.

Rayma's ring tone belted. Her pulse soared, shadows growing smaller. She snatched the phone from her purse.

"Hello?"

"Caitlyn." Rayma's harried voice incited chills down her spine, up her arms, tighten behind her neck.

She pressed a knuckle into her cheek, expecting the worst. "What's wrong?"

"I was talking to my PI friend and found out that Johnson had a twin brother."

Caitlyn's legs buckled. She sat amongst the papers she'd dug out of the file cabinet. Although this was shocking, she'd expected something far worse. "A twin?"

"Yes, a twin."

"What happened to him?"

"We don't know yet. Oh, and Esther was a prostitute."

A harsh sound escaped her. "Keegan's mother?"

"Yep, Keegan's mother. Mrs. High and Mighty Uppity Webb. Was a prostitute."

Caitlyn grabbed a handful of papers and set it in the box. "So you're investigating Johnson and his wife?"

"I'm investigating Keegan more than anything, but they just happen to be a part of his life."

"You can't keep doing this to every boy you meet."

"I don't. I just do it to the boys I don't trust."

"Oh, Rayma. You don't trust anyone."

"Keegan is getting too serious. I have to know I can trust him before I give him my heart. Especially after..."

Caitlyn dropped papers in the box. Maybe it'd be easier to go make copies elsewhere and bring them back later before her last day. Or maybe she wouldn't even bring them back. Would Blake even notice?

She let out another harsh laugh. "Before what, Rayma?

Before you found out Keegan is Wesley's step-brother?"

"You act like it's not a big deal."

"And you act like you have a choice on whether or not you give your heart away."

"I do," Rayma said.

"If only it were that easy," Caitlyn muttered.

Rayma ignored her and continued. "Oh, I've got the guy's name. Jack Forrester."

Caitlyn closed the file drawer and opened the one below. The longer she tried to lecture Rayma on relationships, the more Rayma would blow her off.

She could hear her now. *This coming from the girl who sleeps with the smell of her ex-boyfriend's cologne on her pillow.*

"Jack Forrester, huh?" She hadn't come across that name yet.

"Where are you?" Rayma asked.

"At the office. Doing research. I'll call you tomorrow."

"Be careful."

Caitlyn ended the call and yawned. She stood and placed her hands on her lower back, arching backward, then forward to touch her toes.

What to do next?

Wiggling her fingers, she let out a breath as she rolled upward. Might as well grab the box and get going before she fell asleep in Blake's office. She wasn't sure she'd last much longer, even after Rayma's call, and the last thing she needed was to be found in the morning slumped over Blake's file cabinets.

As she reached for the box, she stopped at the weathered newspaper resting on top. Jack Forrester's name caught her attention. His picture bore a stark resemblance to Johnson.

He was dead. Gunned down in his own home twenty-five years ago after hooking up with some trouble makers in prison. She read the article twice, but Johnson Webb was never mentioned.

Wesley would have been three. The time he said his dad left.

She rummaged through the box in search of the birth certificates. Wesley's, Johnson, Samantha, Jack Forrester.

Yep, he was Johnson's twin, judging by the dates and times.

Disgusted, she dropped the pages, letting them flutter to the box and was just about to grab the lid and go when she spotted the next birth certificate.

Jonathan Keegan Forrester. Son to Esther and Jack Forrester. *What the...*

She fished for her phone, dialing Rayma back. But Rayma didn't answer, so she left a message.

"Hey, call me, it's important."

The only Keegan Caitlyn knew was dating Rayma. Keegan Foster. Esther Foster.

Johnson had married his dead brother's wife? Creepy, creepy, creepy. Wesley said he'd left to search for his family, and Caitlyn wondered if he'd found his family, found that Jack had died, and met his wife then? Maybe they kept in touch and decided to get together after Samantha's death. Maybe they'd had an affair for years. Maybe...maybe...

Too many questions, not enough answers, and not near enough sleep to figure it all out tonight. She locked up the file cabinets, grabbed the box, and made slow and careful steps outside, her minuscule light pointing a path to her car.

She was too much of a damn reporter. Blake told her she should've been an investigative reporter. She couldn't let sleeping dogs lie until she discovered where they were lying, how and why.

Blake used to tell her it was a blessing. She was now positive it was a curse.

***

"Dinner's ready." Tim thumped Wesley on his back.

"Good." Wesley snapped the photo album closed and stood. He fixed his plate, poured dressing on his salad, and sat at the pint sized table. "I feel like one of those giants at a tea party," Wesley said, making fun of the small table.

"It's definitely not a manly table, is it?" Tim said.

"Plus, I'm eating spaghetti and salad. Aren't real men supposed to be eating meat and potatoes?"

Tim shrugged. "Depends on how you label real men."

"True, true," Wesley said.

They ate in a comfortable silence, with silverware clanging against the plates the only sound accompanying them. Even if it wasn't meat and potatoes, it was damn good spaghetti.

They finished dinner and cleaned up the kitchen. "This is what bachelors do," Tim teased. "That's why I urge you to get married."

"Why? So I don't have to do the damn dishes?" he asked. "Why haven't you found someone after Heather?"

"I've dated lots of girls, even seriously. I'm currently dating someone semi-serious, but she's divorced and we both have issues we have to deal with."

"Just another example of why racing and marriage don't mix."

"Oh bullshit." Tim handed Wesley a plate to dry. "Many men in racing are married. It has nothing to do with that."

"I have something I want to show you," Wesley said after they finished the dishes. He retrieved the documents Caitlyn had found; he'd gotten them from his house with the intent of showing his uncle. They sat on the living room floor, and Wesley told Tim everything he knew.

"What can you tell me about my dad I might not remember? I was so young when he left. I remember him coming back when I was six and I didn't have a clue about him. I often joked with my friends about how he must've spent time in prison."

"It took you awhile to open up to him. But then again, it took us all awhile. Samantha understood he had gone through hell. His parents died not long after he'd learned he was adopted. He took it pretty hard. He left to try to find his birth parents, but came back with the news they were dead, too. She forgave him."

"I don't remember my grandparents."

"No. You were young when they were killed in a car wreck."

"You knew his parents?"

"Yeah, they were great people." Tim set aside the family tree but picked it up to study it again. Johnson and Samantha were on there. Samantha's mom and dad and siblings were also included, but Johnson's family was cut off. Almost as if the copy machine or drawing had cut it off. "Johnson was an only child, an adopted child, and it really bothered him when his parents were killed. But his family tree," he handed the paper to Wesley and pointed, "looks like there's another box, a sibling box, beside him. But it's been cut off. See that?" Wesley nodded. "And I can't tell what the name of his parent's say, if it's his adopted parents or his real parents. All I see is a box cut off from the picture."

***

Caitlyn dropped the box of documents in the back seat and locked herself in her car, her heart pounding a ferocious din in her ears.

Rayma still hadn't answered her phone, and Caitlyn wasn't about to call Wesley. Not yet anyway. Not until she knew more.

Wesley didn't care. He said so himself. He didn't want to dwell on it, he only wanted to race.

She spotted a car trailing at a neat distance behind her, but hoped it was only coincidence. After all, she couldn't expect to be the only car out on a night like tonight.

She entered the near deserted I-35 and drove a safe speed, watching the other car behind her. It kept a distance of a few car lengths but stayed in the far left-hand side. She drove in the far right. A few other cars passed her, but not many were out this late. The other kept its distance.

She sped up. The car stayed with her, though far enough back that she could be imagining things. She slowed to a crawl but the car did not pass. At first she thought she was being paranoid so she took the next exit to see what the car would do.

Her body temperature dropped when the car also exited. Coldness gripped her. She turned the heater on high, but her body still shivered. An icy, scary tremble. Her throat closed. She couldn't breathe. The windows fogged, but she was too cold to turn off the heat.

She cracked the window but left the heater on. Maybe the fresh air would help keep her brain functioning. She was going to be sick. Literally she was going to throw up, but she damn sure wasn't going to stop the car to do it.

She took a breath, tried to calm herself, tried to bite back the tension. She was on a road. A lone car couldn't do a damn thing to her.

Except speed up, crash into her, kill her.

The car did speed up, and it didn't appear the driver was being cautious anymore. She frantically searched for her phone, realizing she needed to calm down when she found it where it always was, within an arms distance away. She entered the freeway again. At least he couldn't do anything too stupid if there were witnesses.

The car followed, closer this time.

***

"What in the hell?" Tim studied his sister's birth certificate and wondered why anyone would be interested in having a copy, and where in the hell they got it from. A copy of Johnson's, Wesley's, and another boy named Jonathan Keegan who, according to the birth certificate, was a few years younger than Wesley.

"Do you know this person?" Tim asked, handing the paper to Wesley.

Wesley took the birth certificate and handed Tim one in return. "Check that one out. I don't know that name either." Wesley rolled his shoulders and rounded his neck, stopping when he noticed Keegan's name. He flicked his finger on the name. "Jonathan Keegan. The only Keegan I know is Dad's stepson."

"Look at this," Tim exclaimed. "The one you just handed me belongs to Jack Forrester."

"Who is that?"

"I don't know," Tim replied, "but he's listed as the father of that Keegan guy. Shit..." He threw the papers at Wesley. "Your dad had a twin. The birthdays on this one and your dad's are the same. The time is only four minutes apart."

***

When Caitlyn called a few minutes later, Wesley eyed Tim and stepped away, out of Tim's hearing range.

What was she doing calling at close to midnight? He was still trying to wrap his mind around everything he'd just learned and the thought of speaking to her unnerved him.

"Wesley!" His stomach dipped when he heard her frantic voice. He rubbed the nape of his neck as Caitlyn blurted out the reason for her call. "Rayma called earlier to tell me Johnson had a twin. *A twin.* I went to Blake's office to look over things and found out his twin was killed. His name was Jack Forrester and I believe he's Keegan's dad."

Woah woah woah, she'd gone back to Blake's office in the middle of the night by herself?

He returned to the living room and found Tim amongst the papers. "Where are you?" he asked again, and snapped his fingers at Tim, mouthing '*call your pilot.*' Wherever the hell she was, he was going after her to make sure she was safe.

"Driving down I-35. Someone's following me."

Wesley's pulse nosedived, his head spinning, limbs heavy. He didn't want to be paranoid, but...fuck. "Go to the police. Now. Don't go home. Don't lead him anywhere except straight for the police department. Call them before you get there and let them know what's going on."

"What *is* going on?"

"I don't know. Make sure they know someone is following you and you feel you're in danger. Tell them to send someone. And stay there until I get there."

"Why would I be in danger? Your father's twin is dead. He died twenty-five years ago. I found the obituary."

Wesley puffed out a breath and glanced at Tim to make sure he was making that call. Although Tim eyed him warily, he was on the phone.

He turned away. "Caitlyn," he growled, his voice rough, his body on edge, on fire. He needed to tell her he was sorry. Needed to tell her he wanted to hold her in his arms and never let go.

"I'm calling Rayma–"

"No!"

"She doesn't know the twin could be Keegan's dad."

"You call the police department. I'll call Rayma."

Chapter Twenty-Two

RAYMA PROBABLY SHOULD have left Keegan's house, but she was desperate to understand the lies. Maybe if she was supportive enough, he'd open up to her.

"Let's go," he commanded with a gruff and finished tying his shoes.

"Where?"

"I'll tell you in the car."

"It's after midnight."

Keegan clasped her hands and gazed at her before bumping his forehead to hers. "I know, babe. I have a surprise."

"You seem frantic."

"It's just because I'm nervous. I have something important to tell you."

Rayma followed Keegan out the door, her footsteps sluggish. Oh God, please, please don't let this be a proposal.

Was she making a mistake? Going with him after she'd learned some pretty crazy stuff?

He unlocked her side of the car without saying anything then quickly paced to the driver's side. He started the car, but sat there in silence for a moment, contemplating his next move. He gawked at her almost in desperation and clutched her hands as he pulled her towards him, kissing her.

"Do you know how much I love you?"

Rayma's lips trembled as she forced a smile. She *wanted* to love him, but she wasn't sure she could after three months.

She nodded. "Of course."

Keegan seemed to be the right guy for her. They seemed to want the same things: children, a career that didn't consume their life, time enough to spend together, and a big house with the proverbial picket fence. So what if he hadn't told her his mom had been a prostitute? It wasn't his fault, and it was a long time ago.

Some things, though, a woman couldn't overlook. As long as nothing illegal was going on in his life, or anything that would demean her as a woman, she could overlook many things. But she wasn't ready for marriage.

"What's wrong?" she asked, concerned.

Keegan pulled away from her and tweaked her nose. He slammed the car in reverse and backed out, the faint light from the street lamp illuminating his face.

"My mother was a prostitute," he began. Rayma sagged against the seat and listened, relieved that he decided to tell her. "She met a man and fell in love, and I was born. Later on, but not at first, this man changed her life, helped her to get away from that life. He'd served time in prison before, and he needed to clean up on his own act before he could help her. He wanted to make a life for himself somehow.

"His mother was a crack whore, which kind of explains why he wanted to help my mom out so much. He never knew his father. Come to find out, he had a twin brother he didn't know about. She gave one of them up for adoption and for some reason kept my dad. Maybe she thought it'd help her straighten up her life. I don't know..."

He trailed off in thought.

Rayma didn't say anything nor let on she found this out hours ago. Even though Esther was a total bitch, Rayma admired her for cleaning up her life like that. People made mistakes.

"Are you talking about your mom, Esther?" Rayma finally asked after Keegan was silent. She knew the answer.

He nodded, stopped at a red light, looked both ways, and proceeded to a place he hadn't defined to Rayma. "My father helped her get out of the life she led, and he came into a lot of money so we lived well. Only, he eventually got another family and left us on the sidelines as he tried to better himself in a community he didn't belong to. He didn't forget about us completely, but we weren't allowed to know him as we knew him then. My father... you have to know that before that, my father spent a lot of time in and out of prison. He had a hard life, never had a lot of money, but he found an opportunity and took it. Eventually, though, he moved us with him."

Rayma massaged his neck as he drove, feeling sorry for the childhood he must have had. She wondered if he had ever tasted the sweetness of fixing Christmas cookies with his mother, licking the bowl while he watched them baking in the oven. Small things like those experiences added up to make a person.

"He had a twin brother he didn't find out about until later, when I was a baby and before he changed our lives. His brother came looking for him. He wanted to meet him. Only, my dad had enemies and some of them wanted him dead. They killed his twin brother, never knowing the truth. They thought they killed Jack Forrester.

"My dad stole this man's identity and took over his life. And he continues to help people desiring to change their identity by inventing a new one. People who are running or hiding from something. All it takes is careful skill. He creates their driver's license, birth certificates, and bank accounts. He gives them a whole new life, a career they always wanted. And it's worked for several people, as long as they stay out of the limelight and away from the law."

Rayma heard what he said but it wasn't all sinking in. Her mind was still focused on what he said earlier. They *thought* they killed his father?

"They thought they killed my dad, Jack Forrester," Keegan repeated. "It was his twin, Johnson Webb they really killed."

Chapter Twenty-Three

CAITLYN AWOKE TO stifling heat and darkness. Parched throat. Caked eyelids.

Her head felt like someone had taken it off, packed it with rocks, and twisted it back atop her body, only crooked. Her tight chest made breathing impossible and she opened her mouth, gagging at the smell of ammonia and decay.

Rubbing her eyes, she sat up, but the pain was overwhelming. She placed the heel of her palm on the bridge of her nose and sat a moment, trying to breathe away the pain and figure out where she was.

She was sitting on a concrete floor. A grimy concrete floor. She shook her hands away from her body, then wiped them on her shirt.

Where was she?

She blinked away the gooeyness on her eyes then glanced around. A microscopic light wavered under a door above her, but no steps led up to that door. Besides that light, she faced utter darkness. She guessed this was a basement. A creepy, crawly, soggy basement.

How had she'd gotten here? She remembered being at work, finding the info, being followed.

Johnson She'd made it to the police department and realized Johnson was the one following her. He'd called out to her, and they stood outside as he apologized profusely and begged her to listen. Claimed Blake was out to destroy him, was using her to do it, and he was worried about Wesley. When an officer came out to ask if she was okay, she'd told him yes and agreed to meet Johnson at a twenty-four hour café.

But...Johnson? Was he responsible for this?

She groaned, but that only stimulated the pebbles of sand that seemed to lodge in the back of her throat. She croaked a "hello?" and crawled along the floor, using her hands to find her way around the cold concrete, wincing when she brushed against something questionable. No telling what her hands would have on them if she could see. Judging from the odor, rodents and possibly cats frequented the area. Probably slithery creatures or creepy crawlies. Her clothes stuck to her, hopefully from the humidity and not from blood.

God, where was she? She tried crawling to the door but a spasm of pain kicked her spine and knocked her to her side. She coughed, rested her head against the concrete, and tried again. If she could get to that door, maybe she'd find hidden stairs.

She reached around for her purse but found nothing. Her hand bumped against a hard wall and she tried to walk her way up it. At least that could keep her upright.

Her legs buckled, even with most of her weight leaning on the wall.

Suddenly, the door squeaked open and a blaze of light followed. A shadow of a person, several shadows actually, followed by a scream. She tried to cry out, but the woman's screams and men's hushed voices silenced her and she focused on anything and everything she could. Someone beamed a flashlight, the down strokes making it impossible to see. She heard a screech and a bump before the light was gone and the door closed, imprisoning her once again.

The woman grunted. Caitlyn tried her best to hurry to her but she had to grope around the floor, using the woman's whimpers as a beacon for which direction to take.

"Are you okay?" Caitlyn whispered. She stroked the woman's her hair, once probably soft but now matted into tangles. Something about her was familiar, but without light to guide her, she couldn't guess.

"Caitlyn?" she moaned.

She went weak. "Rayma?" They hugged, and Rayma softly cried. "It's okay," Caitlyn tried to assure her, but was unable to believe it herself. "Where are we?" she asked, hoping Rayma got a glimpse before being pushed into this hellhole.

"In...a basement," Rayma said, having trouble voicing her words. "On Johnson's...land. It's under...his barn. Most people would...never suspect."

"What happened?"

"Oh God," Rayma said. "Keegan, he pushed me in here. I didn't take his news the way he wanted me to."

"What news?"

Caitlyn held Rayma as she told her what she'd learned of Keegan and Johnson. "I should have tried harder," she said. "I should've pretended I took the news graciously. I should have gone along with it. If only I were an actress, I might be able to help you. Now I'm stuck here and there's nothing we can do." Rayma started crying again.

"You wouldn't have known I was in here if you had gone along with his plan," Caitlyn assured her. "It's okay, we'll figure something out."

"They're going to kill us," she said. "They're leaving, they're probably working on their new identity now and if they don't kill us, we're gonna die in here. He offered to take me with him. I should have played along."

Caitlyn crooned to her, passing on false reassurances. No, Rayma shouldn't have played along. Her life would have been in danger no matter what.

Johnson wasn't Johnson?

So Johnson, the real Johnson, had been dead for years? She never truly knew the real Johnson, and neither had Wesley for that matter. He would have only been three at the time.

Had Samantha known? No, no way. She took this man in and thought he was her husband, who had been gone for three years. Wesley said himself she thought he changed, but accepted him. Samantha had never known her husband had a twin brother, had she? She'd wanted her family back, wanted her son to have a father, and was unaware of the evil this man had devised to change his life.

Maybe he did want a better life for himself and saw this as a perfect opening. Maybe he truly did have a good heart but not enough chances to prove it. No, what this man did was wrong, and he hurt a lot of people in the process.

What about Blake? Where did he come into play in all of this? They already knew Chad was Blake's son, and apparently he was killed because he knew what they know now. But why? How was Blake involved?

As time crawled to a stop, Caitlyn tried to keep Rayma awake for fear of a concussion. When she thought it was safe enough, she let Rayma doze. Nothing they could do tonight. It was dark, they were tired. Rest would give them a clear head, to think about what they were going to do and how they were going to get out of here.

Caitlyn couldn't sleep. Rayma occasionally cried out in her sleep, and Caitlyn couldn't tell if she was in pain or if she was having nightmares. She might have broken bones from being pushed, and Caitlyn tried to feel with her hands any unusual lumps or sticky substances to signify a broken bone or blood.

As dawn emerged, light filtered through undersized windows that only a small animal could climb through, but it offered enough light to see the room. The basement was small and cluttered with boxes and shelves. The stairs that lowered to the door were obviously on the other side.

Caitlyn crawled toward the windows, hoping she would be able to stand when she got there. She used the wall as a brace to help herself up but nearly passed out from dizziness. She stood a moment, trying to gain her balance and her bearings then looked up. She reached her arms up, able to touch the bottom of the window.

They had no hope of crawling out.

Rayma woke and called out.

"Caitlyn?"

"Yeah?"

Caitlyn plodded toward her friend. She was sore and had

to stop to regain her equilibrium, but her legs needed blood circulation and it felt good, despite the throbbing in her head.

"Do you have any broken bones? Do you feel okay?" she asked Rayma.

"I'm fine," Rayma said. "We're not going to get out of here, are we?"

"I don't know." Caitlyn sat beside Rayma. "You know Keegan better than I do. You don't think he'd let us stay down here and starve to death, do you? Surely he'll come to check on us, and when he does, he'll to listen to you."

"I don't think so." Rayma sat up slowly and scooted against the wall to rest her back flat against it. Caitlyn did the same. "You should have heard him. He was…different. I think he killed Chad or at least knows who did."

"What?"

"He told me the story then acted almost crazy, desperate. He offered me a new life, a new identity, told me I could live happily ever after if I'd just support him. I should have pretended to go along with it. But I freaked."

"Are you kidding me?" Caitlyn gripped Rayma's hands. "You did what any normal person would have done. And if you had gone with him, how would you have escaped?"

Nodding, Rayma lowered her eyes and licked her lips. "I think they're leaving the country and never coming back," Rayma said as tears fell.

Caitlyn only wished she could cry. Her mind was racing too fast to conjure any images other than apathy for the situation she was in. Fear long since faded, and now a distinct survival mechanism kicked in. What to do? There had to be something.

She crawled around, rummaging through boxes and plastic containers full of old clothes, holiday decorations, books, probably Samantha's or Esther's, and baby toys, probably Wesley's. Or could they have been Keegan's? Rayma soon followed and they searched everything, despite the meager light.

"Is this Esther's home also?" Caitlyn asked, wondering if she was involved.

"No. Apparently he has a clandestine house stashed away

she doesn't know about. She's away so much of the time and they have their home in town, but this one is outside the city limits. No one probably knows about it. We'll never be found."

"She must know what her husband and son are involved in."

"I don't know anything anymore," Rayma said. "I don't think their marriage is anything but legalized by now, and only by paper. I think Keegan's been forced into this lifestyle and wants out, but he'll do whatever he can to protect his father. Plus, what can he do? He has his own new identity. Esther has all she could ever dream of, especially coming from where she came from."

Caitlyn stopped burrowing through the boxes and leaned against the wall again as she tried to stretch the kinks out of her muscles. She wasn't prepared to give up hope, but things weren't looking good for them.

"Let's stack these boxes up to that wall and see if we can reach the door," Caitlyn said.

"It's going to be locked."

"Maybe so. But maybe we can bust it down. It's our only hope."

She opened the lid of a container labeled *Christmas decorations* and thumbed through garland and old Christmas cards that might be interesting to read if all else failed and they had to sit here and wait to starve. Or maybe the cardboard boxes would supply enough sustenance to keep them going a few days. Caitlyn shook the thought aside, angry at herself for even allowing such thoughts to discourage her.

She closed the lid and pushed the container to the door. They'd need at least two or three more.

"I found a pen!" Rayma screeched as if discovering the key to their survival. "I have an idea." She uncapped the pen and scribbled on the side of a box, crying joyously when she discovered it worked. "Let's write something on this, like 'help us, we're trapped in the basement' and throw as many as we can out that tiny window." She tore chunks of pages from a book. "Johnson owns land and doesn't have many neighbors, but if the wind blows enough maybe these notes will travel somewhere. It's a chance."

"Great idea." Caitlyn truly hoped it would work but wasn't as certain as Rayma. She didn't let Rayma see her doubt. She handed Rayma a stack of the cards. "But use these old Christmas cards. The back is blank and maybe it'll catch someone's attention more than a page from a book. And be sure to write Johnson's barn or something, so they'll know where to come."

Rayma scribbled furiously as another idea flashed through Caitlyn's head. "Save one of those cards. I'm going to tie it to the end of this garden and feed it out the window like a flag."

"Dammit!"

"What is it?"

Rayma tossed the pen. "The ink ran out."

"How many signs do you have?"

"Four cards and this page I wrote on." She flapped the paper and handed the cards to Caitlyn. "But this one only says 'help, we're stuck.'"

"It'll work." Caitlyn snatched them and stood.

She reached for the window, but didn't have the force she needed to feed them through the cracks. They stacked boxes so they could reach higher out the window, then Caitlyn climbed as Rayma handed her the cards.

"Let's shovel everything we can out this window. And grab that piece of garland with the card I attached. I'm going to use it as a flag."

"Who in the hell is it going to attract?" Rayma asked. "This house is in the boon docks."

"It's going to work. Meanwhile, we get to that door and push our way out."

***

By the time Wesley and Tim landed at the airstrip in the small country town of Ames where Johnson now lived, Wesley was in a panic. They wasted half a day flying in to Austin and talking to the police, who claimed they'd never seen her. Wesley was afraid to give them too much information lest they want to keep him there, so he and Tim taxied across town to Caitlyn's apartment, talking to neighbors, then calling Rayma to find out she wasn't answering her phone, either.

Something was wrong.

His heart tripped down his spine, cold lancing his body. If something had happened to her, he'd never be able to live with himself.

He wouldn't want to live, period. She was his life, or at least a large part of it, and he wanted to tell her that. He should never have waited this long to tell her that. And now she might be in danger. *Because of him.*

Ames was such a small town that no rental car companies or taxis were available. He barely got phone service. He managed to get ahold of the police, and they told him the same thing. "What the hell am I supposed to do then?" he asked.

"If Frank's there, he sometimes has a truck you can borrow," a police officer told him.

He considered making a report, but didn't have anything to report and didn't want to give the police any reason to be suspicious.

Frank, a balding man with a full beard, toddled over at about that time to see if they needed any help with the plane. Probably in his mid-sixties, he wore overalls with a plaid shirt underneath.

He greeted them with a hefty pump of his hand. "I take care of the airstrip here. Can I help you boys with anything?"

"We need a car," Wesley said. "I didn't realize there was no car rental company around here."

Frank laughed. "No siree. Not much of anything around here 'cept a few gas stations, a grocery store, and some churches. But if you have a place you need to go, I have an old truck I can loan you. We just have to fill out paperwork for insurance purposes."

"That'd be great." Wesley followed him over to the office and watched impatiently as the man shuffled papers around, trying to find one he needed. Why didn't he just keep it in a file cabinet where he'd be able to find it?

"What brings ya'all about here?"

"I'm here to surprise my dad. Unfortunately, he won't answer his phone so he can't come pick me up."

"Who's your dad?"

"Johnson Webb."

"Johnson, huh?" Frank straightened his twisted frame and handed Wesley a stapled document. "You need to sign right here, son. One more place on the next page. Yeah, Johnson's a good man. You look a lot like him."

Wesley signed where he indicated, turned the page and signed again, and handed it back to Frank. "Yeah? How long have you known him?"

"Oh, he's lived here for about, oh eight years or so now I suppose. Got hisself a nice wife and a good law office. Even though he defends those criminals, I know somebody has to do it." Frank handed Wesley the keys and took his money, then guided him to the rental. "He helped out my nephew once. You have it until tomorrow, just have it back by afternoon if you will. If not, give me a call and we'll make different arrangements"

"Not a problem."

"Sorry it isn't much of anything," he said as he opened the driver's side door.

That was an understatement. The truck should have been either retired or upgraded long ago. The seats were worn clear to the inside on some parts, and the few knobs that remained were close to falling off. Rust ate most of the cab, but as long as it got him and Tim where they needed to go, he had no complaints.

Wesley had only met Johnson's wife once and she had seemed distant, like he was interfering in a new life they had created for themselves and he wasn't welcome. That was fine with him—he didn't want to be a part of that life just as much as she didn't want him.

She answered the door and glanced at their shoes before letting them enter. He understood why as soon as he stepped in. Stark white tile lined the entry. Wooden beams arched into an opulent living room filled with white carpeting and pale leather couches. The only hangings on the white-washed walls were colorless.

Wesley couldn't imagine his dad living in this house.

"Your father isn't here," Esther said.

"I need to know where to find him."

Esther shrugged. "We don't keep in close contact anymore."

"You're still married?"

She nodded and took them to a dining area, the only cozy part of the house, and that wasn't saying much. He winced as he stepped across the carpet. She'd be spending the rest of the day trying to get the dirt from their shoes off the floors.

"Where's Keegan?" Tim asked.

Esther glanced at Tim, and Wesley noticed the telltale signs of a blush. "I don't know that either. He doesn't live at home anymore and doesn't call very often."

Tim, discovering he might have an advantage with her, scooted closer and clasped her hands. Her blush thickened.

She was a woman who obviously took care of herself and probably appreciated male attention. He wondered if Johnson gave that to her. Her gauzy black shirt dipped low and was accessorized by a sizeable necklace. The shirt was tucked into a miniskirt too young for her. She might have been an attractive woman if she hadn't been trying to look younger than her age.

"It's important we find Johnson," Tim said. "Or shall I say Jack Forrester?"

"What?" Esther recoiled as if she'd been slapped. She pulled her hands away. Her face blanched as all color drained from it. Tim sat back in his chair, studying her.

"He's been dead for...years," she said, her fingers fluttering at her collarbone.

"And you married his twin?"

"We met when Johnson came to meet Jack but he was married at the time. We dated each other after his wife died."

Wesley shot up and paced the small confines of the room. "You mean you kept seeing each other while he was married?" he asked, needing to know about his dad's fidelity.

"No, no." Esther kept shaking her head and brought a shaky hand to her hair to whisk a piece away from her face.

It was time to get dirty. Caitlyn was missing and the only thing he knew so far was Johnson was the last who heard from her. If he had to drag Esther on their wild goose chase so she'd mess her perfectly coiffed hair, so be it. Not many people got the chance to live a life of luxury, and he was less than pleased with her.

He stopped pacing long enough to stand in front of her and watch the expressions on her face. "Johnson's office was closed, we've already checked there. He's not in Austin, as you surely know he has an apartment there. Where else can he be?"

"Is he in trouble?"

"Should he be?"

Esther shook her head and rose from her seat. "He has a house in the country he uses for his retreat sometimes. Let me get you directions."

Wesley had never visited his father in Ames and didn't even know about this secret home he had, but the countryside was impressive, with rolling hills, large oak trees abounding, and bright yellow flowers on the side of the road. It was small, a town where everybody knew everybody, and he couldn't figure why his dad would choose a place like this as his home. It was beautiful, but Johnson never was the type of man who liked everybody to know his business, and this town struck him as that type of place.

Esther had given them directions with a picture and pushed them out of there as fast as possible. He recognized the house as soon as they drove up. It was an average brick home, a barn almost out of place but probably used as storage off to the backside, and a picket fence surrounding a manicured yard. Johnson owned at least ten acres, but there were a few neighbors nearby.

He and Tim trekked to the house while Wesley studied his surroundings. He noticed trash in the yard by the barn, which was out of place with the rest of the immaculate surroundings.

Johnson answered the door with a wide grin. "What a pleasant surprise," he said, stepping aside to let them enter.

"We didn't come for pleasantries, dad. We're looking for Caitlyn."

"Caitlyn?" Johnson arched his brow. He sat on the couch and indicated they should do the same. Tim stood ramrod straight and glared. "I haven't seen her."

His uncle never cared for Johnson, and now that he had reason to suspect him of something, Tim would be as unforgiving as possible until he proved himself. Wesley sat close to his father and studied every nuance of expression on his face.

"I tried to reach her so I could talk to her about Blake, but I couldn't ever get ahold of her. Have you tried her friend?"

"Her friend is missing, too."

"If Rayma is missing, they probably found a hotel together. Austin is a huge city. They could be anywhere."

"Where's your wife?"

"You obviously ran into her at home. How else did you get directions here?"

"Why do you have two houses?"

"Lots of people have more than one house, son. If you hadn't noticed, Esther's home isn't really a home. I stay there for my reputation's sake, but that's about it. This is home to me, one I can feel comfortable in."

"You're having problems in your marriage?"

"You've seen that house Esther calls a home, what do you think? I need a place where I can kick up my feet. Hell, I'm afraid to even walk along the floors in Esther's home. Excuse me a minute." Johnson rose and moved to another room for a minute. Wesley used this time to explore the living room. It had more personality than the last one, and he understood why Johnson would choose to stay here.

Photos adorned the wall and sat atop some bookshelves, and he was surprised to see him and his mom in some of them. Others held pictures of his new wife and Keegan, his stepson. Other pictures Wesley assumed were Johnson's wife's family.

"Ah, the hodgepodge of my life," Johnson said when he returned and Wesley was studying the pictures. "I brought you some ice tea."

Tim took the tea and sat it on the table, obviously having the same thoughts Wesley did. No way would he drink tea from his dad's hands at the moment. He couldn't conceive of evil within the man who raised him, but he didn't even know him. Not anymore.

Wesley refused the tea and turned to outstare his father. Johnson was a tall man, but his dad had never been able to intimidate him with his height. "When were you going to tell me about your twin?"

Johnson sighed and set the tea glass upon his tabletop, eyed Tim, and glanced back at Wesley.

"You're right. I did have a twin brother. I found out after my parents died. When I tried to find him, he was already dead, too. As you can imagine, I endured a lot of pain and heartache. Blake was a friend of mine, I thought, and I helped him create the business. I've already told you he wanted to buy it and I wouldn't agree to sell. Hell, he even admitted that. He collected information about me and my family over the years. Things that didn't even make sense to me. I didn't know all of this until later, when I discovered he was trying to sabotage my life. He wants the business so bad, he'll do anything. And he wants a story so bad, he'll make something up just to have it."

"What about Keegan?"

"I met Esther when I first met Jack. Later, we became acquainted again and married. Weird, I know, but life works in funny ways sometimes."

"Too coincidental," Wesley whispered. He didn't believe in that many coincidences. Blake's son was killed, and Blake had been in the hospital. Caitlyn was missing, and Caitlyn came across the information Blake kept hidden. Dammit. He couldn't prove anything and sitting here talking to his dad was proving to be a pathetic way to spend his time. He needed to explore around the house, see what he could find.

"Where's your bathroom?"

"Down the hall to the left."

Wesley closed himself up in the bathroom and skimmed the room, but it looked like a normal house to him. Johnson said he met Esther when he first met Jack, but he also said he never met Jack because Jack was already dead.

He was lying about something.

Wesley moved the curtain aside and saw the barn, closer this time. He noticed litter nearby and wondered why Johnson's yard was immaculate except there.

"What's in the barn out back?" Wesley asked when he emerged from the bathroom.

"Oh, I have a car I'm trying to restore, some of my outdoor equipment. I thought about remodeling it for a rent house once, or making it my office, but I haven't yet."

Wesley nodded, glanced at his watch, and said, "We need to get going. You have a nice place, here. Maybe one day I can see that car of yours."

"Definitely." Johnson stood and clutched his son's hand in a shake. "I appreciate you stopping by, even if it wasn't for pleasantries. Maybe one day we'll all be able to get together for a barbecue."

Chapter Twenty-Four

"HEY," JOHNSON SAID when Keegan answered his cell. "They're loading in the truck now, so give it a few minutes. How're the girls?"

"Caitlyn put on a crying show when she found out her boyfriend was here but would never be able to help her. Rayma begged me to let them out. They made a lot of noise but as you know, it's sound proof."

"Are you okay?" Johnson asked, knowing how Keegan felt about this. He was tired of hiding but he'd reached a place in his life where he wanted to be Keegan. Not the son of a whore who never had anything in life.

Johnson didn't want anything to happen to Caitlyn either, but unless he wanted to spend the rest of his life in prison, they couldn't risk letting either of the girls go.

He'd never tell Keegan the girls wouldn't survive. And if there was a snowball's chance in hell they somehow made it out alive, they'd be long gone.

"Let's get out of here as soon as possible," Johnson said, dropping the curtain as Wesley loaded in the truck. "Give it about five more minutes and head this way."

Esther must have given Wesley the address to this house because he never used this address for any correspondence and it remained unlisted. The small town was a good front, him posing as a dedicated attorney and loyal husband. Esther had the life she wanted now. Money, influence, friends. She could travel the world and see things she only dreamed of at one time.

He'd done her a favor really.

Johnson pulled out a suitcase from his closet. He wouldn't pack much, just a change of clothes and his new identity, but he needed to make sure he left no loose ends. Wesley's visit took him by surprise. He hated surprises.

It was odd trying to rid himself of the mindset he'd dedicated himself to for over twenty-five years. He had been Johnson through and through, capturing his personality, acquiring his wife as his own, and regarding Wesley as his own true son.

He knew Johnson up and down, spent enough time with him to know his past and his family before he died, and since then he had been Johnson Webb, not Jack Forrester. Now, it was time to change his identity again, become a new man, an island boy. He would move to the Caribbean, have women dote all over him, and fish all day. He was ready to retire from the hectic life Johnson led.

And now he had the money to do it.

He wasn't sure what the authorities would expect him to do other than what he did do–become Johnson Webb. Should he have called Samantha up and told her that her husband died, then leave the broken widow to raise her son by herself? No, Jack Forrester had no family to miss him. Keegan and Esther might not have approved, but Esther was a prostitute who wanted a life and recognized it to be an opportunity of a lifetime. Keegan was just a baby, too young to know any better.

He had loved Samantha, getting into Johnson's mind frame and loving her more than even Johnson ever would. Samantha's death had almost destroyed him.

Wesley was important to him, too, as a child and a status symbol. People loved attorneys who had a wife and kid. He didn't want to harm Wesley. He had been like a son to him.

Johnson might not have been the most loving father, but he tried to give Wesley everything he needed. Though Keegan was his real son, his feelings for Keegan couldn't hold a candle to the way he felt about Wesley. Wesley was proof Jack Forrester's life had truly turned around for the better.

He feared this would eventually happen and though he

grieved for what he would have to give up, he was delighted he was able to fool everyone for so long. They still would have been fooled if Blake hadn't screwed it up, but he'd never been out to fool anyone. He only wanted to make a new life for himself. Jack Forrester would never have been able to do what Johnson Webb did.

He'd met Blake in prison. Had given Blake a new life, a degree, a business. And when Caitlyn had decided to pursue a career in journalism and Blake loved to write, it was perfect. Caitlyn could remain a part of Johnson's life, and he could keep a close eye on her, without her even knowing it.

Blake should never have kept that information. It should have been burned. Better yet it should never have existed. What was he thinking? Blake was just as in on this as Johnson was. He had his own new identity, posing as the owner of a successful magazine and making lots of bucks doing it. He should be kissing the ground Johnson walked on because he was the reason Blake was able to live his dream of writing.

Oh well, Blake would be left with a lot of explaining to do, and Johnson and his son would be long gone.

***

"I need to check out that barn," Wesley told Tim as they left the house. "It's a perfect place to hide someone."

"You really think your dad is hiding her?"

Wesley shrugged. He had no idea what to think anymore, but he wasn't about to leave without checking it out. He'd search heaven and earth to find Caitlyn and after checking out that barn, he'd visit Blake and pummel him until he talked. He'd come back for his dad if he had to.

His gut quivered as he approached the heavy doors and pulled them open. He realized Johnson was lying as soon as he saw there was no vehicle to restore, no outdoor equipment, and nothing in the way of a remodeling project except one old lawn mower and a large pile of hay. Debris littered the dirt floor, spider webs flourished in the corners. He spotted a small loft in one corner, a door in the other, and was heading toward the door when Keegan shot out of the hay bale.

Keegan held a pistol, which he tossed from hand to hand. "What's going on, brother?"

All the adrenaline building throughout the day, the anxiety and spleen that made him feel like he was parked indefinitely in the pit-stop of Daytona Speedway, came crashing down on him as he paced around Keegan, his fists balled.

Tim stepped in the doorway and hesitated. Wesley surveyed his uncle then his gaze crawled back to Keegan.

"Hey, Tim, good to see you," Keegan said. "You, too, Wesley."

"Don't give me that line of bullshit. What's going on?"

"Now why would you think something is going on?"

"Because your girlfriend and Caitlyn are missing, and you're hiding away in this barn with a gun."

"I'm not hiding."

"Then what are you doing?"

"Hunting rabbits."

The sun glistened through cracks in the wall and highlighted the stifling darkness of the barn. Wesley studied his stepbrother in search of a weakness. So far he hadn't pointed his gun and kept it lowered to the floor.

Tension braided Wesley's spine at the sound of a woman's scream. His toes curled. Without giving his safety another thought, he spun around, ducked, and landed a sweep kick behind Keegan's calf. The man lost his balance but didn't go down. Wesley jumped at him and kicked him in the chest. The gun fell as he hunched over. Wesley captured him around the neck and jammed his knee into Keegan's forehead.

He grunted and fell to the ground, pulling Wesley with him.

Keegan's arms went flying, but Wesley dodged the blows and punched his stepbrother in the nose.

On his hands and knees, he tried to straighten. Channeling his focus and mustering all the training tools he'd learned throughout the years, Wesley karate-chopped him in the spine. Keegan grunted and went down.

Tim seized the gun and kept it trained on him while he went

to the door and wrestled with it. "How do you open this door?"

Wesley didn't care that he'd almost been shot. His only thought was Caitlyn. He glared at Keegan to determine his next move, and heard muffled screaming that shook him to the core.

He grabbed Keegan up by the throat and hurled him backward, pinning him into the wall.

"Where is the key?"

"I don't have it."

"Wesley," Tim said. "It isn't worth killing the bastard."

"It might be," he said. "Call the damn cops."

"I don't think so." Johnson stepped in, leveling a gun at all of them. "Let him go," he told Wesley. He only squeezed harder. "Now."

Wesley, his back towards Johnson, wheeled around to face his dad, pulling his stepbrother with him. He held him upright around the neck then thrust him to the ground. Keegan thwacked his head on the lawn mower. Wesley grabbed him and pushed him toward the lawnmower again.

Johnson leveled his gun at his son's head. "I wouldn't do that if I were you."

Wesley dropped Keegan and stood, spreading out his arm and stepping back. "What are you going to do? Shoot your own son?"

"No he's not going to shoot his own son you idiot." Keegan stood, swiped his hands across his mouth then swaggered over to Wesley and decked him in the jaw. Wesley snatched a hold of him and pushed him toward the wall. Keegan charged again, throwing punches.

"Boys!" Johnson fired the gun at the barn's ceiling, ripping the roof apart. Wood shrapnel fell to the floor. "I don't want to kill any one of you," he said after they stopped fighting. He assessed Tim, his leer suspicious. "Drop the gun."

Wesley thought he was in a nightmare. His dad's gun remained trained on him. He wasn't sure what to expect of his dad and was beginning to wonder if it *was* his dad. It looked like the man he knew all his life, only he had lost some weight in the past few weeks. His face was pale and fraught with tension and his eyes were wide and wild, but that seemed normal considering the circumstance.

His dad's twin, Jack Forrester, popped into his head, but he had seen the man's death certificate. Unless it was phony. Or unless...

"Wesley, you and Tim need to turn around and head to the basement."

Caitlyn. Johnson had a basement under the barn and Caitlyn was in there. He'd gladly go to her, and they could figure out how to get out later.

He stumbled backward, toward the door. "Care to tell me why we're going through this mess?"

"Because you couldn't leave well enough alone."

"I tried to leave it all alone. You're the one who partnered with Blake, who then sent Caitlyn to get a story."

"I always knew Blake was an idiot," Johnson said. "Messing with things he shouldn't have messed with. I should never have let him hire that girl. Tim, drop the damn gun before I shoot your nephew."

"You mean before you shoot your son?" Tim asked.

"He's not my son. I always wished he was, but..." The man shrugged.

"You're Jack Forrester?" Tim asked.

"The one and only. Wesley's father's twin, adopted by another family. When Johnson was killed, I had no choice but to take over his life. I didn't have one, and his wife and son needed me more than my own did."

Keegan stood and spat at Wesley's feet. "Didn't expect that, did you brother?"

An audible click sounded as Tim fired the weapon. Empty. He fired again. Empty.

Keegan laughed. "I never keep bullets in that thing."

"Well, I keep mine loaded all the time," Jack said.

"Good, you're going to need it," Tim said. "I don't know what the fuck is going on, but you're going down. Keegan, open the door to the basement and let those girls out. Then you lock yourself up with your dad. You can both kill each other later."

***

Caitlyn heard gunshots and voices.

Wesley's voice.

Her mouth dried, body aching as she and Rayma clutched each other.

Wesley was out there, searching for her, risking his life for her. She would die if something happened to him. She wanted to shout out and tell him that Johnson wasn't really his dad, wasn't really even Johnson. All these years, since Wesley was three years old, Jack had taken over his twin brother's identity, his life.

How did he do it?

They'd found documents in the barn. Apparently, the man had created new identities for several people over the years.

"What are we doing to do?" Rayma asked.

Trembling, she pulled out of Rayma's embrace and stacked boxes against the wall. She'd build a staircase up to that door if she had to. "We're going to get out of here."

"How do you figure?"

"I don't know but eventually, that door is going to open, and we're going to be ready."

***

"You're funny." Jack stood with his feet wide and planted firmly on the floor, gawking at Tim. All Wesley wanted to do now was get into that barn. If he died in that barn, so be it. At least he would be with Caitlyn.

The love of his life.

Maybe phone service would pick up just enough to dial 9-1-1. He considered yanking his phone out of his pocket and dialing, but he'd have to hide or else he'd probably get shot.

By the man who had playacted his father all these years. He had no doubt the man would shoot him now. He had nothing to lose but his own life, and he wouldn't risk being discovered.

"I'll go," Wesley said. He traipsed backward toward the

door that apparently led to the basement, where Caitlyn had been left to die. If he could just hold her one last time, he'd die happy.

Jack, still pointing his gun at Wesley, tossed a key to Keegan. "Open the door. Make Tim go first."

"Hey," someone outside yelled. Adam roamed in, fostering a knife in front of him. Wesley's gut lurched, fists clenched at his side. He couldn't afford hope. If Adam was here, chances are he wasn't here to save Wesley. How did he know about this place?

"Hey, man." Keegan called. "You sure you want to do this?"

Dread paved a hole under Wesley's skin, tightening every fiber of his being. He inhaled slowly, urging himself not to collapse and let them all win. Caitlyn was still in that barn, restoring his hope. He'd fight to the end.

Adam stared blankly and waved his knife at Keegan. "Please drop your gun, Jack."

"You know if that information is discovered, your life is over," Johnson—no, Jack—told Adam.

"It's already pretty much over," Adam said.

"What are you doing?" Keegan asked Adam.

"What the hell is going on?" Wesley asked.

"Look, I considered taking on a new identity. I could still be Adam, head of a new race team. Maybe even owner. After all, didn't Tim leave the team to me in the event Wesley died before or with him?"

Wesley felt someone was walking on his grave, which could very well be happening soon. His best friend and crew chief was a traitor. His name probably wasn't even Adam.

This had to be some nightmare, or one of those phony thrillers with bad actors.

"You didn't expect that, did you Wesley boy?" Keegan landed a wad of spit at Wesley's feet. "Adam, here, my best friend since God knows when, is, hell what's your real name?" He glanced at Adam, proud of this revelation then shrugged as he returned his glare on Wesley. "Doesn't matter. He'll have a new name soon. And Johnson here, or should I say Jack? Anyway, Dad gave him a new identity. And since he was so good with cars, he devised a way into your race team with the help of us masterminds. He did a good job keeping us informed of your life. Even helped us with Caitlyn when Blake decided to use her to get to you."

"And Chad?" Wesley asked, derision a solid heat in his voice.

"Oh, Chad. Poor Chad. Blake so wanted his life to be like Johnson's. So he convinced his son he should go into racing. Too bad he wasn't smart enough to live Johnson's lifestyle and had to hide the fact Chad was his son."

"Blake shouldn't have given him that information to his son," Adam said.

"You killed him?" Wesley accused.

Adam shrugged. "Had to protect our asses. Including yours, you know. We tried to keep that information from spilling out to your fans and ruining all our lives."

Had everyone Wesley known in his life been a farce?

"What about Derrick?" He asked, trying to keep his voice from cracking.

"Derrick's a smart man. I had to do something about him when he discovered the truth."

"Will you get that knife out of my face now?" Keegan asked.

"Go on now." Jack smacked Wesley over the head with the gun. "Into the basement."

Adam swung around and grabbed Keegan, pointing the knife at his throat and holding him as a shield. "Not so fast."

"What in the hell are you doing, boy?"

"I'm sorry about this, man," Adam told Wesley, ignoring Jack's comments. "I respected the hell out of you."

"You know you can't let Wesley go now, right?" Keegan asked Adam.

"I don't plan to, but I can't go with you and your dad, either. Hell, you'll kill me just like you tried to kill Blake, like you had me kill Chad. I already have the life I want, only this time I'll be owner of a new race team. I've already got my press release ready. Wesley goes crazy, kills his father, stepbrother, and uncle. Even his girlfriend. Before killing self."

Sirens wailed in the distance. Adam stabbed his knife into Keegan's chest. Blood gurgled and spewed out of his mouth, but Adam held up upright, using him as a shield. Wesley dove behind the hay bale.

"Guess I better hurry," Adam said.

"No!" Jack screamed. "No!"

Jack fired his weapon, shattering the barn wood, continuing his tirade in the direction of Adam. Wesley prayed that Caitlyn was safe. He no longer heard screaming, but the heavy beat of his heart thrummed in his ears.

The gunfire stopped.

"Fine," Adam said. "I'll open the door to the barn myself. I'll kill Caitlyn so you don't have to. I'm sure you'll want to kill yourself after that."

Wesley watched as Adam hurried to the basement door. Wesley wondered if there was a drop-off, maybe some steps leading below.

Where had Jack gone?

"Johnson," Adam said. "Oops, I mean Jack. God, it's hard to go back to that name. Well, your son was still alive. Don't know how long he's going to live now that you've shot him up so many times. My story might have to change after that scenario."

Wesley heard Jack whimpering but still didn't see him. He had to trust that Jack wasn't going to shoot him. Not now. He stood and faced Adam. Adam propped Keegan up by the wall near the door. Blood pooled under him. Adam wrestled the door, signifying he'd do whatever necessary to open it and confident he'd live through this.

Wesley would die before he let Adam get to Caitlyn. He stepped out of the safety cocoon of the hay bale, praying Jack's target was now on Adam's back.

Wesley cracked his knuckles. "Come on, Adam. You want to resolve this? Let's do it."

Adam ran forward, wielding his knife. Wesley sidestepped just in time before another gunshot rang out.

Adam's body slumped to the floor. Jack stood in the doorway, body shaking and gun pointing to the ground. Tim rushed toward him and nabbed the gun before he had a chance to turn it on himself or anyone else. He eased Jack to the ground, found the door keys, and tossed them to Wesley.

"Caitlyn," Wesley called as he unlocked the door. "It's me. I'm coming to get you."

And he had no intention of letting her go. Ever.

Caitlyn rushed into his arms, crying and blubbering. He held her tight and nuzzled her neck, not for the last time.

Bracketing her face between his hands, he stared deep into her eyes. "Are you okay?"

Her lips fluttered open. He thumbed her mouth.

"I am now," she whispered.

"Do you know how much I love you?"

She blinked hard and shook her head. He kissed her, then pulled away to study her again "I love you more than anything. I'm sorry for not telling you before."

A smiled beamed across her face. She locked her arms around his neck and rested her forehead on his chest. "I love you, too."

Six Months later

"How's Rayma?" Wesley asked Caitlyn as he strutted into the kitchen wearing nothing but a towel.

"Excuse me?" Caitlyn asked, gleaming. "Why are you thinking about Rayma right now?"

"I heard her leave. Sorry I missed saying good-bye."

"She's okay." Caitlyn locked her fingers on Wesley's jaw and pulled him in for a kiss. "Still dealing with processing the information," she continued, backing away.

"That's an understatement."

They were all okay and getting better every day. Jack Forrester had pled guilty and was sentenced to life in prison with no parole. Adam and Keegan were dead.

It helped that after Tim managed to call the cops, he'd turned on his video. Everything from Adam's confession to Johnson shooting Adam had been recorded. Their names were cleared, and the name of the person who had confessed to Chad's killing was cleared. Jack had admitted to hiring him to confess, and Esther had taken a plea deal and admitted to everything she knew.

Rayma was trying to come to terms with what happened, and Caitlyn stayed in contact with her daily.

Wesley hadn't won the championship. He was taking time off, trying to recuperate, and considered investing in a race team for next year. The biography that Caitlyn had written was set to release next month, and they had set up a book tour around the globe.

Wesley had finally owned up to his mistakes, his worst being blaming himself for his mother's death. Though he would always feel responsible, he realized the memories tainting the perception of his mother weren't worth holding on to. Samantha loved him, he loved her, and she would never have wanted her son to give up because he didn't think he deserved happiness.

He was convinced his mother hadn't known about Jack Forrester, and was somewhat eased by the fact his mother had been happy.

Caitlyn moved away and nodded at his torso. "Don't tell me

you have shorts on under that towel." She tugged on the towel and it fell away. "Damn, you do. Do you need help taking them off?"

Caitlyn reached for Wesley and pulled down his boxers, hoping to see a very ready man. Instead, she found a ring tied to him. The most exquisite diamond ring she'd ever seen.

"Will you marry me?" he asked.

Caitlyn squealed as she leapt into his arms and rained kisses across his face. "Yes, yes, yes," she vowed.

Wesley spun her around the room and joy bubbled out of her. Those ten years spent apart was now worth every moment. Their love still held the same candid sensations it had when they were in the puppy-dog phase of their relationship but it was stronger, wiser, and able to hold fast onto the cambers of life. After surviving the hell they endured ten years ago and the hell they'd experienced a few months ago, nothing would ever separate them again.

"I love you," Wesley growled in her mouth before kissing her senseless.

"So should we start trying to have babies now, or wait until after we're married?" Caitlyn joked.

Grunting, Wesley sat her on the barstool and ravished her neck.

"Hmm," she continued, "Guess that means we better start now."

NOTE FROM AUTHOR

Thank you so much for joining me on Wesley and Caitlyn's journey! I hope you enjoyed reading it as much as I enjoyed writing it, and I'd love to hear what you think! Reviews help authors and are very much appreciated.

Caitlyn and Wesley's story was one of the first I ever wrote, years ago. I published it under the title Holding Fast using my pseudonym, Emma Sanders. The rights were reverted back to me, but it took me a few years of writing other stories before realizing I must rewrite and revise this story. Their story, like their love, wouldn't die!

A bit about me: Many years ago, during my senior year in high school, I was dubbed most likely to write a novel, and that has been my dream ever since my mother read 'Brer Rabbit' to me and my sister so often that my sister was able to recite it me before she could read. I was jealous because I wanted to be able to do that and eventually, I did! I haven't stopped reading since. My mother gave me my first romance story at a very young age. I'm not sure it'd even be legal now, ha-ha! And even though I longed to write, alas, I had to get a read job. Luckily for me, I fell into the perfect job in criminal justice and later became a certified paralegal. When not caring for my small farm or spending time with her husband of two decades, I love to craft, read, go off-roading, and dream of all the places I'll one day visit.

If you'd like to know what happens with Rayma, be sure to visit my website or sign up for my newsletter at www.loveismystery.com. There, you'll also find info about my other published works and upcoming books.

Thanks again, and I'd love to hear from you!

Books by Angela Smith

Burn on the Western Slope

In Burn on the Western Slope, chemistry fires up the ski slopes when an undercover agent and a suspected jewel fence fall for each other.

Fatal Snag

While assisting her cousin plan a wedding, a fashion consultant trades garters for guns as survival when she falls for the groom's sullen brother and ends up on a mission to save him from an organized crime ring.

Final Mend

After his cousin is murdered, a recovering alcoholic-turned triathlete hires a former investigator-turned bartender to help track a missing child.

Visit www.loveisamystery.com/my-books for more info!